PARTIES IN
CONGRESS

By the Author

The Sublime and Spirited Voyage of Original Sin

The Seduction of Moxie

Parties in Congress

Praise for Colette Moody

Advance praise for *Parties in Congress*

"In today's volatile political atmosphere, where you're a hero when you hate and cheered when you practice incivility, Colette Moody steps up to the plate. This politically smart and savvy book takes everyone to task and spares no one. Set in our modern battleground of political wars, Moody manages to weave insightful political drama with a tender, sexy love story, a truck load of common sense, and drop-dead one-liners. I read this and then shared it with some political friends. Because it is so close to things that we have actually witnessed, we laughed until we cried. But it also reminded us of something we often lose sight of in this country's current vitriolic mood. Laughter is a wonderful alternative to outrage and love trumps hate forever."—C.P. Rowlands, author of *Lake Effect Snow* and *Collision Course*

Lambda Literary Award Winner
The Sublime and Spirited Voyage of Original Sin

"Aye. The temperature is steamy. The sun is high. The beach is crowded. And you'll laugh with each splashing wave on the shore as you read *The Sublime and Spirited Voyage of Original Sin* by Colette Moody. The Bold Strokes Book is a bold, comical lesbian romance about pirates, true love, and *Original Sin.*"—*Chicago Free Press*

"[A]n entertaining hybrid of historical flavor, clever repartee from a vintage romantic comedy, and rip-roaring action (think 1940s pirate movie). Some of the banter between major characters suggests the duets in *The Pirates of Penzance.*"—*Kissed By Venus*

"Seamy port towns rife with riff-raff, the stink of unwashed bodies long at sea, and a perilous quest for buried treasure figure in the fast-paced novel, enlivened by nuggets of fact woven through the fiction by the author, a self-proclaimed history buff."—Richard Labonte, Book Marks

The Seduction of Moxie

"This book is hilarious. I snorted and laughed out loud in several places: the dialogue is quick and silly and has exactly the right feel for a story set in the Roaring '20s…What's fun about this book is the cheap gin, the New York Speakeasies, the well-meaning but air-headed roommate, the blowsy landlady, the cross-country train rides, the sexual frustration, and the eventual and quite satisfying end of said frustration. Moody is definitely a writer to watch."
—*Liberty Press*

"Well, I'm satisfactorily smacking my lips after reading Colette Moody's homage to a charming historical romance based in the wild 1930s jaunt-de jour. What a fantastic book! Kudos to the author for her diligence with researching the history and lingo of 1930s, adding whimsicality with the changes taking place in the sexual race of class and morality of that particular time period, and the superb burst-out-laughing hysterical repartee that was generated between the characters. Great romance, great plot, great cameos thrown in with happenstance, fantastic backdrops of New York and then Los Angeles, super sweet, sexy, fun, sensuality, and all based in the 1930s where the author has wrapped the stars of the story around Hollywood's crème de la crème. Great book! We want more. We want more."—*Kissed By Venus*

"I pride myself on having a good sense of humor and absolutely love a book that will make me laugh. This one did that and more… I laughed so much that, like Wil Skoog, I nearly peed a little. And look out for little Clitty! I couldn't put the book down and, at the same time, never wanted it to end. I can't wait until Ms. Moody's next offering. Trust me, if you like a hilariously filthy read with a great set of characters—both main and secondary—Colette Moody's work is some that you absolutely DO NOT want to miss."—*Lesbian Fiction Reviews*

Visit us at www.boldstrokesbooks.com

PARTIES IN CONGRESS

by

Colette Moody

2011

PARTIES IN CONGRESS
© 2011 BY COLETTE MOODY. ALL RIGHTS RESERVED.

ISBN 10: 1-60282-202-6
ISBN 13: 978-1-60282-202-3

THIS TRADE PAPERBACK ORIGINAL IS PUBLISHED BY
BOLD STROKES BOOKS, INC.
P.O. BOX 249
VALLEY FALLS, NY 12185

FIRST EDITION: FEBRUARY 2011

CREDITS
EDITOR: SHELLEY THRASHER
PRODUCTION DESIGN: STACIA SEAMAN
COVER DESIGN BY SHERI (GRAPHICARTIST2020@HOTMAIL.COM)

Acknowledgments

Firstly, thank you, person holding this book. Without your interest (and my neurotic and borderline tragic need to please others), I'd just be the neighborhood loon who drinks entirely too much and mumbles stories into her armpit. But thanks to you, I'm an AUTHOR who drinks entirely too much and mumbles stories into her armpit. The distinction is small, yet significant.

My deep appreciation goes to Cathy, who called upon her close political circle to help me vet this book and ensure that I veered closer to cogent plausibility than I did to deranged idiocy. I like to think we found that happy medium.

As always, I thank the staff at Bold Strokes (and my fellow BSB authors) for their tremendous efforts on my behalf, support, and camaraderie. Thanks especially to my editor, Shelley, for embracing my lunacy and letting it wash over her like a warm tide—though, at times, I imagine it was much like the warm tide that results in an uncomfortable blast of salt water up your nose.

And to Laura, who helps me curb my instances of inappropriate behavior and keeps me out of jail, I'm grateful for your unwavering patience and for all you do (both naughty and otherwise). I love you deeply.

Dedication

This book is dedicated to Congress members Tammy Baldwin, Barney Frank, Jared Polis, and David Cicilline, as well as Houston Mayor Annise Parker and every other politician who bravely and unapologetically serves in public office as openly gay. You are making history.

CHAPTER ONE

B ijal balanced the bags in her arms precariously as she turned her key in the lock. Just as her apartment door popped open, she heard the voice of her roommate Fran from inside.

"Oh, baby. Your ass is sooo tight."

The door swung wide to reveal Fran sitting in the recliner, running her fingertips lightly over a glossy magazine page. She appeared to be caressing the image of a bikini model who was bending provocatively at the waist. "Why is this fucking thing not scratch and sniff?" She absently took another sip of wine and looked up. "Oh, hey. How'd your interview go?"

Bijal exhaled in relief, happy that she wasn't walking in on some sexual hijinks and that her dinner wouldn't have to get cold while she sat dejectedly in the hallway, waiting for Fran and her paramour to finish. She held out her trappings in answer to the question, clutching the neck of a bottle in one hand and a greasy paper bag in the other.

Fran's eyes lit up. "Wow, champagne *and* manicotti? I'm assuming it went very well indeed." She set down her vices and followed Bijal into the kitchen.

"You could say that." Bijal smiled broadly. "I start tomorrow."

"Congratulations. Um, which job was this again?" Fran began picking through the contents of the take-out bag, and her stomach gurgled as though from the sheer power of suggestion.

Bijal sighed in irritation. She was sure she'd told Fran about this position at least twice already. Perhaps if she'd been wearing a bikini at the time, Fran would have paid a bit more attention. "I'm the new research coordinator for Mayor Janet Denton's U.S. congressional race."

"Hmm, what happened to the *old* research coordinator?" Fran asked suspiciously as she pried the lid off the aluminum manicotti container and dove directly into it with a plastic fork.

Bijal struggled to open the champagne. "From what I could glean, he wasn't terribly engaged."

"What exactly does that mean? Not engaged?"

"He wasn't finding enough dirt on the mayor's opponent."

"Ah, so you're the mudslinger," Fran said, waggling her meat sauce–covered utensil in recrimination.

Bijal bristled slightly. "I don't sling the mud. I'm more the person who...harvests it from the earth," she said, finally generating enough force with her thumbs to shoot the cork across the room.

"How very green of you," Fran said, then scowled. "Or would that be brown of you?"

"Is that a racial slur?" Bijal asked, arching her left eyebrow in mock-accusation. She poured the warm bubbly into two coffee mugs, the only clean glassware they owned at the moment.

Fran scoffed. "Oh, please! You think you Indian Americans *own* brownness? For the record, my brown people were in this country getting shit on long before yours were." She indignantly picked up her mug, which sported an image of Jane Fonda from the movie *Barbarella*, replete with tight space suit and ray gun, and took a sip of the champagne.

"Are you saying you want to have a brown-off?" Bijal joked, diving hungrily into her own take-out container.

"You can't bring the brown, Ms. Life of Privilege. And you're getting manicotti on your blouse."

Bijal glanced down at the stain in horror. "Shit!" She put the food down and moved to the sink for a damp towel. "I need to start buying marinara-colored clothing."

Fran laughed and took a seat at the kitchen table. "Okay, so tell me about your new boss. What's she mayor of?"

"Ravensdale, Virginia."

"I think I drove through there once...by mistake."

Bijal continued to dab the sauce from the fabric. "Yeah, it's not a big town. And it's kind of out in the sticks."

"So you're saying she's like the mayor of Mayberry? You're really selling me." Fran drank again from Jane Fonda, who was no doubt providing her with sweet succor.

"Now, now. They have both electricity *and* plumbing," Bijal said, pulling up a chair, her blouse now sporting a huge wet spot over her right breast.

"And newfangled horseless carriages?"

"Maybe one or two. But no one in her campaign is named Goober."

Fran took another bite of the magical pasta. "Here's the real test. Would I hate her?"

"Probably," Bijal answered absently. "She's a Republican."

"I was afraid you'd say that."

"Easy, don't blow ricotta cheese out your nose. My old boss, Dr. Hayes, recommended me and got me the interview. But don't worry. I did some research on Mayor Denton before I even went to meet her. I definitely feel good supporting her candidacy, especially since it'll be my first real job inside the Beltway."

"So, when you say you feel good," Fran said, punctuating the last two words with air quotes, "you mean she's hot? Is that it? She's bangable? Because if so, maybe you need to power down that snatch of yours for a little while, Bij."

Bijal stopped mid-chew to glare, then swallowed what was in her mouth. "My snatch is on screensaver mode already, thanks. But I don't want to sleep with her, Fran. I want to get her elected. Remember, this is primarily a job, but, luckily, I happen to agree with a lot of her political positions."

"So she's for marriage equality?"

"She's for civil unions, which is close."

Fran looked as though she smelled something unsavory. "Well, I'm glad we're all fine with settling for something 'close' to equality," she said sarcastically. "Wasn't it Dr. King who famously said, 'As long as it's close, we're cool'? No, that sounds wrong, doesn't it?"

"Point taken," Bijal said. "But please keep in mind that I said she was a Republican. Being pro–civil unions makes her exceptionally progressive for her party. She considers herself a moderate Libertarian."

"What about on abolishing 'Don't Ask, Don't Tell'?"

"She's not opposed."

"Is that the same as supporting it?" Fran asked, squinting.

"I would put her in the ballpark of not *sponsoring* legislation to repeal it, but she would vote for it if it came to the House."

"Reproductive rights?"

"She supports Roe v. Wade."

Fran seemed stunned. "And is she willing to run on these issues as a Republican in a red state?"

"We may need to downplay her more socially progressive views a little during the campaign to make sure she doesn't alienate the far-right base."

Fran sat and silently stared at her for a moment. "Were you hypnotized shortly after you arrived?"

"Look, we've talked about this before. Conservatism is founded on fiscal responsibility and small government—two things I believe in. I don't happen to support the Republican Party's social platform—"

"Perhaps because it includes your subjugation?"

"And neither does Mayor Denton," Bijal said.

"Uh-huh. And does the mayor know you're a lesbian?"

Bijal looked at the table in discomfort. "It didn't come up at the interview, no."

"But it certainly can't hurt that you're a woman *and* a minority, right?" Fran asked, dunking a piece of garlic bread into her marinara sauce.

Bijal feigned outrage. "Are you implying that I got the job because I'm Indian and *not* because the mayor knows my old boss? How *dare* you!"

Fran chuckled. "So who's the mayor running against? Some old Dixiecrat with his hand in the till?"

"Actually, the incumbent is Congresswoman Colleen O'Bannon."

Fran choked on Barbarella's nectar. "*Openly gay* Congresswoman Colleen O'Bannon?"

"That's the one."

"You're a disgrace to your people."

Bijal shook her head slowly. "Which ones? As a triple minority, I have a lot of people who I can shame."

Fran pushed the manicotti away from her. "I don't know if I can continue to eat your celebratory food."

"Why not?" Bijal asked, slightly hurt.

"With fewer than half a dozen openly gay members of Congress, you, a muff-loving homo, have chosen to work for someone running to unseat one of them?"

"Look, O'Bannon being a lesbian doesn't automatically make her the best candidate. I'm sure she's made plenty of questionable, corrupt decisions in her career that have nothing to do with her being gay. You're generalizing."

"Am I?"

"You absolutely are. Do you vote for every black candidate because you're African American?"

"Do you really want an answer to that?"

"Are you *serious*? Why don't you just vote for all female candidates who share your bra size?"

"Because, as far as I know, there's no active discrimination against 34Cs."

"So you have no problem boiling down a candidate to just their race? Their stance on issues doesn't matter?"

Fran pulled the manicotti back to her and stabbed it, clearly frustrated. "Of course it matters. So does life experience."

"And if Richard Nixon was black, you'd have voted for him?"

"In Bizarro World, you mean?"

Bijal goaded her impatiently. "Just answer the question."

Fran looked at her smugly. "It wouldn't have mattered, because a black Richard Nixon wouldn't have been the 1968 Republican nominee, would he?"

"Aren't you always arguing that being equal means having someone judge you on how well you do your job, and nothing else? Congresswoman O'Bannon's sexual orientation has nothing to do with her ability to create and support effective legislation."

"So if I understand you correctly, you're betting that Mayor

Denton has better ideas and is more ethical than the oppressed lesbian, so that proves we live in a post-homophobic society?"

"Fran, you need a job where you don't spend all day with angry militant liberals at that nonprofit."

"You aren't kidding. They don't pay for shit."

"Hmph. I'd just like this election to bear no resemblance to O'Bannon's last one."

Fran swallowed loudly. "Refresh my memory."

"Buddy Campbell?"

"Oh, shit! *He* was her opponent?"

"That's the one," Bijal replied. Everyone knew exactly who Buddy Campbell was. The Republican incumbent congressman had been doing just fine in the polls until his dirty secret was uncovered less than two weeks before Election Day—the ultimate October surprise. Campbell was a married father of four children and the co-sponsor of the failed Family Values bill, but he was also carrying on a surreptitious sexual relationship with his fifteen-year-old babysitter.

At first, he'd tried to deny it, but when incriminating e-mails, recorded phone calls, and text messages had emerged, it was clear to everyone that his was a lost cause. The Republican National Committee begged Campbell to drop out, even though the election was only days away and they couldn't possibly get another Republican on the ballot. The party dictum was that having no one in the race was better than having a lying, adulterous, hypocritical pedophile, even if he somehow won. After all, how could they even celebrate that without looking skeevy?

But Campbell was deluded enough to think that his constituents loved him so much, no sex scandal was great enough to stand in the way of his reelection—especially since his Democratic opponent was a self-avowed lesbian with no political experience to speak of.

Sure enough, Campbell was the only one surprised when the ballots were tallied and O'Bannon was elected to Congress. But that shock would seem insignificant when stacked up against what came next for him—divorce and statutory rape charges.

Bijal poured herself a refill of champagne. "So hopefully Mayor Denton has been utilizing a little more…"

"Rectitude?"

Bijal nearly choked. "What about her rectum?"

Fran glared. "Rec-ti-tude," she overenunciated.

"Oh, right. That."

"So what else do you know about O'Bannon?"

Bijal wiped her mouth with a paper napkin. "Well, I haven't had much time to look into her voting record, but she's only been in one term, so there may not be much there."

"I suppose you can go the 'What has your congresswoman done for you?' route."

"Precisely."

"Where's the mayor's election office? Is it way out there in East Lower Ballsack, Virginia?"

"Unfortunately, yes. It's nearly an hour away. Though they did put it near the traffic light."

Fran snorted. "Well, sure, you want to show off the town's landmarks. I'm going to hazard a wild guess and say it's also within a block of a restaurant that has the word 'waffle' in the name."

"Wow, you really know your rural Virginia boondocks. You're right. It's across the street from the Waffle Nook, which is just down the street from the book depository and adjacent to the grassy knoll."

"Sounds picturesque."

Bijal had a fresh pang of self-doubt. "I just hope I can pull this off, Fran. This could be big."

"I know, honey. Just try not to sell your soul in the process, okay?"

CHAPTER TWO

B ijal sat at her new desk, jotting down some highlights from Congresswoman O'Bannon's website onto a yellow legal pad. Tallying up the time it took her to drive to the office, pick up her laptop from the office manager, and get situated, she already felt like she'd been working for an eternity. She glanced at her watch and was appalled to see that it was barely ten thirty in the morning. How could that be?

Donna Shoemaker, the mayor's dour campaign manager, a thin, no-nonsense, dark-haired woman sporting a grim, intense expression, walked over to Bijal's desk and perched her flat behind on the corner. If someone she'd known well had performed the gesture, it would have seemed intimate and friendly. But somehow coming from this woman, to whom Bijal had only been briefly introduced at the interview the day before, it seemed both ominous and inappropriate. "So, how're you settling in, Ms....is it Roo?"

"Rao," Bijal said. "Rhymes with 'cow.' Bijal Rao."

Donna's brow furrowed ever so slightly, as she no doubt struggled to process the name to identify Bijal's ethnicity. It sadly was an expression that Bijal recognized immediately at this point in her life and in this rather xenophobic social climate. "Where are your parents from?" Donna asked, rather transparently.

"Philadelphia," she replied, being purposely obtuse. It amazed her that being born in the United States wasn't really good enough for most people if you looked like you were from anywhere east of Baltimore. "And, yes, I'm settling in just fine. Thanks." She forced a smile.

"I see you've already got your nose to the grindstone. Found anything useful?"

"Absolutely."

Donna crossed her arms. "I'm all ears." The way she said it definitely sounded like a challenge.

"Well, I've taken a look at the election results of this district over the last twenty years."

"Yeah, a lot of this district is rural—which is part of the reason we feel so confident that the Republican Party can take back this seat in Congress. It's a red pocket in a red state."

"A red state that's had a number of Democratic governors, where both U.S. senators and seven of the twelve congressional representatives are Democrats," Bijal elaborated.

"Well, that's true."

"And a red state that went blue in the last presidential election."

Donna looked irritated by the facts. "So then you see that we have our work cut out for us," she snapped, her attitude suddenly shifting 180 degrees. "We need to stop the blue tide that's coursing through Virginia, break their momentum. We only lost this seat in the first place because our candidate was a pedophile."

"An insurmountable obstacle," Bijal said with a nod. "But this district has been slowly trending blue for nearly a decade."

"Really?" She sounded surprised.

Bijal pushed through a stack of papers on her desk and produced a graph that she handed Donna. "Really. It hasn't been a radical swing, but a steady one nonetheless. Chalk most of it up to slow urban sprawl in the areas that aren't rural, and the rest to the fact that the median age of residents is much lower than it used to be. Younger voters tend to be more liberal."

"Do we know why they've gotten younger?"

Bijal glanced back to her legal pad. "Palmer College opened several years ago. The district now has several thousand new residents under thirty."

Donna paused and seemed to turn this information over in her mind like compost. "This is good information," she finally said.

"There's more."

"Oh?"

"Congresswoman O'Bannon is very helpful in that she publishes a daily schedule on her website. She definitely has someone tech savvy on her staff, and she seems very interested in transparency."

Donna stood and started eying O'Bannon's website over Bijal's shoulder. "Hmm, that *is* good."

"But after a fairly thorough search, I discovered she's had a surprisingly blemish-free first term in office."

"Here we go," Donna said, rolling her eyes.

"She's co-sponsored a couple pieces of legislature—both of which were very popular and passed easily. She's bucked her own party more than a few times when she disagreed with either aspects of their bills or their questionable methods. I've found no allegations of corruption or impropriety. In fact, many members of both parties regard her quite highly."

"Yeah, I've heard this sermon before." Donna shifted closer to Bijal. "Let me share with you what I told your predecessor. Everyone, and I mean *every-fucking-one*, has dirt. And this woman is no different. We may just need to scratch a little deeper to find it."

Bijal had a sinking feeling in her gut—not just from Donna's inexplicable mood swing or even her disquieting use of profanity. But something in the words themselves seemed to hail back to what Fran had been telling her just the night before. "I'm assuming you don't want to run against O'Bannon's sexual orientation."

"No, a large portion of moderates wouldn't like us making that an issue. So you need to find an issue that we *can* use."

"Um—"

"And whatever you do, don't come back to me later and tell me O'Bannon has never misspoken, never made an error, or never supported a grossly liberal measure."

"Because?"

"Because I'll shitcan you like I did the asshole who sat at this desk before you."

"Riiiight," Bijal rasped incredulously. "Which is precisely why I'd never do that."

"Well, not if you want any kind of career in politics, right?"

Bijal suddenly doubted what she really *did* want. Up until about a minute and a half ago, she'd thought she'd known. "I do, yes. And, on the outside chance this carries any weight with you, my landlord was kind of counting on my paycheck. He's elderly."

Donna straightened her jacket. "Then I'd say we're all working toward the same goal, Roo."

"To keep me gainfully employed?"

"And ensure you a job recommendation, yes—something free of public ridicule."

This was becoming surreal. "Wow, I didn't even realize that public ridicule was an option. Are there any other possibilities that I should know about? Caning? Stoning?"

Bijal's nervous attempt at humor didn't seem to remotely faze Donna. "Here's my expectation, Roo. You're to burrow yourself into the congresswoman like a tapeworm."

Bijal began writing on her legal pad. "Let me just add latex gloves to my shopping list."

"I want to know every person she's misled, every math test she ever failed, and every goddamn check she's bounced. I don't care how insignificant it seems, just bring everything to me. I'll judge what's useful. Don't stop digging until you hit pay dirt."

"Or the digestive tract, apparently."

"Right." Donna glanced back to Bijal's computer screen. "And just what *is* the congresswoman up to?"

Bijal clicked back to the schedule page. "Actually, this afternoon, it looks like she plans to speak at a dedication ceremony for a co-op for the homeless in Richmond."

"That's perfect. I'll get you a video camera, and you can film the whole liberal welfare-fest."

"Actually, that would be useful, since I haven't been able to find any video clips of her. Didn't she ever debate Buddy Campbell on television?"

"No, Campbell was afraid of questions about his indiscretion, so he backed out at the last minute. That guy was an idiot."

"Being an idiot sounds like his best feature," Bijal said, almost to herself.

"Okay, so what time is this thing?"

"Uh, two o'clock."

Donna glanced at her watch. "Then we need to hurry. Get online and map how to get there. I'll have Dan, the office manager, bring you the A/V equipment and give you the rundown on how to operate it. Make sure both batteries are charged."

"Will do."

"Great. You can show us the footage in the morning."

"Sounds good," Bijal said as Donna walked away with purpose. If she'd known how much driving was involved with this job, she might have mulled it over more before she accepted.

She glanced back to Congresswoman O'Bannon's Web page and examined the small picture in the upper right corner. A dumpy woman around the age of fifty stood in front of a group of younger people, probably the staff—the highly technical, motivated, grass-roots staff, the staff she was starting to envy.

"Shit."

She pulled up Google Maps.

❖

Bijal arrived at the event a little early and entered the building lobby relieved that she would have ample time to find the room the congresswoman's event would be in and set up the video camera she was carrying under her arm. If only she felt more confident using it.

As she glanced over to the building directory, she spied a tall, bespectacled woman, probably in her mid-thirties. Though she was dressed as a businesswoman in a blue pinstriped suit with a pencil skirt, something about her emanated a certain androgyny. Perhaps it was her muscular hands with close-cropped fingernails. Maybe it was the casual way she swept her shoulder-length hair out of her eyes, or her strong, firmly set jaw. Whatever the quality was, Bijal found herself appreciating things like the small shock of gray that contrasted so strikingly with the rest of the woman's dark hair.

For some unknown reason, the stranger's head suddenly turned and she made eye contact with Bijal. They shared a polite smile, one that seemed to pleasantly linger. A discernible heat built in their gaze. Bijal found it unmistakable.

Suddenly, a man bumped Bijal from behind and she was forced to turn around and apologize for standing idly in the lobby, blocking the main entrance. When she spun back around, she saw that the object of her affection was now waiting for the elevator.

Bijal bypassed the directory and hustled over to catch the elevator, not caring what floor it was going to. "Nice suit," she said, neither able to keep the flirtation out of her voice nor wanting to try.

The woman surveyed her and, from so close, her green eyes were striking. "Thank you."

Bijal clung to the increasing signs that this attraction was mutual. The warmness in her expression encouraged her. "You fill it out very nicely," she added boldly.

Green eyes fixed on hers again. "Well, obviously that red-dot sale at J.C. Penney paid off for me." The elevator doors opened and they both stepped inside. "What floor?"

The woman's husky voice was all the final circumstantial evidence Bijal needed. This woman was not only a lesbian, but she was clearly flirting back. "I'm not sure. What floor will give me the most time with you?"

"I'm getting out at eleven," she said with an alluring smile. "Do you think you'll be able to maintain your string of come-ons that long?"

"Are you kidding? I once hit on a woman sitting next to me on a plane nonstop from DC to Houston. Eleven floors is *nothing*."

"Impressive," the woman remarked as the doors slid shut. "Tell me, is the camera so you can film it?"

"Huh?" Bijal glanced down, having forgotten she was even carrying the thing. "Oh, no. I'm filming Congresswoman O'Bannon's speech."

"Really? Is it something like a student project?"

Bijal beamed. "What a smooth way to ask my age."

"You think you're the only accomplished flirt in this elevator?"

"I'm Bijal Rao," she said, extending her free hand. "And I haven't been a student in years. I work for the congresswoman's opponent."

"Ooh, so you're a spy? That's kind of thrilling." She held Bijal's hand gently and for much longer than the duration of the average handshake.

"No, nothing as exciting as that, unfortunately. I just do their research—you know, look for weaknesses to exploit."

She seemed intrigued. "I don't know, all that espionage still sounds very…secret agenty."

"That would require a level of smoothness I don't possess," Bijal said, somewhat modestly. "Though I can drive a flaming speedboat over an open waterfall. Don't ask me how I know that."

The elevator emitted a single chime and the doors opened. "Here's my floor."

"Wait, I didn't catch your name." Bijal held the doors open expectantly.

"Congresswoman Colleen O'Bannon, but you can call me…the opposition." She winked playfully.

"Shit," Bijal hissed without thinking, pulling her hand back so the elevator could close and either her embarrassment could abate or she could privately wither away in mortification, whichever came first.

"Good luck, Bijal. It was very nice meeting you."

The doors slid shut, but it was several moments before Bijal realized she wasn't moving. She hadn't hit a button.

❖

As Colleen drove home, her cell phone rang. Pressing the Speaker button, she instantly recognized the number as that of her campaign manager. "Hey, Max."

"Hey, Colleen. How'd it go?"

"Great. We had a decent-sized crowd, local media was there."

"You didn't have any crazies picketing with signs saying 'Screw the Homeless'?"

She laughed. "Not unless you count that guy in the back who was shouting something about soylent green being people."

"Did he look like Charlton Heston?"

"A little…oh, and Denton did send a staffer to film me."

"No shit?"

"None whatsoever. She recorded the whole event."

"Hmm," he said, his voice tinged with suspicion. "And you're sure she's with Denton?"

"Yup, not a doubt in my mind."

"Did she say or do anything to try to discredit you?"

"No, in fact, she was surprisingly friendly. Not to mention easy on the eyes."

"Crafty," Max said. "Send a hot-looking Republican to distract you while you're addressing a crowd. Did she at any point remove her blouse?"

"Sadly, no. She kept her clothes on through the whole thing."

"Whew, you just narrowly escaped with your reputation intact."

Colleen gently slapped her turn signal. "So if I told you I motorboated her while a state delegate was speaking, you'd be mad?"

"Mad *and* jealous, yes," Max replied. "At any rate, I wanted to check on your event, as well as let you know that you picked up a couple of points in the latest Gallup Poll."

"Nice to hear."

"So I suppose we shouldn't be surprised that Denton is getting nervous. They started behind and just keep falling farther back."

"Well, let's not get too cocky, Max."

"What are you, Han Solo?"

"If I only had a tenth of his swagger. Is that all the news?"

"For now, but stay away from bounty hunters."

"Thanks, Max. I can always count on you for the invaluable insight."

"And always check your hyperdrive," he added.

"Yeah, bye, Max. See you tomorrow at the office."

"Bye," he said, chuckling at his own humor.

Colleen pressed End and shook her head. "Geek."

CHAPTER THREE

B ijal was still toiling at the computer when Fran walked through the apartment door.

Fran glanced at her watch, no doubt surprised to see it was nearly one in the morning. "Ooh, good. You're still up." She shuffled over to the refrigerator and took out a chilled bottle of water. "You should have come out with me, girl. Some butch laid the worst line on me *ever*."

Bijal propped her chin up on her fist and blinked tiredly. "Worse than 'you've got beautiful thighs—what time do they open?'"

Fran unscrewed the cap and took a long drink before sitting on the couch. "I'd say so. This short chick with a wallet chain and a leather vest saunters up to me while I'm on the dance floor, leans in, and says, 'My friend over there says you look like you'd taste like chocolate, and I bet her twenty bucks that you taste more like mocha.'"

"Wow."

Fran nodded slowly. "Uh-huh, that's what I mean. Epically bad."

"No one's ever told me that I looked like I taste like anything. So what did you say?"

"We're going out Friday."

Bijal laughed and rolled her eyes. "Damn, you're a real piece of work."

"What? Can I help it if I'm a sucker for leather and shitty pickup lines?"

"Yes. Yes, you can. You just have to *want* to."

"Whatever. What's eating you? Did you get fired today or something?"

"No, but I probably should be," Bijal replied with a sigh.

"Ooh!" Fran quickly kicked off her shoes, ran over to the kitchen, grabbed a chair, and pulled it up next to Bijal at the computer. "Okay, go ahead."

"So I was sent to this dedication ceremony to film the congresswoman."

"Did you punch someone in the back of the head?"

Bijal blinked at her slowly, wondering why that had been the first thing that had occurred to her. "No, but I saw this amazingly hot woman in the lobby."

"Did you miss the whole thing because you were busy fucking some CPA in the ladies' room? Can I just go on the record and say that we, as lesbians, aren't doing ourselves any favors with all the toilet-stall sex? People poop in there, for God's sake."

"There was no toilet-stall sex."

"Well, a public sink isn't much better. People do some filthy-ass things in public restrooms. Just the other day I saw some nasty—"

"Fran, try to focus here. There was no sex of any kind."

"Oh," Fran said softly. "For some reason, I'm kind of disappointed."

"Well, if *that* disappoints you, you may have to take a moment to steel yourself for the rest of this story."

"Hmm, well, let's see if I can figure this out on my own. You saw a hot woman, and because you're Bijal, you hit on her."

"I did," Bijal said with a nod.

"And did she seem receptive?"

"Actually, yes. She was funny and flirty."

"So you made a date with her?"

"No, I can't."

Fran scowled. "Why not? Is she married?"

"No, even worse. She's the congresswoman my boss is running to unseat."

"Shut your fat, sassy mouth!"

"I wish I had," Bijal said, running her hands through her hair in frustration.

"Okay, I'm officially done guessing. What the hell happened?"

"I practically grabbed her tit on the elevator."

Fran couldn't stifle her laughter. "Smooth, as always."

"I bragged to her that I was in the building from Mayor Denton's office to do political reconnaissance."

"Holy crap."

"Then she told me who she was."

"Did she flip out on you and get up in your face?"

"Not at all. On the contrary." Bijal spun her chair back to face the monitor and began fiddling with the video controls. "Check this out."

Fran stood and watched over Bijal's shoulder as she advanced the video player. She suddenly clicked the Play button as a woman at the podium was speaking.

"And part of the moral imperative that drives us should be ensuring that people who are struggling have somewhere to get help. It's unconscionable that our society vilifies people who, in many instances through no fault of their own, have fallen on hard times. And this functional co-op will be the first in what we hope is a series of facilities throughout the country that will reduce the homeless population in our urban cities, assist people currently without access to health care in becoming more mentally and physically healthy, and teach them both marketable and self-sustaining skills. This is the prototype that will turn inadequate welfare into practical, multifaceted rehabilitation and restore dignity and self-sufficiency for those willing to work toward it."

Fran whistled. "Damn, you're right. She's super-brainy hot. I'd like to see her in a Catwoman suit."

"Stop it," Bijal said as she fast-forwarded.

"Does Mayor Denton look this good?"

"No, now watch this."

"Ooh, does she take off her jacket?"

The action on the monitor suddenly started again, this time clearly after the ceremony was over. People were milling about, and Congresswoman O'Bannon approached the running camera and looked directly into it. "Did you get everything you needed, Bijal?"

Off-camera, Bijal's uncomfortable response could be heard. "Um…yeah. Thanks."

"Because I can do it again, if you need me to." Her voice definitely held a hint of innuendo.

"No, I'm good. Thanks," Bijal repeated.

"Well, it was nice meeting you. Tell Mayor Denton hello for me," O'Bannon said with a saucy smile. Bijal's nervous laughter faded as the congresswoman turned and walked out of frame.

Bijal clicked Pause, and she and Fran sat in silence for a minute or two.

"Wow," Fran finally said, her face registering stunned bewilderment.

"Yeah."

"You're going to cut out all that stuff at the end, right?"

"You bet your mocha ass I am. How would I explain that she knew not only my name, but that I was with the mayor's office?"

Fran took another sip of her bottled water. "I suppose that *is* a little incriminating for you. You think she'll out you?"

"I don't know. I hope not."

"Maybe you can divert attention back to her. Can you re-edit that video so she's admitting to being a socialist, illegal immigrant who hates our troops and wants to force you to have a late-term abortion?"

Bijal's sense of humor evaporated. "Is this you helping? Is that what this is?"

"Sorry. Can you use anything in her speech?"

"I'm not sure. I mean, her indictment of the current welfare system didn't sound very capital-D Democratic to me."

"But the little bit you just played that talked about helping poor people didn't sound very Republican either."

"Fran." Bijal sighed. "I've been working today for over twelve hours. My new hyperaggressive campaign manager threatened my job for what feels like will be the first of many, many times, and I practically invited our opponent into my mouth after revealing my intent to destroy her."

"Mmm, that's a full day, all right."

"Can you cut me some slack and not try to pick a fight with me about political ideology, please? Can that be arranged?"

Fran pretended to be completely put out. "I suppose just this once."

"Thank you. I'll edit this down to only the congresswoman's speech, and I'll let the folks at work decide if there's anything useful in it. But I don't see much."

"You know what you really need to find out about her?"

"What?"

"If she's single."

❖

Bijal rolled her index finger along the wheel of her computer mouse as she scanned the search-engine results for something useful. She yawned, then took another sip of her lukewarm latte.

Donna had told her she'd be presenting the video of the congresswoman at nine a.m., and it was now over ninety minutes past that time. Bijal understood that schedules were hard to keep in a political campaign, but she was exhausted from operating on so little sleep.

As she started to mutter another curse under her breath, she spotted an interesting link and clicked on it. Up came an interview with a gay magazine named *QPolitic* from just after the congresswoman's election win. The title was "O'Bannon Pulls No Punches: Congress' Newest Openly Gay Member Tells It Like It Is."

Bijal skimmed it until she spied some of the same questions she herself had.

QP: So with no political experience, you, as an out lesbian, decided to challenge a Republican incumbent in a red district of a red state.

CO: It does sound a little crazy, I guess.

QP: Were you driven by your opposition to Congressman Buddy Campbell?

CO: Partly, but mostly I'm going to Washington to fight for civil rights—reproductive rights, hate-crime legislation, anti-discrimination laws.

QP: That's a very ambitious agenda, especially when the majority of Americans may not support those initiatives.

CO: Four years ago I lost my partner in the bombing of the East Bay Women's Health Clinic.

QP: I'm very sorry. She was a doctor there?

CO: A nurse—one who was doing her job helping women who chose to have abortions as well as those who chose to carry to term.

QP: Was anyone ever prosecuted for that bombing?

CO: No, even though a group who calls themselves Missionaries of the Light essentially claimed responsibility. Three people killed, seven others injured, no one formally charged with the crime. And why? Because legislators in this country are afraid to appear unsympathetic to the far right wing—even the small subset that's filled with lunatic extremists who violate the law, engage actively in intimidation, and ultimately murder people in their zealotry.

QP: That's quite an indictment.

CO: I can tell you that a large percentage of politicians in office who claim to be anti-choice aren't. They're afraid to be labeled as too liberal or not religious enough, and some are simply petrified to break with the established party platform.

QP: But don't the Democrats do that too?

CO: Absolutely, because they're more interested in their futures as career politicians than in standing up for their convictions.

QP: It sounds like you might make enemies on both sides of the aisle.

CO: We'll see. I'd like to think we still have enough independent legislators that we can work together, irrespective of party, to effect some positive change. That's really what people want—not more political posturing and hypocrisy. They want representatives who stand for something, and if ultimately my constituents don't agree with my positions on the issues, or if they feel I'm not effective, they'll vote me out of office.

QP: That's a refreshing perspective.

CO: [laughing] What, honesty?

QP: More specifically, your Lincolnesque acceptance that you can't please all people at all times and your frank refusal to pretend otherwise.

CO: The real tragedy is that we've stopped expecting our politicians to have integrity. We assume everyone is lying, on the take, and operating only in their own interests. It's mind-boggling that with a governmental system so entrenched in favoritism and quid pro quo, and with a stable of elected officials who almost seem to be racing each other to be indicted on corruption charges of some sort, our citizens aren't marching in the streets demanding reform.

QP: Do you think they should be?

CO: The saying holds true that if people aren't outraged, they haven't been paying attention. Americans are disgusted that their politicians openly lie and don't act in the best interests of the public. But instead of galvanizing into a force that can change the system, we've simply stopped participating. People have stopped voting because they don't think it matters since all the candidates are crooked. They need to start holding people accountable. If legislators break campaign promises, then their constituents need to vote them out of office.

QP: Aren't you worried that philosophy might backfire on you?

CO: Not at all. I didn't run for Congress because it's what I've always wanted to do. I was very happy in my previous job. I ran because I was angry. I'm *still* angry. The people we've sent to Washington should be working for us—to ensure our rights are recognized and upheld, and they simply haven't been. I'm not here to embed myself into the House of Representatives. I'm just trying to do what I can to fix things. And the minute I compromise my principles, I'll walk away.

Bijal pushed her chair back from the desk and pondered those comments. A seasoned politician hadn't made them, for sure.

That O'Bannon openly accused members of her own party of pandering was certainly unexpected, but not as much as her call to the people of the United States to unite against their corrupt and duplicitous representatives.

Clearly when she'd heard such vague descriptors of the congresswoman as "unconventional," "straightforward," and "without pretense," this was what people had been referring to. By all rights and means, if they were running a campaign against someone who refused to be evasive, vague, or neutral, then Denton stood a good shot at winning. Mix in the fact that District 12 was more conservative than not, and that their opponent was openly gay and loudly pro-choice, and O'Bannon's odds seemed even steeper.

So why was she currently leading in the polls by five percentage points?

"Roo," Donna called from the doorway. "Come on into the mayor's office and bring your notes."

"It's *Rao*," she mumbled as she stood and tossed her tepid java into the trash can before grabbing her legal pad and pen. Perhaps if this went well, they'd let her go home early and get some rest. She chuckled at such a ridiculous thought as she settled into the mayor's black leather sofa. Donna closed the door so the three of them could speak privately.

"How are you, Bijal?" Mayor Denton asked with a pleasant smile.

"I'm well, Mayor."

"Call me Janet, please. So Donna tells me that you did a little strategic reconnaissance last night."

"I did, yes." Bijal tried to look bright and cheery, not like the half-dead piece of roadkill she felt like.

"Give us a rundown, Roo," Donna said impatiently.

"Rao." Bijal felt the flutter of fresh irritation building within her. "Um, okay. Did you get a chance to read the report I sent you?"

"Huh?" Donna looked caught off guard. "Oh, sure. I glanced at it. But why don't you go ahead and brief Janet?"

"Right." Bijal's irritation now flowered into full-blown annoyance at being lied to. "I attended a dedication of a new homeless co-op in Richmond. Other speakers besides the congresswoman included a couple of state delegates as well as Senator Flynn, who, as you know, is quite popular and has a very high approval rating."

"A co-op?" Janet asked, her voice thick with derision. "That sounds a little hippie/socialist, doesn't it? Can't we make some hay out of that?"

Bijal cleared her throat. "Well, I was thinking that too…at first. But then I got the details. It's actually taking the place of an existing ramshackle shelter in the city that's been limping along on donations and subsidies and just providing beds and meals. The new program works like this. Homeless people are taken in from the streets and given medical exams and assigned beds. Those deemed healthy enough are enrolled in a job-training program. Those who aren't start receiving medical or mental-health care to try to get them healthy."

"Wait, let's not get too far ahead. What kind of job training?" Janet asked.

"Here's the remarkable part. They contacted a series of local

Virginia business owners—contractors, plumbers, electricians, landscapers—and by assuring them local work as well as giving them substantial tax incentives to participate in this program, they agree to employ these people in various capacities at a reduced salary. They train them, essentially. As long as the employer abides by certain requirements—"

"What kind of requirements?" Donna asked sharply.

"The work has to be inspected upon completion. They have to use parts and supplies made in the U.S. whenever possible. There can't be any improper hiring procedures, things like that. As long as they manage that, the city and state guarantee the company work."

Janet groaned. "Which generates local jobs."

"Exactly," Bijal said. "Trainees eventually graduate to living spaces that are more like apartments. The program bought some dilapidated buildings in the city that will be the first projects worked on. Those will become program housing."

"Which revitalizes downtown," Janet said, sounding vaguely impressed.

Bijal nodded. "Right. When they're ready, the participants move in and start paying a small rent, which goes back into the program. On-site people will reside in the complexes to provide assistance and keep an eye on everyone."

"More fucking jobs," Donna hissed.

"And once residents are ready to be mainstreamed, the program helps find them permanent jobs and residences."

Donna scowled. "Who's paying for the medical care you mentioned? The taxpayer?"

"Actually, no," Bijal explained. "The program has partnered with the local medical school and hires the participating local companies to upgrade the school's facilities. The patients then receive treatment from the resident physicians, who demonstrate techniques and medical theory to the medical students. They hope it'll become a state-of-the-art school and a huge draw for medical and nursing students all over the country."

Janet looked defeated. "And in doing all this, they still reduce the number of homeless people on the street."

"Who's paying all the up-front costs?" Donna asked. "Who's backing the construction projects?"

"It's part of the stimulus package. This is considered a shovel-ready project."

"And how many jobs are they estimating this will create?" Janet asked.

Bijal flipped through her notes for the number. "Well, you've got participating employers who'll be ramping up staff, direct employees of the program itself, and medical college personnel. They're estimating a couple hundred."

"If it works," Donna added. "We can still ultimately spin this as bigger government. It shouldn't be a federal job to clean up every drunk on the street. Some of them are there because they're fuck-ups."

"True," Janet said.

"But some are there because they were laid off, defaulted on their mortgages, or had steep medical bills and no health insurance. Democrats can easily spin opposing this as us simply being callous and greedy." Bijal searched for another statistic among her scrawling. "Preliminary poll numbers show Richmond residents are predominantly behind it. It's been sold to them as revitalization, more jobs, economic stimulus, and renewed infrastructure. O'Bannon and the Democrats have done a good job of talking that up and haven't had any strong opposition."

"You're saying roll over on this?" Donna asked incredulously.

Bijal shook her head. "I don't see any way for you to be against this co-op and win points—not now. Maybe if we'd been engaged months ago and mounted a vocal campaign against it."

Janet sighed. "Let's leave this alone unless O'Bannon starts talking it up."

"That's already happened," Bijal said. "She has a new thirty-second radio spot that launched this morning with highlights from her speech."

"That bitch," Donna grumbled. "Did you find anything in her speech that we can use?"

Bijal glanced nervously at the floor as she tried not to look like she was hiding something. "No, I've gone through it several times. It was brief and well-worded. I think our best response is an indirect one—tout a positive measure that you've implemented as mayor of Ravensdale that shows your innovation and commitment to fiscal responsibility."

The silence that fell over the room was excruciating. This was surely not a good sign.

CHAPTER FOUR

Bijal stepped off the Yellow Line train at the Metro transfer station and scanned the crowd for Fran. She glanced guiltily at her watch; she was over twenty minutes late. "Shit." She searched the station again, slightly less hopeful now, and was instantly relieved to see her roommate glaring at her from about twenty yards away.

She hurried over to her. "Fran, I'm so sorry!"

"Yeah, I was giving you five more minutes before I hopped on the Red Line and left your ass behind."

"Our staff meeting ran late—and this whole Park and Ride thing is becoming a tremendous pain in the ass."

Fran's left eyebrow rose critically. "So is my stomach, which has begun to eat itself while I've been stuck here, watching the local crazies talk to themselves. I think some homeless guy took a shit in the corner over there."

"Um—"

"Anyway, we need to decide where we're getting dinner. You can bitch to me about your day once we're on the train."

Bijal's remorse returned. "Fair enough. I made you wait, so you pick."

"Okay, let's hit Hector's Hacienda, then. I'm dying for their pork enchiladas."

"Ooh," Bijal said excitedly. "And a pitcher of margaritas. Let's go."

They boarded the Red Line train on their way to Dupont Circle.

As they took their seats, the doors shut and Bijal sighed tiredly as she set down her messenger bag and rubbed her eyes.

"Okay, you can start dishing," Fran said.

"First, I need your word that you won't turn my venting into an opportunity to lecture me on the perils of conservatism."

Fran pouted. "Oh, come on. That's not fair. You know what joy that brings me."

"I'll buy dinner," Bijal offered.

"Deal. I'll be as nonpartisan as I can manage."

"Good, because I could really use some political advice."

"So what's the problem?" Fran asked.

"I'm starting to suspect that drunken monkeys are running our campaign."

Fran scoffed. "Well, when I volunteered last year for Councilman Jeffries, brain-damaged cockroaches ran our campaign. Drunken monkeys would have been a step up. Congratulations. At least your incompetents have opposable thumbs."

"Yeah, but I'm concerned we won't be able to pull off a win. We don't seem to be making smart moves."

"Hmm, and who's your campaign manager?"

Bijal sneered slightly. "Donna Shoemaker."

"I don't know the name."

"You know her. She played the Nazi dentist in that movie *Marathon Man*."

Fran laughed loudly. "Wow, as cuddly as all that, huh?"

"She's threatened to fire me at least once a day since I started. At first I thought she didn't like me, but now, after only a week, I know she does that to everyone in the office."

"Is this *before* she drills your teeth without anesthetic and asks you if it's safe?"

"After—directly after. But seriously, I'm really worried about how things are going."

Fran appeared to ponder this. "Okay, let's review the facts and we'll see what we can do."

Bijal began digging through her bag and pulled out a ragged-looking legal pad. "I was hoping you'd say that," she said with a smile.

"I am *so* getting dessert for this."

"As much flan as you can keep down," Bijal said.

"So start with your opponent. Give me her highlights."

Bijal began flipping through her notes. "Congresswoman Colleen O'Bannon—thirty-four years old, incumbent representative of the twelfth district of Virginia. Her family owns and operates the Arc of Orion distillery in Fulton County, and has since 1934."

"Ooh, really?"

"Could you try to be a little less enthused, please?"

"Come on, she's young, queer, liberal, powerful, and likes the sauce. She and I are made for each other."

"Is that so?"

"Mmm, I can imagine her licking fancy booze off my cinnamon nipples all night long. And in the morning, we'd talk about universal health care and repealing the death penalty."

"Jesus, Fran. Try and keep it in your pants at least until we get to the restaurant, okay?"

She looked contrite. "Sorry. Go on."

Bijal looked back at the legal pad and brushed her hair out of her eyes. "When O'Bannon was elected, she passed her management position at Arc of Orion on to her younger brother."

"Okay, so she didn't have any political experience before being elected?"

"No," Bijal replied.

"And Mayor Denton has been in office for nearly four years. So with only a single two-year term under her belt, you guys can run on having more experience—an unusual strategy against an incumbent."

"Well, get this. After O'Bannon's girlfriend of three years was killed in the East Bay Abortion Clinic bombing and it yielded no prosecutions, she decided to run for Congress."

"Damn," Fran rasped. "That's heartbreaking and inspiring at the same time."

"I know, and I don't think we can make the experience argument, because all Mayor Denton's currently known for in Ravensdale is promising to cut property taxes and then actually having to raise them after she took office. She has a bit of a credibility problem to overcome."

"Well, that *is* a problem. But O'Bannon can't have accomplished too much in one term."

"Actually, she co-sponsored the O'Bannon-Croft Hate Crimes bill that the president recently signed."

"Oh," Fran said. "She's *that* O'Bannon."

"Now you're starting to see my dilemma."

"I think so."

Bijal consulted her notes again. "She's also co-sponsoring that bill on nondiscrimination in the workplace that's supposed to be introduced early next year. She's a co-chair of the Congressional LGBT Equality Caucus, and a member of the House Armed Services Committee, the Committee on Foreign Affairs, and the House Select Committee on Energy Independence and Global Warming."

"And Mayor Denton?"

"Is struggling to get cameras installed at the major intersection in her jerkwater, pissant town that would take pictures of drivers who run red lights."

"Wow. Well, let me ask you, Bij, what's your personal impression of the mayor? Do you think she's qualified for Congress?"

Bijal thought about that as the train pulled up to their stop and she tucked her notes back into her bag. "I like her. She's very personable."

"Okay," Fran said slowly as the doors opened and they strolled with the flow of the crowd into the station. "Is she smart?"

"She's not stupid."

"Hmm, not what I asked. Let me put it this way. Is O'Bannon smart?"

"Absolutely."

"See that? There's your problem right there. You need to go with the whole 'my candidate may not be very bright, but she's likeable' strategy." They rapidly filed out into the street.

"Well, it's not like that hasn't worked before," Bijal replied.

"Please, don't remind me. Now, tell me about the mayor."

"She's fifty-two and nearing the end of her first term. Before she was elected, she was a member of the city council. Her husband is a minister, and she has three kids that range in age from thirteen to twenty-two."

Fran frowned.

"Yeah, not very exciting, is it?"

"And she doesn't sound like the kind of person who people might find earthy or easy to relate to. She married a minister?"

"Well, someone has to."

"Tell that to Catholic priests," Fran said as they headed toward the flashing lights of Hector's Hacienda.

"It should help secure her the right-wing vote," Bijal said hopefully.

"Girl, you're running against a liquor-peddling lesbian. The mayor could be married to a seven-foot rubber dildo with a Hitler mustache and she'd have the right-wing vote."

"Yeah, but unfortunately, to appeal to moderates, she may have to walk that fine line where she risks losing the support of conservatives. I'm really banging my head against the wall here. I mean, how far to the left is too far?"

"You certainly have your work cut out for you."

"The thing is," Bijal said wistfully, "I'm worried that Donna is a loose cannon who isn't exactly on the ball. Whatever chances we have become even more remote because she doesn't ever seem to know what she's talking about, never reads her e-mail, isn't up on current events or issues, and spends most of her time blaming staff members for things she missed."

"So, don't worry so much about winning this election. Just chalk it up as experience for the résumé."

"You know I don't work that way, Fran. I can't do things halfheartedly. I really want Janet Denton to win."

"Even after everything you just told me?"

"I think she just needs to take control of her campaign—"

"And shitcan her campaign manager?"

"And get back on the right track. O'Bannon may be very involved for a first-term representative, but she's part of the big-government, high-spending movement that most upper- and middle-class folks are tired of. I can help Janet become the right kind of candidate. She can be the socially moderate, fiscally responsible Republican people are looking for."

They stood in the doorway of the noisy restaurant and Fran held up two fingers to the hostess, who waved them through to be seated.

"Well, if that's what you think, then that's what you run on."

"Yeah, I just need Mayor Denton to agree."

Fran looked up at the server who arrived promptly at their table. "We need a pitcher of frozen margaritas, my friend. And two glasses with salt."

❖

Bijal thumbed through the article she'd printed out. She'd been trying to read it for nearly fifteen minutes, but her mind kept drifting to the upcoming debate scheduled between Mayor Denton and Congresswoman O'Bannon.

After only two weeks on the job, she was starting to feel that Janet's campaign was like a runaway freight train that she'd never be able to get back on track. So far, she'd had no success talking to the mayor without Donna there, and Donna was still spending a fair amount of time glaring at Bijal and threatening her job.

She tossed the pages haphazardly on her desk, intending to read them later when she was less distracted. She reclaimed her computer mouse and, out of habit, did a search on "Colleen O'Bannon."

A news entry she hadn't seen earlier was now at the top of the search results. She clicked it and scanned the story with great interest.

Once done, she rose, approached the mayor's office, and knocked on Janet's door, knowing she was ensconced in there with Donna. Swallowing loudly, she listened for a response from within.

Instead, the door flew open and she was face-to-face with a very aggravated-looking campaign manager. "What is it?" Donna barked.

"Sorry to interrupt," Bijal replied softly, staring past her antagonist and speaking directly to Mayor Denton. "But I thought you'd want to know that O'Bannon has responded publicly to the gay-bashing in DC yesterday."

Donna blinked absently. "Gay-bashing?"

"Uh, you know," Bijal explained awkwardly, "the two men who were beaten downtown last night?" Neither Janet nor Donna showed a glimmer of recognition, so Bijal continued. "One was killed? The other's in critical condition?"

Janet finally mustered an expression, and it was apparently confusion. "I must have missed that story."

Bijal was now officially livid. "Um...okay." Did the two of them just sit in the office telling ghost stories and making s'mores all day while everyone else in the office actually worked? How did they both miss such a major local news story? The national press had even run it that morning.

"Did O'Bannon decide to have a big gay press conference?" Donna asked sarcastically. "That can only help us."

"No," Bijal replied curtly. "But the media approached her for a statement since she's both openly gay and a co-sponsor of the hate-crimes bill. I sent you both a link to the story with her full response."

"Great," Janet said brightly. "Thanks." Neither made a move to look at Janet's computer.

A very awkward silence ensued as Bijal became more incredulous that she was apparently the only person in the room who cared about this development. "Because the press may want to get your response as well," she suggested, trying to help them understand. More silence. "Since you're her opponent...and this has become a very visible issue."

"Maybe we could get some free airtime out of this," Janet suggested to Donna.

Donna shook her head rapidly. "We don't want to touch this with a ten-foot pole, Janet. Let's let this pitch go by and we'll swing at the next one. Roo, if anyone calls for a statement on this, we have no comment. Let everyone know."

"You don't think we should prepare *anything*?" Bijal asked, no longer caring that her annoyance was patently audible in her voice.

Janet cocked her head slightly. "What are you thinking, Bijal? Do you have an idea?"

"It's important as a mayor of a small town for you to shift more inside the Beltway."

"What the hell does that mean?" Donna asked, her nose wrinkled in disgust.

"It means that it's more important for Janet to be seen as out front on issues that are national, and even more so on issues within DC—which, incidentally, isn't that far from District 12."

Janet scowled. "Hmm."

"But there's no way to win on this issue, Roo. If we come out as even remotely pro-gay or pro-hate-crime legislation, we risk losing the right."

Bijal suddenly pictured the large Hitler dildo Fran had described. "I don't believe that."

Donna looked stunned. "You what?"

"We need to be appealing to the moderates, not the social conservatives. O'Bannon's already put herself out there as extremely progressive. No matter where you stand on most issues, you'll be to the right of her. We can make real ground by focusing on those in the middle."

"Good point," Janet said absently.

"So if you believe polls and statistics regarding hate crimes, most voters agree with O'Bannon. It's a win/win situation for us to make a public statement. We need to start siphoning voters away from her."

"Right," Janet replied with a nod, sounding only slightly more certain than she had the second before.

Donna glowered. "Okay, Roo. You've given your two cents. Thank you."

"Sure, and it's *Rao*." Bijal refused to break eye contact with her until the door was shut between them.

❖

Bijal seethed for nearly two hours about what a horrendous, incompetent bitch Donna was. Only when the phone on the desk to her right rang did she allow herself to stop visualizing Donna's evisceration.

"No, the mayor has no comment on that," her officemate Kristin was saying to whoever had called. Her face suddenly registered shock, then twisted up. "What? Could you please repeat that? No, she has no comment on that either. No, sorry." Kristin hung up, but her mouth hung open.

"What is it?" Bijal asked.

"That was the *Herald*," Kristin replied, her eyes wide with panic. "They wanted the mayor's response to her husband's comments on hate crimes."

"What?" Bijal shouted the question so loudly that the other half dozen staffers hustled over to her desk in time to see her do an Internet news search on "Reverend Denton." To her horror, an article appeared, as though to taunt her—"Congressional Candidate's Husband Denounces Victims of Gay Bashing." "Oh, shit. Someone go get the mayor."

After some coaxing, both Janet and Donna emerged from the mayor's office, eating Chinese food from the cartons.

"What is it?" Donna asked, her mouth full of lo mein.

Bijal read directly from the Web article.

> Reverend Albert Denton, minister and husband of congressional hopeful Mayor Janet Denton, stated today that the two victims of an assault outside a District of Columbia gay bar last night that left one of the two dead were "inviting that kind of aggressive response" by "defiantly embracing sin."
>
> Rev. Denton, who went on to say that neither he nor his wife "support the gay lifestyle" or any legislation that would "give special rights to people who brazenly engage in immoral behavior," was asked to respond to public statements made by his wife's opponent Rep. Colleen O'Bannon.
>
> O'Bannon is one of only a handful of openly gay members of Congress and is a co-sponsor of a recently passed anti-hate-crime law. Earlier today, O'Bannon told the press that a government that "allows hate crimes to continue without penalty is complicit every time an act of violent discrimination occurs. In a country that boasts 'liberty and justice for all,' we now send a clear message we won't tolerate persecution of anyone. I hope the perpetrators of such a reprehensible act are quickly found and prosecuted fully."
>
> O'Bannon's opponent, Janet Denton, currently mayor of Ravensdale, VA, was not available for comment via her

campaign spokesperson. However, her husband readily responded to press inquiries regarding both the recent crime, as well as the related O'Bannon-Croft hate crimes legislation.

Rep. O'Bannon, contacted with Rev. Denton's statements, said, "While I have no interest in starting a feud with either Mayor Denton or her husband, I'm horrified that anyone would imply that two people walking down a sidewalk somehow 'invited' a brutal beating and murder. That kind of bigoted and incendiary rhetoric is precisely the problem, and frankly, it's an outrage."

Bijal spun around in her chair and scowled at Donna.

Janet shook her head. "God damn it, Albert." She looked at Donna apologetically. "I had no idea they'd try to talk to him."

"Bastards," Donna spat.

"So now what?" Janet asked. "Do we release a statement?"

Donna grumbled loudly. "We'll have to. Roo, pull Albert's comments in their entirety and print me a copy. We'll have to parse his words so it looks like what he said was just taken out of context. Kristin, brew a new pot of coffee. Janet, call your husband right now and tell him that if he utters another syllable to anyone, I'll personally cut his nuts off."

❖

"Hello?"

"Hey, Fran. It's me." Bijal sighed into her cell phone as she got into her car and shut the door. "I got your voice mail."

"Holy shit, girl! What's going on over there? I thought I'd turned on the movie *Footloose*, but instead of John Lithgow preaching about the evils of dancing to bad eighties music in a barn, it turned out it was just your boss's husband on MSNBC. And in case you don't know yet, that jackass is *all over* the blogs."

Bijal rested her forehead on her steering wheel and closed her eyes. "I know, believe me. If they'd just responded to O'Bannon's comments proactively, like I fucking suggested, the press probably wouldn't even have contacted that idiot."

"Wait a second," Fran said, the indignation evident in her voice. "You suggested they respond earlier and they didn't?"

"Yup. Remember when I mentioned how useless our campaign manager is?"

"That does sound familiar. Well, I hope your foresight got you something."

"Oh, it did—a series of very nasty looks and an extra"—she paused to peer at her watch in the darkness—"two and a half hours at the office trying to do damage control."

"Damn, that sucks. Are you on your way home?"

"Actually, I need you to do me a favor, Fran."

"What?"

"Can you go online and find me a lesbian bar, anything within a forty-mile radius? I've spent a large portion of my day listening to people talk shit about gays, and I need to cleanse myself."

Fran laughed softly. "I hear you. It just so happens that I'm online right now…and you're in luck, sister."

"Thank God! I knew I couldn't be languishing in this fucking Stepford town all alone. What's it called?"

"You're gonna like this—The Klit N' Kaboodle."

CHAPTER FIVE

B ijal had no problems finding The Klit N' Kaboodle because Fran had given her excellent directions. She was surprised to see that the place wasn't small and unassuming, like so many queer establishments tended to be—especially one in such a rural area. Had Bijal been in a better frame of mind, she would have found their neon sign featuring a sassy-looking cat flicking its tail utterly hysterical.

Though the sun had set long ago, it was still far too early for any crowd to have gathered, which was fine with her. She wasn't there to socialize or dance. She was there to have a stiff drink and ponder if she had possibly made a mistake in accepting this job.

Hardwood floors and brass railings made the place seem a bit like an old nautical fish house. The lights had not yet been dimmed, and in the corner DJ equipment sat next to an area that was clearly a dance floor when they got busy. The blue patio string lights draped across the ceiling gave the place a rather charming feel.

She shuffled up to the bar in the center of the establishment— rectangular and surrounded by dark bar stools. Behind the bar was an expansive collection of liquor, overseen by a female bartender, graying and a little paunchy, who was wiping down the glasses with a linen napkin.

Bijal took the seat 180 degrees away from the only other person seated at the bar—a thin, sinewy woman wearing a Western cowboy shirt with mother-of-pearl snaps and a bolo tie. Bijal had no desire to speak to her, or to anyone, for that matter.

The bartender smiled at her and nodded. "What can I get you tonight, honey?"

"Um...do you have a happy-hour special?"

"The specials are right there," the barkeep said, pointing to a small acrylic menu holder several inches to Bijal's right.

"Great," she said, scooping it up and perusing it. "I'll have the... um...hmm." The drink names sounded foreign yet disturbingly familiar. "I'll have the pink twatini."

"Good choice." The bartender grabbed a bottle of vodka haphazardly by the neck.

"And I suppose I'd better get some food, since it's been about nine hours since I've eaten. Do you have a menu?"

"Flip it over, sugar," the bartender said as she prepared the astoundingly X-rated-sounding drink.

Bijal's weary brain didn't immediately know how to process the instructions, but the right synapse suddenly fired and she flipped the drink menu over to study the bar food. The last thing she needed was to be too drunk to drive home on a Thursday night.

As she scanned the modest selection of cuisine that fell under the heading Cunt-ry Cooking, she was struck by the same issue she had with the drink specials. "Hey, um, can I ask you a question?"

The bartender set down a very pink-colored drink in a traditional martini glass, garnished with a maraschino cherry with the stem tied into a knot. "The name's Sue," she said with a flirty smile. "And, sorry, but I'm taken."

"Good to know, but I actually wanted to ask you about the names on your menu."

"Oh, that," Sue replied, crossing her arms. "Here's how I see it. I'm getting pretty goddamn tired of women, especially lesbians, being called nasty names and made to feel like we're somehow not as good as other folks. So in the way the African Americans have reclaimed the N-word to take away its power over them, I'm doing the same thing... in my own little way."

Bijal blinked a couple times and reassessed the bill of fare. "Okay, I understand the muffaletta—that makes perfect sense. So do the fried clams. But what's a 'blooming pussy'?"

"It's a deep-fried Vidalia onion with special dipping sauce."

"Special *vaginal* dipping sauce?" Bijal asked, completely amazed that she was having this conversation.

Sue put her hands up playfully. "Hey, what you do with your nosh is completely up to you. We don't judge here."

"Clearly. And what exactly is 'areola pie'?"

"Taken literally, it's the best of both worlds. In this context, though, it tastes a lot like pecan pie."

"Uh-huh," Bijal muttered. Sue was very possibly totally fucking insane. When Bijal unintentionally caught the eye of the brawny cowdyke across the bar—who then nodded at her and smiled—she quickly directed her attention back to the menu, hoping that would effectively send a leave-me-alone message. "Then I'll forgo the 'dick-free oyster platter,' which is…kind of confusing. I mean, I'd hope that *everything* is dick-free. I'll just get a basket of the 'faggity-ass french fries.'"

"You're in luck," Sue said, keying the order into the register. "We just put new grease in the fryer."

"Today?" Bijal asked.

"Well, no. Not today, but recently. In the last month."

Bijal couldn't contain her frustration any longer. "Wow, and to think that just this morning when I accidentally spat toothpaste into my hair, I thought that meant I would have a *bad* day."

"Things are looking up." Sue was apparently oblivious to the sarcasm.

Bijal exhaled loudly and blew her hair out her eyes. Remembering why she'd stopped here, she tasted her twatini, which was actually pretty good. She took another sip and closed her eyes. To her chagrin, when she opened them again, the brawny cowdyke picked up her mug of beer and sauntered toward her.

Could this day get any worse? Would her brazenly gay fries perhaps come with a side of labia remoulade and pickled clitoris?

"Hello, beautiful," the brawny cowdyke said in a voice that sounded like she gargled with ground glass in her free time. Remarkably, somehow Bijal had expected her to sound like that.

"Hello," she answered flatly, not even trying to hide her lack of enthusiasm.

"I'm Flayme. Flayme Coverdale."

"Hi," Bijal said, purposely withholding her own name. She stared back at her drink and tried to figure out what she had done that she was now paying so dearly for. Was it that lost night in Manhattan?

"You've never heard of me?" Flayme asked, seeming genuinely surprised.

"Are you the lead singer of Whitesnake?"

Flayme looked confused. "So you're not here for the signing?"

"Someone plans to interpret this conversation for the hearing impaired? Can we just tell them not to bother?"

"*Christ*, but you're sassy," Flayme rasped with a grin. "It complements your hotness nicely."

Bijal stared at her, unimpressed. "Does this usually work for you?"

"What?"

"This carpet bombing of flattery and flirtation."

Flayme leered and the left corner of her mouth rose. "I'm an author, and I'm here to sign some of my books. I thought you might be here for that, given the early hour, but I hadn't factored in that you might just be a hardcore alcoholic."

"We're a much maligned minority, the hardcore alcoholics," Bijal said, lifting her glass in salute. "Cheers." She allowed the fruity beverage to slide coolly down her throat. A quick glance showed that Flayme was still staring at her. "So what have you written? Anything I might know?"

"Well, right now I'm promoting my new lesbian romance *You Fist My Heart*."

Had she called it a romance? "Wow, that *does* sound romantic," Bijal said in a deadpan voice. "You could have gone with *You Heart My Fist*, but I guess that just wouldn't pack the same wallop, huh? No pun intended with the word 'pack.'" She took another sip of her drink and prayed for tipsiness.

"It's a tearjerker," Flayme explained.

"Sounds like it could be if you're not relaxed enough, yeah."

"This may come off like a line, but your flippancy and indifference really turn me on."

Bijal propped her chin on her fist. "Something tells me that if I kicked you in the back of the head, that might turn you on too."

"Baby, you can read me like a book."

"A book with the word 'fist' in the title?"

Flayme gave what Bijal assumed was her best come-hither look. "I won't lie. I like to get a little freaky."

"Quite frankly, I'm shocked," Bijal replied sarcastically.

"Hold on for a moment." Flayme walked back over to the opposite side of the bar and returned with a small cardboard box full of paperbacks. She grabbed a copy and handed it to Bijal. "This is for you, sweetie. I want to do pages seventy-three to seventy-five with you." She winked brazenly.

Bijal was caught somewhere between horrified and curious. She had to admit, this was at least a new approach. She took the book, which had a rather angry-looking fist on the cover bursting violently through a pink papier-mâché heart, and opened it to page seventy-three. "Wow…which one of us brings the bowling pin?"

"I have one." Flayme sounded smug.

"I had a sneaking feeling that you just might. My God! Is this part about the cantaloupe even possible?"

"Would you like to find out?"

"You know, I'd have to say that by design the vagina is plenty sticky on its own without shoving various fruits up there."

"Hear, hear," came a voice from behind her.

Bijal turned to see who agreed with her and gasped when none other then Colleen O'Bannon pulled up the bar stool to her right. She was instantly overcome with nausea.

"Hi, Bijal," Colleen said with a smile.

"Fuck," Bijal breathed, the lone syllable protracted for several seconds in her nervousness. "Is it possible for us to ever meet under respectable circumstances?"

"Ooh, *Bijal*," Flayme repeated. "That's a great name. Mind if I use it?"

"I think I might, yes."

Flayme's sexual interest in Bijal seemed to utterly dissolve at that very instant, and her eyes narrowed as she scrutinized both Colleen and Bijal—perhaps trying to deduce the nature of their relationship. She extended her hand across the corner of the bar to Colleen. "Hi, I'm—"

"Flayme Coverdale," Colleen said, shaking her hand enthusiastically. "You wrote *Leaving the Handprint of Love: Spanking Stories for Very Naughty Girls*."

Bijal stared, catatonic—unable to move anything except her eyelids.

"Always nice to meet a fan," Flayme said through an alabaster grin. "Would you like an autographed book?"

"I'd love one," Colleen replied.

Flayme snatched back the book she'd given Bijal and picked up a pen, which she clicked with great flourish. "Who am I making this out to?"

Colleen began spelling it for her. "S-p-y-x-i-e. It's pronounced 'spicy.' Spyxie Sugarbottom."

"That's a very sexy name," Flayme said as she scrawled feverishly across the cover page.

Bijal was still agog. "Wow, naughty, spicy, *and* sexy."

"I have many layers," Colleen said, with the slightest hint of a smirk.

A group of four women walked in, clutching books to their chests and looking very eager. It was apparent they were here for Flayme.

Bijal glanced back to Colleen, noting how her appearance had changed now that she was wearing more casual clothes. In faded low-rise jeans, a crisp purple blouse, and a buttery-soft-looking leather jacket, she was absolutely stunning.

"Here you go, Ms. Sugarbottom," Flayme said, handing over the paperback but not releasing it right away.

"Thanks. What do I owe you?" Colleen asked.

"Nothing, sweetheart, but I did add my phone number. If you're feeling appreciative later, give me a call." Flayme turned and nodded at her fans, who were milling around a table in the corner with copies of her other titles. "Sorry, ladies, but the throng awaits." She stood, picked up her box of books, and moseyed away.

Bijal tried to read the inscription but couldn't without leaning into Colleen's space. "What's it say?"

"'To Spyxie. When you get tired of the sarcasm and disdain and are ready for a night you'll never forget, call me.' Then she put her number. Do you think she's referring to you?"

The humor in Colleen's voice somehow helped Bijal feel more at ease. "Yes, but I'd just like to go on record that before *you* sat down, she said my sarcasm was a turn-on."

"I didn't…interrupt something, did I?"

"Just an unwelcome sexual advance. You're a fan of hers?"

Colleen began flipping through the book. "No, I'd never heard of her before."

"So you just happened to know all about the happy red handprint of love, or whatever it was? Who do you think you're fooling?" She took a large swig of her drink.

"It's on the poster on the front door. I saw it when I got here," Colleen said discreetly. "And, come on, that's a pretty unusual title."

Bijal grinned. "Please tell me that Spyxie Sugarbottom is your chat-room name."

"If only. But it sounded like she was looking for a provocative one."

"More like a pornographic one. I hope you won't be upset if that's the name of the protagonist in her next book, *Up to Her Elbow: Reaching for Love*."

Colleen's mouth curved in amusement. "Is that the sequel to *I've Had You Up to Here*?"

"Maybe so."

"No worries. Perhaps I gave her something she could use."

"So it was just political subterfuge?"

"It's really more an attention to detail, though I prefer the term 'sorcery.' It sounds more mysterious." Suddenly, Colleen stumbled across a passage that changed her expression to one of horror. "Oh, my *God*!"

"Wait till you get to the part with the bowling pin."

Colleen closed the book and pushed it away from her. "Leave it to a lesbian to figure out a way to mix sex with bowling."

Sue reappeared from the kitchen with a basket of fries and set it in front of Bijal. "Here you go, honey. Hey, Col. You want your usual?"

"Please. Ah, I see you're reclaiming your femaleness by ordering from Sue's post-pejorative menu."

Bijal blew on a fry to cool it. "Do I ask for ketchup or menstrual relish?"

Sue chuckled. "I'll bring you a bottle of Heinz and a maxi pad. Do you two know each other?"

"We do, yes. Sue, this is Bijal Rao. She's in the business."

Bijal was impressed that Colleen remembered her full name, then dismissed it as more sorcery.

"Aw, that's a shame," Sue said, setting a glass of something amber-colored in front of Colleen. "You seemed like a nice kid."

"I used to be," Bijal replied dejectedly as she ran her finger along the rim of her martini glass.

Sue leaned on the bar. "Have you had to sell your soul, sweetie?"

"Not such a good day, huh?" Colleen asked.

Bijal scoffed. "Noticed that, did you?"

"Maybe," Colleen said, reaching into a paper bag beside her and retrieving two liquor bottles. "But perhaps this will help."

Sue looked ecstatic. "You brought them!"

"Of course I did," Colleen said. "I keep my campaign promises."

Bijal looked at the labels curiously. "What are they?"

"Last week, I was telling Sue that the whiskeys she stocks are complete crap," Colleen explained.

"Even though I carry Arc of Orion," Sue said defensively.

Colleen shook her head. "But your well drinks all taste like paint thinner. Orion is your only top-shelf brand, which isn't much in the way of variety."

"You're insufferable, Colleen—and you always have been."

Bijal considered Sue's words. It was clear these women were close and had been for a while. Were they romantically involved? Sue had, after all, already mentioned that she was "taken."

"So I agreed to bring Sue some of Orion's other products so she can taste the difference for herself. Are you game, Bijal?" Colleen asked.

"I'm not sure. I don't know much about whiskey."

Colleen glanced at the remainder of the pink twatini in Bijal's hand. "What's your usual drink of choice?"

"Um…anything served with a tiny umbrella, a plastic monkey, or a swizzle stick shaped like a naked woman."

"Sounds *fancy*," Colleen said jokingly.

"I'm a woman of modest means and tastes," Bijal replied.

"As are most of the women who come into the K and K," Sue added. "Which is what I was telling Colleen the last time she brought this up."

"I'm not suggesting that you stop carrying economical brands, just that you give the patrons a few more options. Let's have a few shot glasses, Sue, and a bottle of your crappy stuff. We'll have a little Whiskey 101."

"Okay," Bijal said with a shrug. Why did the thought of Colleen and Sue together bother her so much? Was she stupid enough to want a little fling with her opponent? As she watched Colleen open the bottles and pour three small shots for Sue and three for her, with eyes strikingly green and hands strong and capable-looking, Bijal decided that yes, she was indeed that stupid—perhaps even more so.

"All right, ladies," Colleen said. "Before we start, there are three aspects of tasting to consider. The first is the nose, or aroma of the liquor. Before it ever hits your lips, don't just sniff it for the overall scent. Rather, close your eyes and try to pick out different fragrances. You might smell things like different spices, herbs, or fruits."

Bijal and Sue each reached for the glass on her far left and brought it near enough to investigate its scent.

"Shit!" Sue coughed. "I think I burned my nostrils!"

Colleen chuckled. "Don't inhale it, Sue. Just breathe in."

"I smell petroleum," Bijal said. "And asphalt," she added before setting it down.

"Hmm," Colleen murmured. "Okay. So the next thing is the palate, which is what you get when you initially take a sip. After that, you get the finish—the flavor that comes after you've swallowed, like a second, smaller taste. Go ahead and take small sips of the one you've smelled."

They both drank and paused before Sue said, "Varnish with sort of an old tube-sock finish."

Bijal slammed her empty shot glass on the bar dramatically. "I second the varnish, but to me, the finish was more like airplane glue."

"Nice," Colleen said. "That was your trusty well liquor, Sue."

"Oh."

"Now try the glass in the middle. That's Arc of Orion's Single Barrel Ten-Year-Old Bourbon."

As they had before, Sue and Bijal closed their eyes and inhaled. But Colleen had been right that this was a far more complex smell.

"Um, caramel?" Bijal asked.

"Very good," Colleen replied. "What else do you smell?"

"There's kind of a fruity scent," Sue added.

Colleen nodded. "Yup, some say apricot. You may also get leather and spice."

"Yeah, I get the spice," Bijal said. "Can we taste?" Colleen nodded, so they both sampled the bourbon. The disparity from the last glass of swill went well beyond the nose, that was certain. "Wow, I got sort of a nutmeg and wood flavor."

"That's the oak casks it's aged in," Colleen said.

"Yeah, exactly," Sue said. "And a finish that was like a sort of vanilla heat."

"Right," Bijal said excitedly.

Colleen appeared pleased with their responses. "The last one is our small batch reserve. We call it Betelgeuse."

"After that weird movie with Michael Keaton?" Sue asked, breathing in her final sample.

Bijal laughed, perhaps louder than she should have. "It's probably named after the *star* Betelgeuse, which, if memory serves, is in the constellation Orion, right?"

"Correct," Colleen replied. "You get bonus points."

"Wait," Sue said mockingly. "Don't I get any points for knowing the movie starred Michael Keaton?"

"Only if you can somehow tie it in with bourbon or some other whiskey product," Colleen said with a cocked eyebrow.

Sue stopped and thought for a second. "Well, that movie made me want to drink," she explained weakly.

Colleen and Bijal looked at each other and laughed. "Sorry," Colleen said. "Nice try, though. So what do you get on the nose of this one?"

"I get apple and vanilla," Bijal said.

"Totally," Sue said. "But oaky."

"You guys are getting really good at this."

After tasting the final whiskey, Bijal found she liked this one the best by far. "Ooh, there's clove."

"And something kind of sweet," Sue said. "Like molasses or honey."

Bijal nodded. "And the finish is like a toasted…nutty flavor." She finished it off. "This stuff kicks ass."

"So am I hearing that you'll carry more top-shelf brands?" Colleen asked.

"All right, all right." Sue sighed. "I'll carry your snobby, highbrow, artsy-ass booze."

"Good," Bijal replied. "Then can I have some more of the Winona Ryder reserve?" She extended her glass, and Colleen filled it generously.

Sue cleared away the remaining empty glasses. "So, Bijal, do you work on Capitol Hill?"

"No, I'm a campaign worker."

"Yeah? Whose campaign? Anyone I might know?"

Bijal noticed that Colleen was now fiddling with her cell phone, blatantly disengaged from the conversation. "Mayor Denton," she replied softly.

Sue moved closer. "I'm sorry, who?"

"Mayor Denton."

Sue immediately fell into hysterics. "Shut your cheeky muffin hole!"

"I should go," Bijal said, feeling instantly self-conscious again. She slammed back her whiskey and set the glass on the bar.

Colleen set her hand on top of Bijal's before she could push away from the bar. "I'm not here to chase you out, so how about this? Let's just not talk about anything remotely strategic—nothing about the campaign that could even be interpreted as sensitive."

"Okay," Bijal replied skeptically.

"And if one of us says something unintentionally, the other will politely stop the conversation and disregard whatever it was."

"You think we can do that?"

Colleen smiled. "Well, if not, I'll have to stop talking to you. And, so far, I was kind of having fun."

"I suppose I'm willing to try if you are."

Sue was still softly chuckling to herself. "This is going to be awesome," she said before crossing to the other side of the bar to take someone's order.

"So, may I?" Bijal asked, pointing to her empty glass.

"Certainly." Colleen pushed the bottle over to her. "Do you mind if I ask you a personal question?"

Bijal filled the shot glass again. "If I get to ask you one too."

"That's fair, I suppose. Are you out at work?"

"That depends on if you're one of those gays who thinks it's her duty to out everyone."

Colleen shook her head. "Nope, this is all off the record."

"As in, do they know that while my candidate's husband is spewing hate speech about gays, I'm secretly hoping he's struck by lightning? I don't think they have a fucking clue."

"That must be really challenging."

"It is, in a way," Bijal said. "But I'm not defined solely by my sexuality, just like I'm not defined by being a woman, or Indian, or a Capricorn."

"Good point."

"You know, I've never agreed with any candidate on a hundred percent of the issues."

Colleen sipped her drink. "But isn't equal rights a pretty major issue to compromise on?"

"*All* issues are important. I can't cherry-pick. And it can't be much easier for you. Being out in Washington makes you a very conspicuous target."

"Yes, but I couldn't have done it another way. I refused to run for office while trying to keep it a secret."

"Too many people already knew?"

Colleen's eyebrows furrowed for a moment. "Well, that, but, more importantly, I would have been sending a message that I was ashamed of who I am. And I'm not. My entire campaign message was that no one deserves to be marginalized."

Bijal watched Colleen's middle finger as it lazily traced the rim of her glass. "So do I get my personal question now?"

"Sure."

"Are you and Sue...wait...let me reword that."

"Just so you know, I'm not a genie. It doesn't need to be worded in a precise way or something horrific will happen to you."

Bijal thought back to Fran's earlier question for the congresswoman. "Are you single?"

Chapter Six

Colleen smiled as she held eye contact with Bijal. "I am, as a matter of fact. Sue and I are just old friends. We went to high school together."

"That's nice," Bijal replied, the relief that this fascinating and sexy woman was unattached warring internally with her common sense.

"It is, yeah. She's done a lot to organize the statewide LGBT community not to just be more politically active, but to work on both my campaigns. They've been very supportive, and their involvement has proved invaluable."

"So, do you date?" Bijal asked, feeling emboldened by her deepening connection with Colleen. Heat surged through her, and while she wasn't exactly sure just how much the alcohol had prompted, she was determined to do a little research on the issue.

"I date, I just haven't recently."

"Do you think your election could handle that?"

Colleen's gaze traveled up to the ceiling for a moment. "Are you implying that I'm a more palatable lesbian when I'm single?"

"Exactly," Bijal said, pouring herself another whiskey. "You're kind of like an unloaded gun—an antique one with a fancy pearl handle."

"Should I stop this simile before you start speculating on how I might feel in your hand?"

"No, I mean everyone knows how a gun works, what it does. And as long as there aren't any bullets in it, even someone who doesn't like guns can admire one without feeling threatened."

"While that may be, I'm firmly opposed to pretending or hiding something to get votes. I'm more the open-book type."

Bijal took another sip of her drink. "You must drive your campaign staff crazy."

"I think they appreciate my frankness," Colleen said, putting her chin in her hand.

"You don't constantly decline their ideas and tactics?"

"My staff understands that I have a philosophy of no pandering. I'm not capable of it, even if I wanted to—which I don't. So when you stop and look at it *that* way, I'm refreshingly reliable in my opinions. It makes strategy sessions much shorter and keeps the flip-flopping to a minimum."

"Yeah, believe me, I know. I've dug through your record with a microscope."

"See?" Colleen asked. "If I'm pissing y'all off, I must be doing something right. But we should probably stop talking about this."

Bijal felt a small pang of guilt for crossing over the agreed-upon threshold of what they could discuss. "You know, it's infuriating how likable you are."

Colleen sipped on her straw. "Would it make it easier for you if I was a violent bitch?"

"I'm not sure. Would you leave the red handprint of love?" Bijal punctuated the question with her best attempt at a leer.

Colleen covered her mouth with her hand in what appeared to be a polite attempt to hide her amusement. "I hope you didn't drive here. You took a cab, right?"

"No, I drove," she replied, finishing her drink. "Why?"

"You may be just a *little* tipsy."

"Yeah, I probably should have eaten more of my faggity-ass fries." Just saying the words cracked Bijal up, and she giggled for several seconds while Colleen simply watched. "It's all right. I'll just call my roommate. She'll come get me."

Removing her cell phone from her pocket, she dialed her home number and was frustrated when she got their voice mail. "Hey, Fran. It's Bijal, and I'm sitting here at the bar with none other than my opponent, who has been very commodious…um, wait. I don't think that's the right word. Anyway, I need a ride home, so spit out that snatch and come and get me." With that, she closed her phone and slipped it back into her pocket.

"Well," Colleen said with a smile. "How can she refuse a sweet, helpless request like that?"

Bijal continued laughing. "Was that rude of me?"

"Only if she actually listens to that voice mail while she's servicing someone. In which case, I think she'd have you beat in the rudeness department."

"Oh, good point."

"Do you live nearby?" Colleen asked.

"No, I live in DC."

"How about I give you a ride?"

Bijal considered the offer. "But I called Fran."

"But you didn't reach her. What if her phone is off? Or the battery is dead? Come on, I can't leave you all the way out here. It'll take her at least forty-five minutes just to drive out here, and just as long to get back."

Bijal was warming to the thought of being alone with Colleen in a car for an hour or so. "Well, if you don't mind."

"Not at all. It's partially my fault that you drank so much, so it's only right."

Bijal stared at her for a moment. "You're so fucking fair, it's just wrong."

"Maybe I'll make that my e-mail auto-signature," Colleen said, standing and removing two twenty-dollar bills from her pocket and tossing them on the counter. "Hey, Sue, she needs to leave her car here, okay?"

Sue approached them slowly with a smirk. "Sure thing. What kind of car is it, sweetie?"

"A blue Subaru." Bijal stood up and realized she was a little less sure on her feet than she'd expected. "Um, what do I owe?"

"It's all taken care of," Colleen replied.

"Wait, that's not right. I can't let you pay for me."

"You can buy the faggity-ass food next time, okay?"

Bijal started to nod, then stopped suddenly. "Wait, are you okay to drive?"

"Yeah, I've been drinking iced tea."

"You two have a good night," Sue said, clearing the counter. "And don't forget this." She held out the autographed copy of *You Fist My Heart.*

Colleen snatched the paperback from her with a grin. "Thanks, Sue. See you next week."

Sue waved. "G'night."

Bijal followed Colleen outside, past a small group of women smoking, and started scanning the parked vehicles to see if she could pick out which one was Colleen's. Not seeing anything particularly unusual, she turned back and saw Colleen undoing the bungee cord on the back of a sleek silver motorcycle. "That isn't yours, is it?"

Colleen was unfastening two helmets secured there. "You think you'll be able to hang on?"

Bijal's fuzzy brain couldn't process much beyond the image of riding behind Colleen, plastered to the back of her like a hot towel. Suddenly, as though God himself had intervened, her cell phone rang. Still operating on autopilot, she pulled out the phone, opened it, and hit the Speaker button. "Hello?"

"Bijal?" She instantly recognized Fran's voice as it boomed into the night air. "Are you telling me that you're with that hot piece of congressional ass, and you didn't immediately call and invite me out there so I could throw myself at her and try to dry-hump her on the dance floor?"

"Uh..." Bijal felt like her mind was processing a million pieces of information simultaneously, yet she was still unable to form a single word for a coherent response.

"Now hold on," Fran continued, her voice blaring across the parking lot. "Can you not speak because your mouth is full of—"

"Ahh!" Bijal snapped the phone shut in a fit of panic. "I...think we got disconnected," she explained weakly.

Colleen was looking at her with what seemed to be a mixture of amusement and pity. "Maybe you should call her back and tell her that you have a ride home. But don't talk to her on speakerphone this time."

"Right." Bijal moved several paces away and dialed. "Fran? Yeah, sorry. No, I'm getting a ride home. Uh-huh. No. No. No! I'm hanging up. Here I go. Bye, Fran. Bye. Bye!" She closed the phone again and slipped it into her pocket. Before she could fabricate what would undoubtedly be a ludicrous explanation, she shifted her gaze to Colleen astride the motorcycle. Her leather jacket was now zipped up, and she had on her helmet and a pair of black gloves. She looked exceptionally sexy. "Oh, dear Lord."

Colleen held out the other helmet. "Are you ready?"

"More than you know," Bijal muttered, taking it from her and studying it. The sound of the bike starting up startled her enough to make her jump.

"Hop on."

Bijal put the helmet on and began fiddling with the chin strap. "Just give me a second to get my pants off."

"What did you say? I didn't catch that."

"I have no idea. So just climb on back here?"

"Yup, and hang on."

Bijal slipped into the seat behind Colleen and put her feet on the rear pegs. The vibration of the motor was disturbingly stimulating. "Um, hang on to what?"

"Me. Hold on to my waist. I don't want to leave you behind on the pavement." Slowly, Colleen began backing the bike out of the parking lot as Bijal tentatively slid her arms around Colleen's midsection.

"Is this okay?"

Colleen laughed. "Just keep it above the waist."

"I'll do my best. You know, this is a great jacket. It's so soft." Bijal caressed the leather like a long-lost lover.

"Keep that up and it'll have some good things to say about you too." Colleen opened the throttle and the bike took off.

Much to Bijal's chagrin, the helmets coupled with the engine noise made conversation very challenging. She was able to give Colleen directions, but any additional small talk was out of the question, and Bijal had been looking forward to a little more playful discourse.

But she hadn't been prepared for the sensation of flying through the evening on a motorcycle, which was absolutely exhilarating. With the wind whipping her face, she sobered up soon, though she was still enjoying hanging on to Colleen, perhaps a little too much. Colleen felt solid, and while Bijal had anticipated some awkwardness in their forced intimacy, a surprising ease replaced it very quickly.

Of course, none of this diminished the carnal sensations induced from the pulsing motor between her legs. The feel of her breasts rubbing on Colleen's back was beyond arousing. She tried to focus on enjoying the ride, but her libido frequently pushed her mind back to a ride of a very different nature. By the time they pulled up outside Bijal's apartment, she was relieved that she could now simply take a cold shower and the battle would be over.

Colleen shut off the bike as Bijal stepped onto the sidewalk and started to undo the chin strap on her helmet.

"So, would you like to come up?"

"I'd better not. What would your roommate think?"

Bijal pulled her helmet off. "Before or after she tries to dry-hump you? I mean, she's a big fan of yours—she's a Democrat."

The corner of Colleen's mouth rose slightly. "Yeah, we Democrats are big dry-humpers. It's in our blood."

Bijal bit her lower lip. "I'm sorry. That was so badly worded."

"Maybe a little."

"Well, thanks so much for the ride."

"Anytime," Colleen said.

"Do you go to Sue's bar regularly?"

"Bijal, we probably shouldn't do this."

"Chat in the street?" Bijal looked around uneasily. "I know it looks like a sketchy part of town—"

"No, I mean the other 'this'—flirt, get involved with each other. At least while this election is going on."

"Is that what we were doing?"

"Well, that's what my jacket thinks." Colleen's voice softened. "Look, I really like you. You're becoming one of my favorite Republicans."

Bijal felt herself blushing and couldn't remember the last time that had happened. "I'm flattered."

"You and Teddy Roosevelt are my short list, though you're far cuter."

"Um, thanks."

"Well, he had an adorably pert nose," Colleen said.

"With all due respect to Teddy, I think I have the better ass."

Colleen chuckled but her eyes quickly raked over Bijal, causing a quiet moment of heat between them. "I thoroughly agree."

"So what were you saying before you stopped to ogle my ass?"

Colleen snapped back into the conversation. "Oh, right. I was saying that if we saw each other before the election ended—even if we promised not to talk about politics—it would still be a problem."

"Ethics are so goddamn inconvenient."

"Which is precisely why so many politicians choose to ignore them."

Bijal handed the helmet back. "I guess I'll see you around, then."

Colleen took it and secured it to the back of the bike. "Yeah, I have a feeling you will. I'd tell you that tomorrow will be better for your campaign, but that'd be bad for me." The smile she flashed made Bijal's breath catch.

"Thanks anyway."

Colleen started the motorcycle. "Good night."

"G'night," Bijal answered, giving a quick wave and heading up the steps. As she unlocked her apartment door, she heard Colleen riding away.

Fran walked out of the kitchen with a tall glass of orange juice in one hand and a bottle of Evian in the other. "I just want you to know how disappointed I am in you," she said, passing the water to Bijal.

Bijal opened the bottle and drank as she flopped onto the sofa. "I know. I didn't intend to flirt with her. I've completely compromised my integrity."

"No, I mean I can't believe you just let her bring you here and drop you off. I'd have given her directions to the Sheraton and asked her to walk me to my room." She sat down next to Bijal and crossed her legs.

"Subtle, Fran. Were you watching out the window?"

"Hell, yeah. So are you going to sit there and tell me that you didn't find her and that motorcycle hot?"

Bijal laughed. "Oh, my God! She's so sexy it's ridiculous. She may be one of the hottest women I've ever met. My whole body is throbbing."

"Ooh, there we go. Tell me all about it."

"She's so confident and smart. She started teaching me about whiskey and bourbon, and I could only stare at her mouth while she was talking."

"Hmm, and is that how you ended up too drunk to drive? Or did you just pretend so you'd have to catch a ride on her pulsing pelvic torpedo?"

"There was no pretending, though I am feeling strangely thankful that I drank too much."

Fran brushed the hair off her forehead. "So have you decided to quit your job?"

"What? Why would I do that?"

"Because you want to fuck your opponent, and honestly, that's the first thing you've done in the last two years that I completely understand."

Bijal slowly absorbed the words and turned them over in her mind. "Look, I have no intention of quitting just because I think Colleen is attractive or because I like her as a person. There's personal and there's political, and those two things can and should be separate."

"So you honestly think you can actively work for a candidate with an ass clown for a campaign manager, while secretly banging the opposition?"

"There was no banging...just a little jacket fondling."

Fran cocked an eyebrow. "Was she *wearing* it while you fondled it?"

Bijal nodded, then put her face in her hands. "I'm going to take a shower."

"I'll just bet you are."

Bijal stood and yawned. "And if you're nice, when I get out I'll tell you about the author I met tonight at the bar who hit on me."

"No shit? What was her name?"

"Um, I think it was Spanky McFisterson."

"Nice."

CHAPTER SEVEN

Bijal stepped out of the taxicab in The Klit N' Kaboodle parking lot and was happy to see her car waiting patiently for her. Contrary to her fears from the night before, she had no signs of a hangover and was feeling surprisingly good.

Perhaps she'd been right that she had just needed to blow off a little steam. Though it would have been even better if she'd ended her evening rolling around naked with a certain hot congresswoman, she was still riding the remnants of the adrenaline rush from their flirting, coupled with the intimate ride home.

As she unlocked her car door, she saw a piece of paper jammed under the windshield wiper blade.

"If that's a parking ticket, I'm going ballistic." She slid it out and unfolded a piece of notebook paper that sported handwriting she didn't recognize.

Bijal~

I enjoyed chatting with you last night a great deal, and I hope we can do it again sometime. You never know when our paths may cross again, after all. If not sooner, perhaps we can plan something in a couple months. (I'm thinking sometime after the first Tuesday in November).

Here's wishing you a better workday today, though obviously not too good.

Take care,

Spyxie

Bijal chuckled as she ran her fingers lightly over the signature before folding the note back up and slipping it into the sun visor. She started the engine and pulled out into the road, headed for work.

It had been nearly a year since Bijal had seriously dated someone, and even longer still since someone had conjured butterflies in her gut the way Colleen did. In the absence of someone who was the irresistible force to her immovable object, she'd dated women she found physically attractive, but unfortunately hadn't experienced any deep personal connection. As a result, nothing more than casual sexual relationships had developed, and she was surprised by the unforeseen pang of loneliness that now came out of nowhere. Had she really been missing something deeper and just hadn't noticed until now?

Perhaps so, because these new feelings seemed somehow foreign and exciting, though of course the least convenient person possible had sparked them. That was so classically Bijal's bad fortune—sort of like being rescued from a burning building by a large razor blade. She laughed softly to herself. The only thing worse than her luck was her penchant for crappy similes.

As she waited for the red light to change, she considered Colleen's offer of a post–Election Day date. True, that was many weeks away, but in the grand scheme of things, it wasn't all that long, she supposed.

Of course, this might be just some elaborate, fucked-up strategy to distract Bijal from properly doing her job. Her stomach sank a little. If Colleen thought that Bijal's heart wasn't completely in this fight, it might be a form of passive sabotage—and perhaps Colleen found that political game more palatable than simply outing Bijal to Janet Denton and the rest of the campaign staff. Mind games, instead of something overt that could be construed as hypocritical.

As Bijal pulled into the parking lot of the mayor's campaign office, she was surprised to see a dozen or so people standing outside with picket signs and a van from the local news affiliate.

"What fresh hell is this?"

Though at first they seemed to be mostly leaning and sitting on the ground, as Bijal parked and turned off her ignition, they all sprang to life and started waving their signs, which read things like "Liberty and justice for ALL," "Civil rights aren't special rights," and "I am NOT a second-class citizen."

"God damn it." Bijal braced herself for this confrontation. And she had nearly sustained a good mood for a few hours too. She leapt out of her car and tried to move briskly past the crowd to the office entrance.

The news crew began filming as the picketers began chanting, "Let us be! Let us be!"

"Excuse me," Bijal said, trying to push her way through the protesters.

"Tell the mayor we want an apology!" a dark-haired woman said, her face twisted in anger.

"From her and her husband," an unseen voice behind her demanded.

Bijal tried to swallow and found it a challenge. "I'll pass that along." She continued her slow progress toward the building.

A blond newscaster shoved a microphone in Bijal's face. "Do you work for the mayor's campaign, ma'am?"

"Um…yes."

"Is Mayor Denton planning to apologize for her husband's remarks?" the reporter asked.

Bijal was starting to feel queasy. "The mayor made a public statement yesterday."

"She didn't apologize for her husband saying that we deserved to be gay-bashed," someone shouted, prompting other members of the crowd to loudly agree.

Bijal's pulse quickened in fear. This couldn't possibly end well. She just needed to get inside without saying anything to anyone. "I'm not authorized to make any formal—"

"We're not subhuman!"

The reporter tried again. "What's the mayor's response to this protest?"

"Just let me—"

"We want to see the mayor!" a protester shouted.

"Yeah, send her out!"

Bijal was close enough to the front door that she could finally touch it. Now if she could just gracefully duck inside without looking like she was fleeing from an angry mob. "Look," she began, casually resting her hand on the handle, "I'll definitely s—"

The office door flew open, cracking Bijal in the left side of her face. "Shit!" she snapped, recoiling and covering her throbbing jaw with her hand.

She looked up to see Donna glaring at her before she leaned in discreetly. "Roo, what are you doing out here? You're not authorized to make any statements."

"I was trying to get to my desk," she hissed back defensively.

"Well, get inside, for Christ's sake, before something regrettable happens."

Bijal's blood was boiling. "I'm pretty sure it's too late for that."

As though sensing the shift in the power dynamic, the blond reporter shoved her microphone at Donna. "Where is Mayor Denton? Will she be addressing this crowd?"

"Mayor Denton isn't here today," Donna said, looking into the camera as though she was trying to seduce it. "She's at a fund-raiser."

"Well, does she plan to respond to this protest?"

Donna chuckled smugly. "Honestly, I don't even think she's aware of it. If I speak to her, I'll let you know what she says."

Bijal couldn't watch any more and, sensing her opportunity, she slunk into the building and headed to her desk. Before she was even able to sit down, Kristin intercepted her. "Holy shit, Bijal! What happened to you?"

"The great diffuser out there hit me with the door. Is it bad?"

Kristin eyed Bijal's jaw and grimaced. "We'd better get something cold on that. Come on." She pulled Bijal into the office kitchen and began tossing some ice cubes from the freezer into a plastic baggie.

"Kristin, how long have those demonstrators been outside? It's eight a.m., for Christ's sake."

"When I got here half an hour ago, they were already here. Channel Nine must have showed up some time after that. As soon as Donna saw the media arrive, she called Janet and told her not to come in."

"What? Where is she?"

"Ooh, this is already starting to swell," Kristin said, lightly applying the ice. "Remember that NRA rally Donna said it wasn't necessary for Janet to attend?"

"Wait, she sent Janet to the NRA rally that we already declined?"

Kristin released the plastic bag to Bijal's firm grasp. "That's exactly what she did."

❖

Colleen hit the Pause button on the remote. "Her," she said, pointing to the television. "That one right there."

Her campaign manager Max crossed his arms as he scrutinized the Denton aide the local news affiliate had cornered on her way into the office. "The one getting clocked in the face? Or the one doing the clocking?"

"The recipient," Colleen said, sitting on the edge of her desk.

Max laughed. "Well, she looked good *before* that blow to the face, sure."

"Stop."

"You said you ran into her at the K and K?"

Colleen nodded. "Uh-huh, but I met her at the shelter dedication in Richmond first."

Max snapped his fingers. "She was the one in the back of the room filming you."

"That's her."

"I have to say, I underestimated Denton. It's a smart move for her to have an openly gay campaign staffer. It doesn't endorse anything, but it implies a tacit tolerance."

Colleen strode behind her desk and sat. "Well, it would if she was actually out."

"Shut up," Max said excitedly. When he saw her expression, his face fell. "You won't let me leak that, will you?"

"Of course not. It's her business, Max. So I don't want it leaving this office. I'm not trying to get her fired or turned into a headline."

He scowled and sat down facing her. "Sometimes I just want to shake you. After Denton's husband spewed his anti-gay diatribe, we could bust them as hypocrites here."

"I know, but I like her too much to do that."

"Denton?"

Colleen laughed and hit Play on the remote. "No, not Denton."

"You mean your hot young Republican there?"

"She is hot, isn't she?"

"I'd say so," he said, watching the rest of the news coverage. "Even though it's completely wrong for us to even be discussing this."

"True."

"Col, are you sure she's not a plant?"

"Like a ficus?"

Max rolled his eyes. "No, not that kind of plant. I mean, are you sure she's not some hired seductress whose sole purpose is to expose to the public the fact that you're a poonhound?"

Colleen paused the DVR again and rested her chin in her hand. "You know, I considered that for a second. Not that I'm in any way admitting to being a poonhound."

"You don't need to convince me. You haven't gone on more than a few dates in the three years I've known you. If you're a poonhound, you're a very bad one."

"Thanks for that, Max. But I don't think she was hired to seduce me. Number one, she admitted that she was doing reconnaissance for Denton while she was hitting on me. I'm ninety-eight percent certain she didn't know who I was."

"Not very smooth." Max propped his feet on Colleen's desk and crossed his ankles. "Though it's possible she's either not a very good seductress...or she's so good that seeming closeted and bungling—"

"Adorably bungling," Colleen added.

"—is all just part of her master plan."

"Aren't you giving the Denton campaign a little too much credit? I haven't seen much evidence of a plan, period, much less a master plan."

He seemed to consider this. "True."

"And don't you think that since I'm already an out lesbian, they'd have a little more to lose if it became known that I was dating one of their female staffers?"

Max's eyes narrowed for an instant. "You've really got it bad for this girl, don't you?"

Colleen contemplated the question. "I love how you like to sum everything up as though it was a Bruce Springsteen song."

"Well, he *is* the boss."

"All I can say at this point with any degree of certainty is that I like her a lot. I find her outrageously sexy, in a brainy, earnest way."

"Uh-huh."

"And so what if I purposely made a couple of wrong turns taking her home last night? It was a nice evening for a bike ride."

"Well, I'll be damned. You *are* a poonhound. Can I assume that you'll be able to keep it in your pants until after Election Day?"

"Come on, Max. Give me a little credit. It's not like I'm a man." She pressed Play again and listened as the network bleeped Bijal's expletive. Her assailant then eyed the camera like it was a lover and blatantly lied her ass off. As Colleen watched the picketers chant, she was suddenly struck by an idea. "Max, do me a favor."

"What?"

"Get one of those mobile lunch trucks to head out there to feed those protesters—on me."

Max beamed. "You're brilliant."

"Let's see if we can make this protest just a little bit bigger. And let them know that Denton's staff is welcome to the food too."

"I'm on it."

❖

Bijal touched her jaw again and flinched. The knot there felt enormous, like the size of a grapefruit. Between that and being generally pissed off, she was finding it difficult to be productive.

"Rao," Donna called from her office. "Come in here, please."

Kristin smiled. "See? She must feel bad about hitting you. She got your name right *and* said please."

Bijal had lost both the ability and the will to craft a pithy reply, so she stood up and shuffled morosely to where she was beckoned.

"Shut the door and have a seat," Donna said. Across from Donna sat Paige, a plump and overly friendly coordinator who was in charge of the volunteers. Bijal had no idea how this day could get any worse, but she felt certain it was about to.

"Paige here tipped me off to something I think we can use against our opponent," Donna said smugly.

"Really?" Bijal was intrigued.

"Yes," Donna replied. "Apparently, O'Bannon's dating some local woman."

"She is?"

Donna cocked an eyebrow. "You look surprised."

"Oh…well, it's just that I looked into that—her personal life—and nothing came up." And the fact that Colleen had told her as much just last night contributed to her bewilderment. What was the other thing she was feeling? Was it disappointment? Perhaps a tinge of jealousy?

"Well, obviously she's been hiding it," Donna said. "I mean, election time isn't exactly the best time to flaunt a lifestyle that the majority of your constituents disapprove of, you know? What we need are some pictures or video to remind people just how uncomfortable it makes them."

Bijal was stunned. "Are you serious?"

"As a fucking heart attack. And guess who's going to tail her?"

"What?" Bijal's quick outburst hurt her jaw, and she protectively brushed it with her fingers.

Donna appeared unmoved. "It's research, Roo. And it's what we pay you for."

Feeling fairly certain that Donna had nothing else she wanted to hear, Bijal turned her attention to Paige, who was still sitting quietly. "Can I ask what this tip was?"

"Well, my sister-in-law went to some book signing last night, and apparently she saw Congresswoman O'Bannon leave with some woman."

Bijal was stunned. "Um…what kind of book signing?"

"Some romance writer or other," Paige replied dismissively. "My sister-in-law is forever complaining that my brother's not romantic enough for her. So I guess she gets what he can't give her somewhere else."

"Clearly," Bijal said softly. It would seem that romance wasn't the only thing he wasn't giving her.

"This is all inconsequential," Donna said, the irritation evident in her voice.

Bijal remained undaunted. "How does she know this woman was O'Bannon's date? Maybe she was a friend or relative."

"Apparently she was outside smoking when they both walked by her. She said she immediately recognized O'Bannon from the news earlier in the day. One of them yelled something about humping the other one's ass and they jumped onto a motorcycle and sped away. Apparently the date was groping O'Bannon like she was testing a melon to see if it's ripe yet."

"Holy shit," Bijal wheezed.

"Exactly!" Donna slapped the desk with her palm. "And that's what we need to show the rest of the twelfth district. I can guarantee they'll stop talking about Albert Denton's fire-and-brimstone speech then."

"So you actually want me to follow her and film her?" Bijal asked, worried that she was noticeably blushing.

"Well, someone's got to."

Bijal's stomach clenched. If they hired someone else to tail Colleen, they might see something between the two of them—a knowing look, a wink, perhaps another drink at the women's bar up the road. "I'll do it," she blurted.

"Good," Donna said. "Go grab the video camera and make sure you have charged batteries and plenty of blank DVDs. You can head out now. Then you can follow her straight from her campaign office."

"So I'm working all night?"

A muscle in Donna's cheek twitched. "You can stop when you get something good."

"What if nothing good happens tonight?"

"Then sleep in and start again tomorrow night. This is more valuable than any work you could be doing in the office."

Bijal was both insulted and disgusted. "So now I'll be like the paparazzi?"

Donna cleared her throat. "No, you can't be that overt."

"What if last night was just some random hookup?" Bijal asked.

"Then she'll no doubt do it again," Donna replied. "She'll give in to her wanton cravings and you'll be there for it."

Bijal pondered that thought. "With any luck." Had she just said that out loud?

Kristin rapped on the office door before timidly poking her head inside. "Donna, sorry to interrupt, but you wanted an update on the protesters outside."

"Have they finally dispersed?" Donna asked.

Kristin's gaze dropped to the floor. "Um, no. There are more of them now."

Donna's eyes took on a crazed glassiness that scared Bijal. "What? Why? I sent the mayor to an NRA rally in Hereford and told the press she wouldn't be here today."

"It seems that Congresswoman O'Bannon made a statement to the press about the protest and sent a catering truck full of free food. It's out there now serving everyone. People are coming from all over for a free lunch," Kristin said sheepishly.

Donna leapt to her feet. "Are you fucking kidding me?"

"No," Kristin whispered, her voice apparently frightened away.

"All right, we need to get these bastards off the premises." Donna was clearly losing her grip. "Call the cops. Someone needs to pepper-spray those fuckers!"

"But we don't own this property," Bijal said.

"So what? We pay rent," Donna shouted.

"If they're not obstructing anything, and they're peaceful, then you need to get the landlord to ask them to leave. Do we even know who that is?"

A silence fell over the room as they all looked at each other expectantly.

"Roo," Donna said. "Find out who it is."

"I don't know. That kind of research might cut into my 'hiding in the shrubbery' time."

Donna's eyes narrowed. "You're just not a team player, are you?"

Bijal was rapidly becoming worn out. "Look, why don't you have the mayor address the crowd and give them what they want? Let her condemn the violence of that assault."

"And risk alienating her conservative base? Are you crazy?"

Bijal bristled. "The conservatives aren't going anywhere. Don't you think most people would agree with denouncing an unprovoked assault?"

Another awkward silence followed that question as Donna seemed to mull something over.

"Kristin, find out who owns this building."

Chapter Eight

B ijal sat in her Subaru across the street from Colleen's house and pressed the Zoom button on the camcorder to try to see anyone through the living-room window. She was thankful Colleen lived in a rural area, since that reduced the risk of any vigilant neighbors noticing her voyeurism.

When her cell phone rang, Bijal set down the camera only long enough to put the call on speaker. "Hello?"

"Bijal," Fran said, "I just wanted to let you know that the lab results came in today. They confirm that you're completely fucking crazy for keeping that shit-ass job."

"Thank God," Bijal replied, picking up her lukewarm fast food. "When you said 'lab results,' I was afraid you'd say that you picked up crabs from one of your late-night bar trysts."

"Ooh, someone's a testy little stalker, I see. Are you outside her place right now?"

Bijal sighed. "Yes."

"Is your hand down your pants?"

"No, it's holding my quesadilla."

"Is that a euphemism?"

Bijal was rapidly losing her sense of humor. "Fran, did you just call to give me shit, or did you have a real reason?"

"Well, personally I think that giving you shit is a real reason, but I wanted to ask if you'd seen the latest polls on your girl."

"Yes," Bijal replied, taking another bite. This food would have been so much better if she'd eaten within the first thirty minutes of purchase.

"So you know that y'all have dropped another three percentage points since Adolph McHatespeech's little 'hetero über alles' tirade?"

"Unfortunately."

Fran continued, undeterred. "Couple that with the embarrassment of Mayor Denton being snubbed at an NRA rally—"

"They didn't know she was coming."

"And having them, instead, introduce a performer who made balloon animals."

"He was on the posted schedule," Bijal explained lamely.

"But Pigglestink the Clown isn't running for office, Bij."

"Well, I hear he went over great with the kids." Bijal set down her rather unappetizing food and looked through the camera.

"Uh-huh, I'm starting to think your candidate couldn't beat O'Bannon in a dick-sucking contest."

Bijal couldn't stifle a chuckle. "Only because her husband would first declare it immoral. Then she'd probably show up on the wrong day."

"Or she'd show up at a preschool, by mistake. So what's your campaign's plan to recover those voters?"

"I wish I knew, Fran. I've been out of the office for the last three days following Colleen around like some kind of international spy."

"Or someone on that scuzzy TV show *Cheaters*."

"Jesus, can't you let me have *anything*? Not even the delusion of mystique around this demoralizing fucking job?"

Fran's tone seemed to take on a hint of concern. "Do you think Donna just wants you out of her hair?"

"You know, I've considered that. I haven't ruled it out yet."

"So how much longer do you plan to waste your nights sitting in your car with your fingers smeared with quesadilla…juice?"

"First of all, quesadillas don't have juice."

"When they're euphemisms, they do."

"I call Donna every morning and tell her that all Colleen did the day before was work and go home. Although someone's at her place with her right now."

"Really?" Fran sounded intrigued. "Like a hot woman?"

"I'm not sure. I was starving so I went through a drive-thru on the way here."

Fran laughed loudly. "You're the shittiest international spy I know."

"Well, so far Colleen has had a very boring, predictable routine. And I was really hungry."

"Uh-huh."

"Anyway, when I got here, there was an extra car in the driveway."

"Is it a lesbian car?"

"What's that?" Bijal asked.

"You know, does it have any classic lesbian iconography? Like a rainbow sticker that says Vagitarian or Indigo Girls…maybe a picture of a penis with a slash through it?"

Bijal zoomed in on the car. "No, it's just a black four-door sedan. Wait, the bumper has a sticker that says Amnesty International. Damn it."

"Yeah, those damn anti-torture, bleeding-heart bastards," Fran said sarcastically.

"No, I just mean that it's not very helpful."

"Bij, if I didn't know better, I'd think you were actually bothered."

"Maybe a little," she said softly.

"And why is that?"

She blew her hair out of her eyes. "Well, partly because I think this whole thing is ridiculous. It shouldn't matter who a candidate sees in his or her free time, unless it's a prostitute, a drug dealer, or a minor."

"Or maybe someone working for the opposition," Fran added. "So what's the other part?"

"Colleen told me she wasn't seeing anyone. I'd be kind of sad if she lied to me."

Fran scoffed. "Because politicians are renowned for being so honest and trustworthy."

"I know, I know. But for some reason, I got a different kind of vibe from her. She seems somehow…authentic to me."

"Hmm, and maybe you just really want her to be single."

Bijal watched a smile slowly creep across her face in her sideview mirror. "Maybe."

"Well, nothing impresses a woman with scruples and a rigid moral compass like spying on her from her rose garden. Just add stealing her credit cards to the mix and you'll have her in your bed in a second."

"As much as I'd love to listen to you berate me, Fran, it looks like someone's moving around in there. I have to let you go."

"All right, but be careful," Fran said, exasperation evident in her voice. "I need you back as my wingman."

"I'll bet."

"I'll get your bail money ready. Call when you're in custody."

"Will do."

"Bye, sweetie."

"Bye."

Bijal saw someone move past the window, though she couldn't make out anything more than an adult of indeterminate gender. Colleen was tall enough that it might be her.

If only Bijal was looking into the window from the side yard, she'd have a much better view. She evaluated the possibility of getting out of her car. There wasn't a street light nearby, and no fence to try to jump. She'd just need to hop over the drainage ditch and walk about twenty-five yards to have a perfect view into the house and see exactly who Colleen was entertaining…and how.

It seemed reasonable, so she quietly got out of the Subaru and began to creep across the street with her camcorder. She hadn't factored in the recent heavy rain and the resulting mud. She carefully navigated the soft ground and got past the ditch before she stopped to zoom in on the window again.

Bijal could see two people embracing, and she felt like someone had just punched her in the gut. They quickly separated and moved out of her line of sight.

Suddenly the front door opened, and she panicked. A round bush large enough to shield her was directly behind her, and she lunged for it. Not taking the deep mud into account, she lost her balance as her foot slid backward, sending her into the drainage ditch, the cold water and thick mud cushioning her fall in what she imagined was probably the worst way possible.

She was motionless on her back as she heard Colleen say, "Okay, Max. I'll see you at the office tomorrow."

A man's voice (presumably this Max) answered with, "Right, have a good night," followed by what sounded like Colleen going back into her house and shutting the door.

Bijal heard him start his car, back out of the driveway, and speed off into the distance.

This was easily her most humiliating moment, though, admittedly, there had been some real doozies. She sat up in the mud and tried to get to her feet without losing her footing again. How long would she need to wait before Colleen went to bed and she could leave? Had the mud ruined the camcorder? How the hell would she be able to get in her car without getting the interior completely filthy?

Could she make it home without wearing her pants? What were her odds of being pulled over while she was driving in nothing but her underwear? Would that help or hinder her chances of getting let off with just a warning?

She finally stood, but then heard the front door creak open again. She dove back into the ditch, this time face-down as she heard a jingling sound and rolling footsteps approaching. Apparently a wild animal was coming for her.

True to her terrible luck, she heard the animal stop near her and start barking. She looked up, and that's when she saw the werewolf, or the coyote, or the hyena, or whatever the fuck it was. It clearly wanted to eviscerate her and then roll in her entrails.

She put her head back down in the futile hope that the beast would lose interest if it couldn't see the fear in her eyes. It only continued to bark at her.

The door opened again.

"Callisto! What is it, girl?"

New, non-animal footsteps approached as the hellhound continued to bark.

"Did you find another possum, girl?"

Bijal recognized the voice as Colleen's. She revised her previous assessment of her most humiliating moment as the beam from a flashlight came to rest on her as she lay in the ditch.

"Um, hello," Bijal said, looking up. She silently prayed for a bolt of lightning to strike her and instantly turn her to a smoldering pile of cinders.

"What the hell?" Colleen asked. "Bijal? Is that you?"

"I'm sorry to say it is."

"What are you doing in my front yard wallowing in mud?" Colleen scanned the area with the beam of her flashlight. "Ah, it's all becoming clearer now. Is this your video camera?"

"Yes," she answered dejectedly.

"I'm...I'm speechless. Are you hurt? Can you stand up?"

"I'd rather just lie here and continue to die a little inside."

Colleen held her arm out. "Come on. Let's get you cleaned up."

"Please don't be nice to me," Bijal implored. "It only makes this more mortifying."

"Well, maybe if you're lucky I'll kick you in the chest later. Now take my hand."

❖

"Here," Colleen said, offering a steaming mug of something to Bijal before taking a seat beside her on the sofa.

Bijal sniffed it. "What's this?"

"Hot tea—to take the chill off."

Bijal grabbed one side of the terry-cloth robe she was wearing and pulled it tighter around her. She couldn't recall a time when she felt quite as guilty or out of place as she did at this moment—now that she was naked underneath a borrowed polka-dot robe, sitting in the living room of her boss's campaign opponent, whom she had been caught spying on while cowering in a mud-filled ditch. If she was ever to stumble across the definition of the word "disgraced," she was certain that a picture of her, dejected in polka dots, would be right next to it.

"You're being exceptionally nice," Bijal said softly.

Colleen showed no hint of a smile. "Well, if it makes you feel any better, it's requiring a monumental amount of effort."

"Nope, that doesn't make me feel better."

"Get comfortable. Your clothes are in the washer."

"Thanks," Bijal mumbled. As though Colleen's dog could sense both the tension in the air and the utter sadness in Bijal, she approached her and nudged Bijal's hand with her head. Bijal complied and scratched the dog between the ears. "You look a little like Lassie," she told her as she stroked the animal's ears.

"She should," Colleen said. "She's a collie."

"But she's not all fluffy like a collie."

"Callisto's what they call a smooth-coated collie. She can still rescue a little boy from a well. She just sheds less when she does it."

Bijal sipped her tea. "She sounds handy. So her name, is that Greek?"

"Uh, yeah. My late girlfriend and I were fans of *Xena: Warrior Princess*. Callisto was a character on that show." Colleen looked a little sheepish.

"Really?"

"That's how we met, actually, on a Xena message board. You know, back in the dark ages before Facebook and Twitter."

"Wow, I thought lesbians only met in women's bars, or through their exes."

Colleen smiled. "Nope, that's a myth. Don't underestimate the drawing power of a spirited debate about which character's development was more critical to the arc of the story—Xena or Gabrielle."

"And you think it was…?"

"Gabrielle, of course," Colleen explained calmly, with a wave of her hand. "She evolved from a meek victim to a fierce warrior wielding multiple weapons with fluid dexterity. You can't stack her progression beside a flicker of personal redemption that took seven seasons and think they're even remotely comparable."

Bijal stared back at her.

Colleen laughed self-consciously. "You don't have the foggiest notion what I'm talking about, do you?"

"Well, no. But I think they're both hot. Does that count for anything?"

"It might, in a different argument. I guess you didn't watch it."

Bijal shook her head slowly. "No, sorry. But had I known I could meet women through it, I would have."

"Wow."

"What?"

Colleen leaned back and put her feet on the coffee table. "You know how they say dogs are food-motivated? You're apparently snatch-motivated."

"I know it may seem that way, but I'm not really. Now, my roommate Fran is a different story."

"The dry-humping Democrat?"

"Um, yeah. Can we forget that happened?" Bijal asked with a wince.

"Which part?"

Bijal mulled the question over for a moment. "You know, every time I meet up with you, something humiliating happens. Can we rewind all the way back to the beginning and start over?"

"But then how would I explain you naked in my living room?"

The only sound audible for nearly a minute was the loud ticking of the clock on the wall.

"This is really good tea," Bijal finally said.

"I'm glad you like it."

"What brand is it?"

"I think it's called subject-changer tea."

Bijal chuckled as she swept her hair behind her ear. "I could have used this years ago. So, look. You're remarkably gracious and nice, Colleen. Most folks would have shot someone crawling through their yard toting a video camera in the middle of the night."

"Luckily for you, I support gun control."

"Of course you do. May I assume that I'm safe from being executed by lethal injection while I'm here as well?"

"You may."

"That's a relief."

Colleen crossed her arms. "So, let's get right down to it, now that you know that all you're potentially at risk of is my refusal to use fabric softener on your clothes."

"Okay, I really have no excuse. I was clearly violating your privacy—"

"As well as trespassing."

"Right," Bijal said. "But I bet you'll be surprised when you find out why."

"Because you work for my political opponent and she wanted you to get dirt on me?"

"Well…yeah. But surprisingly, I was the catalyst for that."

Colleen scowled. "So this was your idea?"

"No, not like that. Someone saw you and me leaving the bar together the other night and called it in to the mayor's office."

"That I was socializing with a member of her staff?"

"No one knew who I was, apparently. But it was enough to spark the rumor that you're seeing someone." Colleen seemed transfixed as Bijal spoke. "Our idiot campaign manager decided we should stake you out and try to get video of you…in a romantic situation, shall we say."

Colleen held her hand up. "Wait, I want to make sure I get all the layers here."

"There's a lot," Bijal said. "It's like baklava."

"Baklava made of spite and shit, perhaps."

Bijal's voice became a near whisper. "I've never had that particular kind," she murmured.

"So even though you knew I wasn't seeing anyone, and even though you realized that the person they suspected was my 'date' was actually you, you went along with their idea of spying to get some R-rated video of me in the privacy of my own home?"

"Boy, it sounds a lot worse when you say it. Look, I didn't want some stranger peering through your windows."

"Because having someone I've flirted with peer through my windows is somehow better? A gentler violation?"

"No, because I wasn't planning on actually invading your privacy. I just intended to go through the motions because I genuinely feel like you deserve better than that."

Colleen's expression was inscrutable. "Then what changed between your initial intentions and when Callisto found you slinking through my ditch like a water moccasin?"

"You had someone over." Bijal looked evasively at the floor.

"My campaign manager, Max."

"Well, I couldn't tell it was a man from my car. And I suppose I wanted to make sure you'd been completely honest with me the other night."

"When I told you I was single?"

"You two hugged right in front of the window," Bijal explained. "I became…mildly curious. I wasn't actually filming you."

"I know," Colleen said, the edge no longer in her voice.

"You looked at the DVD?"

"Uh-huh, while you were changing. The last thing you successfully recorded was a menu board at a Taco Rojo drive-thru."

"I stopped and got a quesadilla."

"You're a terrible undercover operative."

Bijal nodded and held her mug in both hands. "You're not the first to tell me that tonight. This wasn't exactly how I pictured my future in politics, you know? I envisioned being in energetic strategy sessions, traveling to candidate appearances, writing press statements."

Colleen rubbed her lower lip lightly with her thumb. "And instead you're shimmying up drain pipes for a quick peek at someone on the toilet."

"Just to be clear, there was absolutely *no* toilet surveillance," Bijal replied adamantly. "Or anything of you in the shower."

"How long have you been spending your work shift watching me?"

"Just a few days."

"Did it, at any point, occur to you to decline this particular assignment?"

"I'm not sure where you think I fall within the hierarchy of the campaign team, but it's slightly below a houseplant. I don't really have that kind of relationship with my boss. It's more like she barks at me and threatens my job, and then I thank her."

"That sounds really fulfilling."

"Yeah. Can I ask you something?"

Colleen seemed to think about it before finally nodding. "Okay."

"Is professional politics this utterly shitty all the time? I mean, will it always involve people lying and cheating and treating everyone else like crap? Is it nothing more than a gaggle of strutting, competitive, cannibalistic bastards? Does it at any point get better?"

"It does. There are brief bursts of time that don't suck, surrounded by long periods of partisanship, shouting, deception, and shameless self-aggrandizement."

"But that sounds horrible." Bijal felt tired.

"There's that potential, sure. But in those fleeting moments where you do something substantial and really think you make a difference, you suddenly remember why you ran for office. It feels good."

"I guess this just isn't what I'd envisioned."

Colleen nodded quickly. "Unfortunately most politicians aren't as interested in effecting change or contributing, as much as they are in gaining power and notoriety. Those types will always be the lowest common denominator."

"Lowest common denominator?"

"Sure, those people—the ones who grandstand the loudest and point fingers at the opposition for everything that's wrong in the world—they bring down the caliber of the rhetoric. They go negative, and then everyone feels like they're forced to. They stop talking about the measurable merits of a piece of legislation and spew out a few buzzwords like 'socialism' or 'tax increase,' and it drags everything constructive to a screeching halt. It's like trying to have a discussion about tax reform with a rabid wolverine."

Bijal wondered if Donna was one of those rabid wolverines. She'd certainly seemed on occasion to froth a bit at the mouth—particularly when she was shouting. Perhaps her presence in the campaign was infecting everyone else with hydrophobia.

Colleen seemed now to be studying Bijal close enough to make her feel even more uncomfortable. "Colleen, look, I'm really sorry."

"So how's your jaw?"

Bijal's hand flew to her face reflexively. "Christ, did you see that on TV?"

Colleen chuckled softly. "I may have DVR'd it."

"Shit." Bijal put her face in her hands.

"It seems to be healing nicely."

Bijal wouldn't open her eyes as she tried to somehow will herself into a different reality. Would there be no end to this humiliation? "Can I do anything else to make you think any less of me? Tuck my skirt into the back of my pantyhose and then visit the children's ward at a hospital? Or maybe I could push your grandmother down a flight of stairs after I shit my pants?"

"Wow, you really think big. No wonder you went into politics."

Colleen's lighthearted tone made Bijal curious enough to steal a glance at her, and sure enough, she looked amused. "You don't sound like someone who hates me."

"That's because I don't."

"Is this more of that monumental effort you mentioned earlier? Are you secretly fantasizing about exacting some kind of revenge on me?"

"No. Sorry, Bijal. I don't hate you yet."

"No?"

"If I did, I would've called the cops and made sure the press got the story that a member of Mayor Denton's campaign was arrested outside my dining-room window filming me. I don't think that'd look too good for y'all."

"No, that would very likely damage us…irreparably."

"Instead, I'm washing your clothes, letting you use my shower, making you tea, and inviting you to join me in watching an old movie on TV."

Bijal decided to drop the talk of revenge and hate and embrace the offer of the olive branch before Colleen recanted for some reason. "Any old movie in particular?"

"One of my favorites." Colleen picked up the remote and turned on the TV. "It's *September Moon*, starring Violet London and Wil Skoog."

"I've never heard of it—or either of them, for that matter."

"Well, when I said 'old,' I wasn't kidding. It's from the early thirties—not long after the advent of sound." She changed the channel and raised the volume slightly. "Violet London was a lesbian pioneer."

"Really?"

"Yup, she was a Hollywood gay long before it was trendy. Back before the public found it titillating."

"Before women made out with each other on reality shows because men found it arousing?"

"Exactly," Colleen replied. "Violet was the real deal. By the way, would you like something a little more fortifying than a fast-food taco?"

"Quesadilla."

"Whatever it was. I have some spaghetti, meatballs, and garlic bread if you're interested."

"You know, that sounds wonderful."

❖

"So emmy get tiss tate," Fran slurred incoherently, shifting her toothbrush to reach her back teeth.

Bijal rested against the bathroom doorway, clutching a steaming mug of coffee in the vague hope that it would make her feel whole again. "Sorry," she said, stretching. "I'm too tired to understand you if you don't use consonants."

Fran spat and rinsed. "So you're telling me your political opponent found you skulking outside her window in the mud, armed with a video camera with which to spy on her in her own home, and instead of calling both the cops and the local newspaper, which incidentally I'd have done in a New York fuckin' minute, she invited you in, washed your dirty clothes, let you rinse off your filth, vice, and shame in her shower, and then fed and entertained you?"

"Did you even take a breath during that question?"

Fran began applying mascara in the mirror. "Air-flow control is the only positive thing I gained from seven years of playing bass clarinet."

"Impressive."

"Thanks, but stop changing the subject, Bij. Was my run-on synopsis accurate?"

Bijal sighed. "Yes."

"So when did y'all fuck?"

Bijal nearly shot java out of her nose. "There was no fucking, Fran."

"Why not? I mean, I know it's not your personal integrity holding you back, Ms. Crawl-around-in-the-goddamn-dirt-like-a-Peeping-Tom. Does O'Bannon have scruples? Is that the problem?"

Bijal rubbed her eyes wearily. "I'm too tired and demoralized for this line of questioning."

"Look me in the eye and tell me you didn't size up that tall Irish potato and imagine jumping on her like a hot chive."

Bijal stared back at her blankly. "Tall Irish potato? Really?"

Fran's face lit up. "Aha! I knew it. And I couldn't think of anything else Irish, so shut up."

"There's no moral compromise in being attracted to someone and not acting on it."

"Is that something you heard from Oprah? 'Cause please enlighten me. When have you ever *not* acted on an attraction?"

"Hey, I'm not some compulsive sex addict who rubs up against strangers on the Metro. I can keep it in my pants, thank you. Besides, did you just get a little taste of something bitter in the back of your throat as you were saying that? Know what that is? That's hypocrisy, baby."

"Just because *I'm* slutty doesn't mean your behavior can't appall me."

"I guess I assumed that your inherent narcissism would keep you from noticing."

Fran glared. "You are so lucky you're right, because otherwise I'd be hurt. So do you plan to go back to the office to talk to Frau Blücher and tell her your cover is blown?"

"You're kidding, right?"

"Why?"

Bijal was incredulous. "You want me to tell my sadist boss that the surveillance she asked me to do, that was a direct result of my drunken flirting with our adversary, is now pointless because I was caught red-handed trespassing on her property? Which of my many fuck-ups do you think I should start with? I mean, I wouldn't want to lose the flow of the narrative."

"So you're just going to keep wasting your time?" Fran asked, propping her hand on her hip.

"What choice do I have?"

"Well, don't take this the wrong way, because I'm not remotely rooting for your side to win, but shouldn't you be spending your working hours doing something that might help Denton get elected?"

Bijal took a deep sip of her coffee. "Are you implying that spending the evening watching old movies and eating pasta didn't help Janet's polling numbers?"

Fran's eyes narrowed. "If I didn't know better, I'd almost think you want O'Bannon to win. Thus, you don't so much mind spending your workdays on useless endeavors."

"What?"

"I mean, it's certainly easier to reconcile working against someone you like when you're not working against them at all."

"I can't just be motivated by not wanting to be fired?"

"You tell me," Fran replied with a shrug. "If Denton loses, will you feel guilty that you didn't do more?"

Bijal considered that question for a moment. "I hate it when you have the high ground."

CHAPTER NINE

Colleen sat at the desk in her congressional office going through her e-mail when a deep voice called from the doorway.

"Hey, Colleen. Do you have a minute?"

She looked up to see House Majority Whip Luke Sherman grinning at her. He was known by the entire District of Columbia as a smooth talker and a tough negotiator—two attributes that made him very good at his job.

"Sure," Colleen replied. "Come on in."

He shut the door behind him and took a seat across from her, his posture exuding comfort and cockiness. "How's everything been going for you?" he asked. "Good?"

Colleen scoffed. "You know I like you, Luke. But you never just drop by for chit-chat."

He flashed another insincere-looking smile and simply shrugged.

"You want to talk about the Patient Access Reform Act, I assume." Colleen pushed her chair back so she could see him better.

"I do admire your bluntness."

"Hmm, I don't think you really do, but why quibble? I can't vote for the bill as it currently reads, Luke."

He rubbed his chin. "Because of Congressman Saturday's amendment, I'm guessing."

"Absolutely. It restricts women's accessibility to abortion and sex education. How could I possibly vote for that?"

"Maybe indirectly," he said slowly. "But in the end, that will only affect a small population of women."

"The poor—the ones who need it most."

"This bill does a lot of good things that will impact everyone," he said, without addressing her point.

Colleen adjusted her glasses on the bridge of her nose. "So you're telling me that the right to a legal medical procedure for some poverty-stricken Americans is just collateral damage? That's a price you're willing to pay for the rest of that reform bill?"

He shifted in his chair. "Look, you know that this reform, both comprehensively and in small pieces, has been on our agenda for a long time."

She nodded.

"And you know that politics is nothing but compromise."

Again she nodded.

"Now I agree that this bill isn't perfect, but what bill ever is? It's important to the Democratic Party to move this into the win column, especially with Election Day weeks away. Am I right?"

"Actually, no. You're not right."

Luke looked incredulous. "What? Where did I lose you?"

"You left out a few critical facts."

His eyebrow arched. "Such as?"

She grabbed a three-ring binder sitting on her desk and flipped to a page near the back. "Such as the minor oversight that the formal platform of our party says we 'strongly and unequivocally support a woman's right to choose a safe and legal abortion, regardless of ability to pay, and we oppose any and all efforts to weaken or undermine that right.' Remember that? It's a pledge to the American people."

"Come on, you're making a mountain out of molehill."

Colleen was officially becoming irritated. "You think so? Well, I suppose you could try to rely on the charisma and appeal of the amendment's sponsor. Oh, wait. I guess that might be a challenge since Congressman Saturday is an eighty-three-year-old former segregationist."

"Ancient history, O'Bannon." Luke's calm façade seemed to be faltering.

"Perhaps it is to you. Maybe not to me, or to a lot of African Americans. Between the two of us, Saturday doesn't have a lick of compassion in his whole body. Is he really who you want portrayed as the face of the Democratic Party?"

"This isn't about Saturday."

"You're right, Luke. It's about the fact that this amendment would restrict non-abstinence-only sex-education programs that would actually *reduce* unwanted pregnancies. And it would limit abortion access for the women who are poorest. To totally abandon them like that is unconscionable."

Luke rolled his eyes, his schmoozy demeanor now gone. "So forget the large majority of people who'll benefit from the other reforms in the bill? Are you saying you care less about them and more about the minority? Don't the needs of the many outweigh the needs of the few?"

"That depends, Mr. Spock. Are you selling the few down the river to claim a token victory for the many?"

"Look—"

"And one more thing you may have overlooked," Colleen said, "is the teensy little detail that our party ran on the principle of progressive reform, and we won. So when the voters realize that not only did we *not* advance any significant progressive reform while we were in the majority, but we actually diluted some rights that they started with, do you really expect to be reelected? I mean, what's your campaign strategy there? Next time we'll screw you over less?"

Luke stood and started to pace. "So you think it's better not to pass anything and have nothing to show come Election Day? Your strategy is 'Sorry we didn't accomplish a goddamn thing. We were trying to get it perfect, but we couldn't stop screaming at each other long enough to make that happen'?"

"I think it's better to keep your word. What does it say if we can't accomplish all the reform we promised because so many of us are afraid to upset our corporate donors and actually vote the way we said we would? What part of 'No, we didn't do anything useful for you like we pledged to, but here's something watered-down and moderately regressive that we'd like to take credit for' sounds truly inspired to you?"

A muscle in Luke's cheek twitched. "Funny you should mention reelection, O'Bannon. How's your campaign coming along?"

Colleen eyed him suspiciously. He was like a completely different person now. "Fine."

"That's good. It must be hard running as a far-left liberal in a red district. I'd imagine you need a lot of support from the party—political endorsements, financial contributions."

"Are you threatening me, Luke?" She rose, letting the edge of her desk support her, surprised at the turn in conversation.

"Goodness, no!" he replied disingenuously. "How could I? I'm certainly not involved in the decisions of the DCCC." He crossed his arms and stared at her confrontationally.

Colleen was speechless. Was he trying to extort her vote on this bill by withholding assistance from the Democratic Congressional Campaign Committee? "Oh?" She was disappointed that she couldn't manage a more pithy response.

"Well, I can't help that my peers consult my opinion from time to time. I suppose you could consider that a form of influence. And if you were to ask me what I thought you should do right now, I'd suggest that you slide a little closer to the center. Stop thumping your chest so hard and let the party help you. Don't fight us. After all, if you don't work toward the party's goals, how can the party work toward yours?"

She looked at the floor. "So my vote on this bill will directly affect the party's involvement in my campaign."

"I didn't say that."

"Didn't you?"

"I don't have that kind of power," he lied. "I'm just…encouraging you to consider the potential ramifications of voting against this bill. It might look bad for you. You might seem obstructionist, which, I have to admit, is particularly off-putting in a woman—you know, to voters."

"Just as veiled threats can be off-putting in men—you know, to everyone."

Luke laughed and straightened his tie. "Well, on that note, I'll leave you to chew on what we've discussed."

"Thanks. Just so you know, it tastes a little bit like shit."

She could hear him cackle as he headed toward his next destination.

❖

Bijal walked into campaign headquarters and saw Kristin sitting at her desk, working furiously on her computer. Bijal loudly pulled up a chair across from her and got comfortable.

"Well, hey, stranger," Kristin said with a smile. "How's the night shift been?"

"Lots of junk food, somewhat demoralizing, chilly. It's like I'm dating again."

"Trust me, I'm married and it doesn't sound much different."

Bijal couldn't deal with the thought of any more small talk. "I got your message, Kristin. Lay it on me."

"Honestly, I can't believe you haven't heard."

"I was on my way to an O'Bannon rally in Bankshire, but when I saw that your text included the word 'catastrophic,' I decided to stop by so you could explain exactly what happened."

Kristin began queuing something up on her PC. "Slide over here and I'll show you. I don't think I'd be able to fully do this story justice anyway."

Bijal moved her chair so she could see Kristin's monitor. "Was the whole rally bad? Did the crowd turn on her or something?"

"No, and to be honest, it was going really well until the very end. I thought Janet related well to the audience, and she got a good amount of applause throughout." Kristin continued to fiddle with the video player.

"Did angry liberals disrupt it? Protesters?"

Kristin grimaced and shook her head. "It was more of a…wardrobe malfunction."

"Like her fly was down or something?"

"Here it is. Check this out."

Kristin pressed Play and Bijal watched as Janet stood before a podium at the local fund-raising event just a few hours earlier. The crowd was clapping enthusiastically, and Janet was obviously beginning to announce her departure. "Thanks so much for taking the time to come, everyone," she said. "I appreciate your time and your questions. But most of all, I want to thank you all for your interest in government and in your representatives. Have a great day, and God bless!"

Janet waved wildly to the attendees as she walked off the stage and into the wings, out of view of the camera and audience. "Thanks,

thanks," she said, her voice just as clear as it had been moments earlier when she had been addressing the crowd.

Bijal's hand flew to her mouth as she realized that Janet must have still been wearing the remote microphone clipped to the lapel of her jacket. "Oh, no."

"Oh, I know," she was heard to say to someone. The people at the fund-raiser appeared puzzled by precisely what they were hearing booming over the PA system. "Yeah, that guy in red is a real asshole. No argument. Hey, can we stop at the ladies' room? That Thai food from lunch is galloping through me like a freakin' thoroughbred. Huh? Oh, sh—"

A shrill surge of feedback interrupted the final expletive, and the murmurs of the attendees grew louder before Kristin finally pressed Pause.

"Oh...my...God," Bijal gasped.

Kristin nodded. "You see how 'catastrophic' might be the first word to come to mind?"

"Has it gone viral?"

"And then some. It's already played on CNN. I expect it to be in heavy rotation by late tonight."

"Holy shit," Bijal said, stunned.

Kristin started loading another clip. "It gets better. The local affiliate who filmed this little gem decided to find the referenced 'guy in red' and get a comment from him. The news is running that video too."

Bijal cringed as she watched the footage of a fidgety fat fellow in a red sweater beginning to speak. "I guess she had a problem with me asking her for specifics on what she'd do about unemployment," he told the newscaster. "I thought it was a perfectly reasonable question, but I don't see anyone else here in red. So I guess that makes me...well, the—"

The network bleeped the man's final word.

"Why?" was all Bijal could say. "God, why?"

"Because apparently no one thought to remind Janet that her mic was both live and still attached to her."

"It's not because we're cursed?"

Kristin chuckled. "Sometimes it feels that way."

"Where's Janet now?"

"Actually, she's here. I think she's hiding in her office while Donna gives interviews to the press trying to minimize the impact."

Bijal blinked repeatedly as she let that sink in. "Because Donna is a master of reason and public relations."

"Right," Kristin said sarcastically. "And because Yosemite Sam was busy."

"Maybe this is my opportunity to talk to Janet one-on-one."

Kristin shrugged. "Just don't take it personally if she's not in a very good mood."

Bijal stood up and looked at her watch. She had a little time before she needed to head over to Colleen's rally. She started toward Janet's office. "Nah. I'll just assume the Thai food caused her surly disposition, not me."

Bijal was surprised that not only was the mayor in her office alone, but that the door was open, revealing her going through her e-mail.

"Janet?"

"Hey, Bijal." Janet smiled warmly. "I haven't seen you in a while."

"Well, I've been busy doing the surveillance work Donna assigned me to."

"Surveillance?"

Bijal had a sinking feeling in her gut. "Yeah, you know. I've been following Congresswoman O'Bannon around in the evenings. In fact, I'm headed off shortly to her event at the Sheraton."

"Come on in and shut the door."

Bijal did as she was asked and took a seat. This was starting to feel increasingly weird. "Didn't Donna tell you about my assignment?"

Janet shook her head. "What is it you're hoping to see?"

"Donna heard from someone's brother's cousin's college room-mate that O'Bannon was dating someone."

"So you're following her around hoping to catch her in a late-night clinch with some UPS driver?"

"Basically, yes."

"Hmm." Janet seemed bothered.

"May I speak freely?"

"Please do, Bijal."

She cleared her throat and sat up straight. "I want you to know that I really do support you as a candidate. I agree with your ideals, and I'd love to see you win."

"I suppose I shouldn't assume that all my paid employees feel that way."

"But I have some concerns about Donna and some of the decisions she's made regarding the campaign."

Janet entwined her fingers and reclined in her chair. "For example?"

"Not releasing a proactive statement to the press regarding the gay-bashing. Attempting to court the right wing when the vast majority of our undecided voters are moderates. Making me waste my time focusing on O'Bannon's personal life, instead of allowing me to research demographics, issues, and polling. Sending you to an NRA rally that you'd already declined to attend."

"I think I'm starting to get the idea."

Bijal worried if she'd already crossed a line. "Perhaps if you get a consensus before acting," she proposed tactfully.

"Things aren't going too smoothly, Bijal. I'm well aware of that. Did you see what happened this afternoon at my fund-raiser?"

"I may have heard a murmur or two."

"And exactly how would you have me respond to this current embarrassment, if it were up to you?"

Bijal thought for a moment. "The public does appreciate accountability—it's something they rarely see in politics or corporations. So, first, I'd have you contact the guy in red directly and apologize to him."

"Make it a photo op, you mean?"

"No, because inviting the press immediately cheapens it and makes it seem contrived and insincere. I mean just you and him. Let him know that you're genuinely sorry for your remark and that you don't think he's an asshole. If he continues to do interviews, he'll likely share that you not only took responsibility for your comment, but that you were gracious and earnest about it."

"That's good."

"And then I'd have *you* out talking to the media, not Donna.

There's nothing appealing about an employee publicly taking the heat for something her boss said or did."

Janet was looking at Bijal through squinted eyes. "And what else would you have me do? How might we shift momentum?"

"Well…I think we'd stop ignoring the fact that you're a moderate and talk about social issues, and we'd start painting O'Bannon as someone who is very far left of center. This is still a red state, and the people here are more conservative than not. We could easily build support among people who may not be comfortable with O'Bannon's extreme liberal stances. Instead, we're spending all our time doing damage control. You can't score any points if you only play defense."

Janet stared at Bijal intently, all the while her only visible moving body part seeming to be her thumbs.

"Have I said too much?" Bijal asked, suddenly aware of her pulse throbbing in her forehead. "Because I thought we were just sort of informally—"

"Impressive," Janet interjected, stopping Bijal mentally in her tracks. "You clearly have a strong grasp of the issues and the way politics works in general."

"Um, thanks."

"And I do appreciate those things, Bijal, regardless of how things may sometimes seem."

"I certainly don't mean to question that."

"I know. All your points have merit. Everything you've said makes sense. I'll talk to Donna in the morning and we'll discuss some of them. I'll let you know what she says."

"Okay." Bijal wasn't sure what Janet was telling her. Was she saying she intended to run her ideas by Donna? Who was really in charge here?

"And I'll let her know that I think you're far more valuable to this campaign working in the office than creeping around outside O'Bannon's house."

Bijal coughed nervously.

"So go on to the rally," Janet said. "But I'll expect you back in the office starting tomorrow."

"I'm officially off spy detail?"

Janet scowled. "Well, not yet. Not until I can get Donna to agree. But it's important that you're here in the morning, especially since the head of the National Republican Congressional Committee is stopping by to see us for a strategy meeting. I'd like you to attend."

"Charles Hammond is coming *here*?"

"Mmm-hmm, so make sure you have your game face on. I expect he'll have some critical things to say, based on some of the setbacks we've encountered."

"I'm honored, Janet. Thanks so much for this chance to prove myself."

"You're welcome. Just be ready to work your ass off."

Bijal inwardly winced. If she had to work days *and* nights, she had no doubt that would be exactly the end result—no pun intended.

CHAPTER TEN

Bijal sat in her car and sulked, shivering from an unforeseen chill. She had left the Sheraton's fancy banquet room when the event began to wind down, and she now waited for Colleen to come out this back entrance to her vehicle, staking her out like she was a gangster's moll in a cheap detective novel.

It had been disheartening to see how impressive Colleen's event was. The catering was amazing. Her speech had been exceptional. The supporters had all seemed energized and generous with their time, money, and support.

This was not at all the way Janet's events had been trending. Why, not once all night had Colleen insulted a constituent and announced to the crowd her urgent need to defecate.

The hotel back door suddenly opened and out came Colleen, now changed from her formalwear into a pair of faded jeans and a crisp button-up shirt, hefting a garment bag over her shoulder. Walking with her was a rather tall man, one who Bijal assumed was Max, the campaign manager who gave hugs and made house calls. With them was also a shorter woman who Bijal recognized as the dumpy woman from Colleen's website—the one she'd originally assumed was Colleen.

They looked tired, and after stopping for a moment or two to chat, the man and the woman each embraced Colleen, then headed to their respective cars. Colleen shuffled to her own sedan and began loading her clothes into the backseat.

As Max and his coworker both pulled out of the parking lot and drove off into the night, Colleen shut the back door of her car and looked over to where Bijal sat observing her. Colleen's eyes narrowed and Bijal was certain she'd been spotted. Of course, by now, she saw no point in either hiding or feigning innocence.

Bijal waved.

With a lopsided smile, Colleen zipped up her jacket and approached Bijal's Subaru. When she reached the driver's door, she knocked politely on the window and Bijal rolled it down. "Hey, I thought that was you."

"Where else would I be? You might be out somewhere doing something...lesbian."

"Like shopping at a hardware store?" Colleen asked.

"Yes, or watching sports. Absolutely scandalous."

An awkward pause settled between them, punctuated by lingering eye contact.

Colleen propped herself casually on the fender. "You were inside, right?"

"I was. It was quite the little shindig. Very impressive."

"Thanks. Did you get enough to eat?"

"Yeah, I have to admit you Democrats definitely have superior catering."

"Hmm, you think so?"

Bijal nodded. "The stuffed mushrooms were delicious, and the bacon-wrapped shrimp were so good they compelled me to stuff three in my mouth at one time."

"That's quite a resounding endorsement, despite coming from a woman who's been subsisting entirely on cold drive-thru food."

"Well, at Janet's rallies we serve chips, dip, and Bagel Bites."

Colleen grimaced. "Yum."

"Our events have more of a...mid-city soup-kitchen feel."

"Look at the bright side. You'll never be accused of being elitist. Hey, I'm starving, so I need to stop somewhere."

"You didn't eat any of that amazing food?" Bijal asked.

"When you're the hostess, it's hard to stop talking long enough to chew anything. You want to join me for a quick bite?"

"Are you asking me to dinner?"

"Well, technically I figure you'll be there either way. It'd just be more enjoyable if you actually came indoors where I could talk to you, instead of staring at me through the window like I'm some prize Christmas goose."

Bijal rubbed her steering wheel. "Wait, does that make me the Ghost of Christmas Past?"

"If I'm the goose in the window, then you're the boy who gets half a crown for buying the goose—or perhaps you're Tiny Tim's crutch. Regardless, what do you say?"

"It *is* kind of cold outside."

"Downright arctic."

"But we can't go anyplace we might risk being seen together... again."

"Fair enough. What about the K and K?"

"I thought you said you wanted food."

Colleen was obviously amused. "I think Sue might be willing to make me a BLT if I ask her nicely."

"Or if you can think of an utterly filthy name for it?"

"Right. And at this point, I wouldn't turn down a drink either."

"Neither would I," Bijal said.

"Sounds like we both had a crappy day."

"That may be an understatement. You want a ride?"

Colleen checked her watch briefly. "You and I arriving at a lesbian bar together might be a bad idea. Someone might call your office to report that I was in the company of..." She stopped to look around the parking lot suspiciously. "A *lady*."

Bijal chuckled. "A decidedly gay activity, to be sure. How about I follow you there?"

"I like that you suggested that as though you didn't intend to follow me anyway," Colleen said wryly.

"Shh, I'm trying to convince myself that I have a normal job that doesn't involve things like stalking and trespassing."

Colleen beamed as she spun her key ring around her finger. "Well, enjoy your denial. See you there."

❖

Colleen was somewhat relieved to see only a few people in the bar. It was still relatively early, after all, as well as a weeknight. She eyed the patrons, wondering if any of them were likely to recognize her and dash off to gossip to any Republican who'd listen that she was out in bars, picking up harlots.

"Fuck 'em," she muttered as she pulled up a bar stool.

Sue spun around and brightened when she saw who it was. "Hey, chica. How's it going?"

"I've had better days."

The door swung open and in walked Bijal. Sue's eyebrow arched in that familiar manner that Colleen now clearly recognized as silent accusation. Bijal ignored Colleen completely as she took the seat right next to her and smiled sweetly at Sue.

"My goodness," Colleen exclaimed in feigned astonishment. "Why, it's you! What are *you* doing here?"

Bijal's jaw dropped melodramatically. "I, like you, am *shocked* that you're here. Shocked, I tell you." Her attention shifted back to Sue. "Can I get whatever light beer you have on draft, please?"

Sue's gaze darted back and forth between them as the corner of her mouth curled upward. "Um…sure." She withdrew a frosted mug from the cooler and pulled the tap handle to fill it. "You know who y'all remind me of?"

"Who?" Colleen asked.

"Remember that cartoon with the wolf and the sheepdog who were friends until they punched the clock? Then they spent their workday fighting each other?"

Bijal turned to Colleen. "Which one am I?"

Colleen propped her chin in her hand. "Based on circumstances, I'd say you're unequivocally the wolf."

Bijal picked up the beer as Sue slid it in front of her, and she took a sip. "That's fair. And I *do* have that line of credit with Acme."

"Avoid the rocket-propelled roller skates," Colleen said as she read over the meager menu card, looking for something that wouldn't sit in her gut like quicksand.

"Thanks for the tip."

"They're inferior imports."

"Then I'm canceling that order first thing in the morning," Bijal said with a nod.

"Glad to hear it."

Sue crossed her arms and continued smirking at them. "What are you having, Col?"

"I haven't eaten in about twelve hours. What do you have that's tasty but doesn't go through the fryer?"

"Besides condiments?" Sue asked.

"Yeah, the last time I filled up on mustard, I regretted it the next day."

Sue propped an elbow on the counter. "How about a grilled cheese and a cup of soup?"

"You're a lifesaver. What kind of soup?"

"Well, today's soup du jour is 'whatever's in the Cup-a-Soup box bisque.'"

"Perfect," Colleen said emphatically. "You're a gentlewoman and a scholar, Sue."

"Yeah yeah yeah," Sue grumbled, keying the order into the register. "Don't get too excited. I'm charging you up the ass for it. What are you drinking?"

Colleen pointed to Bijal's frosty brew. "That looks good."

Sue seemed surprised. "A light beer? Really?"

"Empty stomach," Colleen said with a shrug. "And I have to drive home so I can curl up in the fetal position and weep." She checked her watch. "I'd like to be weeping by eleven, so shake a leg, sister."

Sue began to fill another mug. "Jesus, Col. What happened? Did your thingie tonight go south on you?"

"On the contrary," Bijal said. "I thought it went great."

"*You* were there?" Sue asked.

Bijal took another swallow. "I'm essentially a political operative."

"Well, it's very obliging of you to be so…up front about it," Sue said with a hint of confusion in her voice. She set Colleen's draft on the bar.

Colleen chuckled. "It's less that she's up front and more that she's just astonishingly bad at it."

Sue nodded in understanding. "Which is why you're the wolf."

"Among other reasons, yes," Bijal replied guiltily.

"Okay," Sue said. "So then why so glum? The person spying on you sucks at it. Your event went well. Or are you not at liberty to say?"

"No, I can say. It has nothing to do with the campaign. Well, other than that I'm being pressured to vote a particular way or I'll lose my party's support."

"Ouch," Bijal said. "It's the Patient Access Reform Act, huh?"

"That's the one," Colleen replied.

"Is it the Saturday Amendment you have a problem with? The abortion restrictions?"

"Uh-huh. But you know what really chaps me?"

"What's that?" Bijal asked.

Sue rolled her eyes. "Oh, Lord."

Colleen proceeded undeterred. "That this system is so flawed when it comes down to actually serving the people."

Bijal turned her bar stool toward her in interest. "What do you mean?"

Sue began shaking her head rapidly at Bijal and mouthing the word "no" repeatedly, but Colleen ignored her and elaborated.

"The vast majority of elected officials don't give two shits about voting their conscience. They're too busy trying to fly under the radar and avoid controversy so they can win reelection, so they knowingly vote *against* the public's best interest or their own party platform without hesitation. And not only are they morally bankrupt enough to base their every decision on this masturbatory philosophy of narcissism—"

"Wow," Bijal said, looking stunned.

"But they're not fully satisfied until they've browbeaten the handful of people genuinely interested in voting on the legislation's merits into compromising their values too. So now I'm supposed to abandon my principles because the party wants to sell out so we can push any old steaming turd through the congressional anus, then spend the rest of the year patting ourselves on the back about it, all the while pretending we don't smell shit."

Sue glared at Bijal. "See? I told you to leave it alone."

Bijal continued to stare at Colleen unblinkingly. "That was...*hot*," she rasped.

"Christ," Sue said. "Like *that's* gonna help."

Adrenaline surged through Colleen, and as quickly as her rant had been flowing a few seconds earlier, words now evaporated from her brain. "Actually, that does help a little." She tried to gauge Bijal's expression. "Are you serious?"

"Yeah," Bijal replied softly, with a slow nod. "Integrity is a major aphrodisiac for me."

"*Well*," Sue sang with obvious discomfort. "I'd better check to see if your order is up." She stepped out from behind the bar and darted into the kitchen.

Bijal's rather sexy declaration had Colleen's pulse pounding, and her lingering eye contact was exacerbating the effect. "You know, if that's your aphrodisiac, then you picked a rather cruel career. Were you planning to try celibacy?"

Bijal shook her head slowly. "It's quite possibly the result of some deep-seated form of self-loathing."

"I suppose you think hitting on me will curry favor, wear down my professional resolve? Don't think your deep chocolate eyes, your striking features, your…lithe, hypnotic curves have taken me in."

"I admire your resolute restraint," Bijal said, punctuating her words with a sultry smile.

"Thanks. And I admire your dimples."

"I'd tell you how amazing I find your ass, but that would be utterly inappropriate."

"Completely," Colleen replied.

"So I won't."

"Good. Then I won't mention how adorable you are."

Bijal seemed to be regarding her as though she was an overachieving contestant in a wet T-shirt contest. "So I guess we'll just continue to look at each other inscrutably."

Colleen half laughed and half choked. "Is *that* what you're doing right now?"

"You don't see the haughty detachment in my eyes?" Bijal asked in a voice that could just as easily been pleading with Colleen to remove her panties with her teeth.

"It must be hidden behind your seduction beam."

"Which is just to the right of my growing infatuation," Bijal said, filling Colleen with a surge of internal warmth.

"I'll have to take your word for it."

"Did it just get really hot in here?"

Colleen exhaled with some relief that she wasn't the only one feeling an unforeseen influx of volcanic waves. "Like a goddamn sauna."

Sue appeared in an instant and deposited Colleen's dinner on the bar, effectively breaking the spell. "All right, you two. Press Pause on the flirting. Grilled cheese is here and—you're going to like this—the soup is tomato."

Colleen bit into a golden corner of the sandwich. "Sue, this is fantastic. Thank you."

"Well, it was a challenging dish," Sue said. "We had to somehow get the cheese slice *between* the two pieces of bread—a little-known industry secret."

"Bravo," Colleen said. "Bijal, I'm going to stuff my face now, so it's your turn to vent. Why did your day suck?"

Bijal took a long swallow of beer. "You didn't hear about Mayor Denton's town hall today?"

"Mmm," Colleen said as she chewed. This was perhaps the best grilled cheese she'd ever had. "I did hear a whisper or two."

"About what?" Sue asked. "What happened?"

"Just a couple of minor indiscretions," Bijal replied morosely.

"Denton called a constituent an 'asshole,'" Colleen explained.

"A slip of the tongue," Bijal explained, rather unconvincingly.

"Then announced to the crowd that she was about to shit her pants," Colleen said.

Bijal cleared her throat. "Technically, she was wearing a skirt."

Colleen nodded deferentially. "I stand corrected."

Sue laughed. "Come on, stop joking around. What really happened?" Both of them looked at her blankly and said nothing. "Holy crap. No way!"

"So my workday began with that knowledge," Bijal said.

Sue's jaw sagged. "You mean it gets worse? Did she back over a troop of Girl Scouts with her car on the way out?"

"No," Bijal replied. "But I took the opportunity to tell her all the ways I think her campaign manager has screwed the political pooch."

Colleen was surprised. "Ooh, ballsy move. How did she respond?"

"By leaving me on my evening spy duty and adding a full day shift to it."

Sue winced. "Damn."

"Yeah," Bijal said. "I can only view it as punishment for speaking up."

"You really think that?" Colleen asked.

Bijal stared into her mug for a moment. "I suppose not. I mean, Janet's smart and very nice. But watching her let Donna screw her into the ground at every turn and then take no action, well, it makes me doubt her judgment."

"More than the pants-shitting does?" Colleen asked.

Bijal seemed suddenly self-conscious, as though just realizing she had shared too much. "I shouldn't be talking about this."

Sue scoffed as she wiped down the bar. "Are you kidding? Until now, I thought politics was boring. You, my friend, have made it fascinating."

Colleen grinned as she stirred her cup of soup. "Sue excels at finding silver linings."

"And peeling the wrap off American cheese slices," Sue added.

"Honestly, I was a little concerned when you said the soup was tomato," Bijal said.

Sue looked wary. "Why?"

"Based on the naming conventions of your menu, I was hoping it didn't come with a tampon in it," Bijal replied matter-of-factly.

"Ooh! Instead of a spoon," Sue said excitedly, snapping her fingers.

Colleen shook her head as her BlackBerry vibrated. "Sue, stop. That's completely and utterly vile."

"You gotta have a gimmick," Sue explained.

Colleen scrolled to the text message she'd received. "Considering that you're trying to sell food, your gimmick probably shouldn't be anything that makes people nauseous or reminds them of cramping."

"That sounds like sound business advice," Bijal said.

"Hmm, looks like I'll be on TV tomorrow night," Colleen declared, happily changing the subject.

"Really?" Sue asked. "Local network?"

"Actually, I'll be on a cable news show debating a state senator from Alabama."

"Which cable news show?" Bijal asked.

"*The Tank Guzman Show*."

"I can't stand that guy." Sue sneered. "He asks questions, but he never lets anyone answer them. It's like he just invites people on so they can listen to him drone on and on."

"He *is* a bit of a douche," Colleen said before ingesting a spoonful of soup.

Bijal snorted. "No offense, but calling Tank Guzman a douche is an insult to Massengill. What will you be speaking about?"

"Alabama has proposed a piece of legislation making it illegal to allow gays to adopt children."

"Nice," Sue said sarcastically.

"And you don't think it's a bad idea to put yourself on TV arguing for an LGBT issue so close to your election?" Bijal asked. "Isn't that like wearing a big sign that reads, 'I'm a liberal'?"

Colleen thought before she answered. "I suppose I should care about stuff like that, but so few politicians are willing to stand up for our community that I can't bring myself to turn my back on them. Even if I wanted to say it's better for the LGBT movement for me to get reelected so I can keep working for equality, I can't. It's the same with the Patient Access Reform Act. It'll get voted on in this session, before Congress adjourns. It won't wait for my election."

"Attagirl," Sue said. "Just for that, your Kotex soup is on the house."

Colleen glared at Bijal. "See what you've done?"

CHAPTER ELEVEN

B ijal settled into the cushy corner of Janet's campaign office sofa. She clutched her latte and tried to blink the fatigue out of her eyes. A glance at her watch showed she was exactly on time for the meeting with Charles Hammond, yet even though she'd been out late, she was still the only one here.

Why was punctuality such an uncommon quality? For some reason, she'd assumed that since a candidate's success was based on how he or she chose to present himself, people might actually try to be on time.

She took another sip of coffee. She should have gotten an extra shot of espresso.

Donna halted dramatically in the doorway, as though seeing Bijal waiting there made her question if she was in the wrong room. "What the hell are you doing here?" she asked abruptly as she shuffled in. "Get out, we have a meeting scheduled."

Bijal was simply too tired for Donna's bullshit and didn't bother to feign politeness or even respect. "I know. I was asked to attend."

"Is that so?" Donna sat on the edge of Janet's desk—presumably to be higher than Bijal, a typical alpha-dog trait. "Then I'll take a decaf with two sugars and a doughnut—a jelly one—if any are left."

"Well, perhaps if any volunteers are left who you haven't been shitty to yet, they'd be willing to get that for you. What do you think the odds are?"

Donna's gaze narrowed in obvious irritation. "Did I miss the e-mail that went out saying you suddenly matter, Roo?"

"It's Rao, and considering that you don't bother reading your e-mail, I imagine you've missed a lot of things."

"I don't know who the fuck you think you are, but here's the deal." Donna's voice had dropped an octave and made the journey from smarmy and oily to sinister. "You're going to shut up and leave—" Janet entered the room in time to hear the end of Donna's directive. "Or you're fired."

"No, she's not, Donna," Janet said dismissively. "Bijal is here because I value her knowledge and instincts. I want her involved in our strategy sessions from now on."

Donna seemed incredulous. "You *what*? Why don't we invite the homeless guy that picks through our Dumpster too?"

"Good idea," Bijal said. "Maybe he'd be willing to get you your coffee."

Janet put her hands up. "Ladies, please. Let's try to be constructive. We have quite a steep climb ahead of us, and sadly it seems to be getting steeper every day. Bijal, have you had a chance to see what the blowback of yesterday's little microphone gaffe is?"

"The video is all over the Internet, and it certainly didn't help that CNN and every show in MSNBC's evening lineup ran and openly mocked it. So I still support the game plan of calling the guy in red to apologize to him, then you making a separate statement to the press personally."

Donna sucked air through her teeth, making a sound Bijal decided was perhaps more annoying than a car alarm set off by the loud pealing of a pod of whales as they ran their barnacle-encrusted fins down a blackboard. "Oh, please, people don't care about silly shit like this. They care about the issues—why they can't get a job, inflation, taxes, homeland security."

"You're joking, right?" Bijal asked. "Have you not been paying attention for the last couple of decades?"

"What do you mean, Bijal?" Janet asked, taking a seat at her desk.

"I mean that the people in this room are politically minded. But most Americans aren't. Do you think C-SPAN is pulling in a bigger share of viewers than VH-1 or MTV? Sure, people have concerns about the economy and terrorism. But most would rather watch someone get drunk on a reality show and vomit off a balcony, or see who gets voted off the bus, the island, or the house full of tequila and stripper poles."

Donna crossed her arms. "That's simply not true."

"No?" Bijal asked in amazement. "The average voter spends nearly fifteen times the amount of time that they spend watching or reading the news, on social networking sites. Nearly one-third of high-school graduates won't read a single book after receiving their diploma."

Janet's jaw sagged. "Holy shit. Is that true?"

Bijal nodded. "Unfortunately, yes. Statistics can be very depressing. For example, in the last dozen years, only one in three registered Virginia voters has bothered to vote in mid-term elections."

"So first you say the American people are stupid," Donna said with a sneer. "And now you're calling them lazy as well."

"No, I'm giving you facts, and you're attributing your personal biases to them."

Janet leaned back in her chair. "So you're saying we need to be energizing Virginia Republicans more."

"Exactly," Bijal replied. "We should be showing them why it's important to get out to the polls and vote for you."

"Well, there's a shock." Donna snorted. "I can see why you're here now, Roo. We never would have recognized that we need to appeal to voters in our party. That's genius."

Bijal turned her attention directly to Janet. "Do you see now why Donna should *never* be the public face of this campaign?"

Donna's eyes flashed with anger. "Now look here, Ms. Diversity Hire—"

Whatever the insulting end to that sentence was going to be, Bijal wouldn't hear it, as in strolled NRCC Chairman Charles Hammond with another gentleman, both wearing crisp suits and grim expressions.

Hammond closed the door behind him and surveyed everyone morosely. "Hello, Mayor Denton."

"You can call me Janet."

He eyed Bijal and Donna suspiciously. "And who are these ladies?"

Janet sprang up suddenly. "Oh, I'm sorry. This is Bijal Rao, my researcher and recently promoted strategist. And this is my campaign manager, Donna Shoemaker."

Hammond pursed his lips for a moment and looked at his associate. "Ah, then I suppose you both should stay. Ladies, this is Eliot Jenkins. I imagine you all may have some idea why we made the trip out here to meet with you in person."

"Things haven't been going well," Janet offered.

Hammond scowled. "What a huge understatement."

Donna clearly shifted into defensive mode. "Excuse me?"

He looked at her as though she smelled of rancid cabbage. "Do you disagree, Ms. Shoemaker? After all, as the campaign manager, you've been steering this sinking ship, have you not?"

Donna stood. "It's not a dictatorship, Mr. Hammond. There's plenty of blame to go around."

Hammond obviously disagreed. "While that may be true, that doesn't diminish your role in this fuck parade."

Janet blinked twice. "Fuck parade?"

"Would you prefer 'shit sandwich'?" Hammond asked.

"So you're making me the scapegoat," Donna hissed. "Is that it?"

"In addition to replacing you, yes. That's where Eliot comes in. He'll be your new campaign manager, effective immediately."

Donna's face no longer registered rage, as it was instantly replaced with shock. "What?"

Janet's eyes flashed in concern. "Chairman, I think you may be overstepping your bounds."

"Oh?" Hammond seemed unfazed. "Mind if I use your dry-erase board to illustrate my point?"

"Go right ahead," Janet replied.

Hammond removed his suit jacket, folded it neatly, and draped it over the back of a chair. He uncapped a blue marker and drew a large grid with three columns. "Okay, three candidates are in this race—you, the Democrat, and a conservative Independent." He wrote the names in the top row. "Now, please tell me if I get anything wrong. Let's look at the issues. The Republican Party is against abortion. Of our three candidates here, which one agrees with the party platform? Certainly not the Democrat and, remarkably, not you. Just the Independent."

He put a check in the Independent's column. "Interesting, right? Gay marriage or civil unions?" He again put a check in the Independent's column. "Oh, look—same thing. You and the Democrat have the same opinion. Don't Ask, Don't Tell? The same. Climate change? The same. Cap and Trade? The same." He added three more checks. "Do you see a trend here?"

"In that handful of issues, yes," Janet said.

Hammond spun around to face Bijal. "Me too. Ms. Rao, do you have the latest polling data?"

Bijal cleared her throat nervously. "Yes. As of this morning, O'Bannon is up with thirty-eight percent, we're second with twenty-three percent, seven percent goes to Phillip Taylor, the Independent, and thirty-two percent are still undecided."

Above the candidate names, Hammond wrote the polling numbers. "This is still statistically a red district, right?"

"Yes," Bijal replied.

"So if voters were considering no factors other than party affiliation, we'd expect to win, right?" he asked.

Bijal shifted uncomfortably. "Well…"

"I mean *no* other factors. Not name recognition for the incumbent, not advertising, not stated political opinions, not announcing that you have to take a dump on local television. If all the voters knew of the three people running was their party, *would we win?*"

"Yes," Bijal replied softly.

"Thank you," Hammond said with an air of superiority. "So let's look at what you've done, Ms. Shoemaker. You took an inherent lead and pissed it away. You've positioned yourself as just as moderate as your opponent. You've snubbed the NRA, insulted your constituents, and wasted your time sucking up to the eleven centrists that live in this district. What the hell kind of strategy is that?"

"I've been trying to convince her that we need to move to the right," Donna whined.

"You've been *trying?*" Hammond asked. "Let me tell you what I see, Ms. Shoemaker. This campaign has been a bag of flaming horseshit for months. And if we weren't working so hard to gain the majority in the House, or if you'd managed to fuck this up just a little *less* spectacularly—perhaps fewer embarrassing YouTube videos, no televised protests in your parking lot—then I might not be here now. But in addition to becoming a regional laughingstock, you've been catapulted into the national spotlight, so now the stakes are raised."

Donna stared at Janet imploringly. "Are you going to let him come in here and insult us all and...and *fire* me?"

Hammond put the cap back on his marker. "Yes, she is. And let me tell you why. Let's go back to our whiteboard." He pointed to each column again. "So as the chairman of the NRCC, who here looks like the candidate I should be supporting? And which one do you think has the better chance of energizing the conservative base and increasing voter turnout? You may have won the primary—"

"We ran unopposed," Bijal said without thinking.

"That explains quite a bit," Hammond replied. "However, I have real doubts that, if you were elected, you'd work with us to support the party's agenda."

Janet was clearly unnerved. "What happened to conservative fiscal policy being a plus? I thought the economy was our priority."

"It is," Hammond replied calmly. "But I'll be honest with you, Mayor. You may just not be far enough to the right for us. If this were Massachusetts, having a centrist candidate would be more acceptable. But you're in Virginia, losing by double digits to an avowed liberal lesbian. That can't continue."

"So, what you're saying—" Janet said.

"I mean, it would be a real shame for your party to drop you. Because not only would you lose this congressional race, but I can't imagine you'd win reelection as mayor here in rural Ravensdale. You know?"

"Yes," Janet said slowly.

"So I'm understood, then?" Hammond asked, putting his jacket back on and adjusting his cuffs.

Janet conceded. "You are."

Donna was rabidly livid again. "I suppose you don't think I'll go to the press with this? You'll all come off like a pack of incompetent liars."

Hammond looked nonplussed. "I anticipated that. We'll keep you on the payroll through Election Day, but we don't require your services here any longer. Lay low, and we'll find a place for you at the beginning of the year. Go to the press, and I'll guarantee that you're so savagely discredited that you never work another day in politics."

"Oh," Donna said flatly.

"Do we have an agreement?"

Donna swallowed loudly. "Yes."

"I'm glad. You may go now."

Bijal watched in astonishment as Donna rose and left the office, clearly defeated in posture and pace.

Hammond handed the marker to Eliot. "Now, Eliot will step you through your new strategy paradigm. And once I'm confident that you both grasp the direction, you'll need to call your press secretary in so we can address yesterday's amateurish bungle, as well as your staff restructuring. Any questions before I give Eliot the floor?"

"No," Janet and Bijal said in unison.

"Good." Hammond flashed his first smile of the morning. "We're making real progress."

❖

Bijal opened the apartment door with her shoulder, awkwardly closing it behind her with her foot as she balanced the many take-out bags she was holding.

Fran was sprawled on the sofa, watching a reality show of some kind. "Holy shit," she said, without loosening her grip on the remote. "You still live here?"

"Yup," Bijal replied, heading for the kitchen.

"When I hadn't seen you in a couple of weeks, I assumed you'd either moved out or been arrested for trespassing."

"Sweet of you to think of me. I guess you're not interested in the Szechwan chicken I have, then, since you've already written me off as a part of the local penitentiary chain gang." She deposited the goods and began hungrily sorting through them.

Fran's face lit up like a bonfire. "Ooh…Did you go to Happy Panda Pagoda?"

"I did."

"Did you get spring rolls?"

Bijal held a greasy paper bag aloft. "Little fat-soaked firecrackers of death, yes."

Fran leapt up and nearly flew into the kitchen to snatch the oily hors d'œuvres from her. "These are *awesome!*"

Bijal continued to unpack the food. "Yeah, they gave me a spring-roll punch card too. After two dozen, you get a free referral to a cardiologist."

"Don't worry, once I gorge myself I'll drink some juice. That undoes all the damage." Fran inspected a black plastic bag mixed in with the others, but clearly not from the restaurant. "What do we have here?" she asked as she pulled out a bottle of whiskey. "Bij, did you get fired? Is that why you're home tonight? 'Cause as a little FYI, you can drink yourself to death with cheaper shit than this."

"No, *I* wasn't fired, but Donna Shoemaker was."

"The Nazi dentist?"

"Uh-huh," Bijal answered with a nod.

"Got shit-canned?"

"I prefer 'flushed away.'"

Fran bit her lower lip. "Very poetic. So what does that mean for you?"

Bijal fished out the plastic utensils. "It means I have a new boss with a totally different campaign strategy, new job functions, and now I only work eleven hours a day instead of eighteen."

"Um…congratulations?"

"Thanks, I don't know what I'll do with all my new free time. Maybe sleep…or wash myself."

"Such a luxurious life of leisure," Fran said before biting the end off a spring roll and scrutinizing the whiskey label. "Hey, this is made by Arc of Orion."

"Yeah, I tried it a couple weeks ago and it's really good."

"The night you couldn't drive yourself home, perhaps?"

"Um…I don't recall, Senator."

Fran stabbed a piece of sweet-and-sour pork with her fork. "Of course you don't, Drunky McHotpants. So is the booze to celebrate the termination of your evil sea wasp of a campaign manager?"

"What the hell is a sea wasp?"

"It's a kind of jellyfish—one of the most venomous animals in the world. Sweet! Shrimp toast."

Bijal dumped some Szechwan chicken onto a paper plate. "You know, that's a perfect description of her. Because Donna has no brain, and she does nothing but float along full of poison, stinging anyone in her path. But no, it's not a celebration."

"Why not? Did another aggressive invertebrate replace her?"

"He's a damn sight smarter. I'll give him that."

"But?"

"But the NRCC placed him there solely to move Janet further to the right."

Fran glowered. "How far to the right? Like 'women should be subservient' and 'gays should be jailed' kind of right?"

"Well, they didn't mention repealing the Nineteenth Amendment, but they did say that if Janet doesn't begin to appear more conservative, the party will publicly endorse Phillip Taylor instead."

"What?" Fran coughed. "That man's *crazy*."

"I know."

"Isn't he the lunatic who wants to bomb China?"

Bijal skewered a bite of food. "That's him. He also thinks all welfare and entitlement programs should be done away with and is running on the platform of laying off everyone who works for the government except for the military…oh, and the politicians."

"Naturally."

"He's suggested more than once that all private citizens should be armed."

"I'm guessing he really means only the white ones," Fran said.

"And he's openly declared his hostility toward most countries in Asia and the Middle East."

"Come on. The NRCC wouldn't endorse that guy. I don't buy it. It sounds like a bluff."

Bijal swallowed. "I think so too. And I told Janet as much when we were alone."

"What did she say?"

"Hammond scared her too much. Before today, she was just worried she'd have to stay mayor of Ravensdale if she lost, but she figured that at least it would get her name out there for next time. Now she's worried that the Republicans will drop her completely and put someone to run against her in her reelection campaign."

"That sounds a little paranoid."

"Normally, I'd agree. But they were nice enough to go ahead and imply that's what they plan to do."

"Damn."

"Yeah, so now I have to go to work every morning for a woman who's pretending to support some issues that I abhor. So again, no, not really a celebration."

Fran walked back over to the couch and sat with her Chinese food. "Maybe it's a sign that you need to get the hell out."

"I don't know," Bijal said, following her. "Part of me wants to stick with it. How will it look on my résumé if I quit the first real political position I get as soon as I take on a bigger role?"

"I'm assuming that while you're revising it you won't put 'once I got promoted, I gave my boss the finger.'"

"Well, no. But even if prospective employers don't know that I quit, *I'll* know." She stared at the television, fixating on the two buxom blondes doing shots of liquor from each other's belly buttons. "What the hell are you watching?"

"*The Love Jungle*," Fran replied eagerly. "They put a bunch of women with fake boobs out in the rain forest with nothing but a thatched hut, a stripper pole, and an open bar."

"What's the point?"

"They're all competing for this hunky Tarzan guy. Every week they have physical challenges. You missed the redhead who was wearing an outfit so tight she looked like a busted-open can of biscuits. She was way too drunk to do the vine-swinging shit she was supposed to, and she puked all over the platform and some big chick who punched her dead in the face. It was beautiful."

Bijal glanced at her watch. "Oh, crap, it's later than I thought. Hey, O'Bannon's supposed to be on *The Tank Guzman Show* in a couple minutes. Can we change over real quick if I promise to immediately come back to the drunken women with low self-esteem?"

Fran shrugged. "I suppose. But if I miss somebody crying or peeing themselves, I'm gonna be mad at you."

"As well you should be," Bijal said, taking the remote and

changing the channel. "Though you never know—someone might pee themselves on this show too."

"I'm gonna hold you to that," Fran replied, waggling a forkful of pork.

Within a couple of minutes, Tank Guzman was introducing the guests in his typical nasal manner.

"Tonight, joining us from the Alabama State House, is State Senator Caleb Prescott, cosponsor of a bill that would make the adoption of children by gay and lesbian parents illegal in his state. On the other side of the debate, we've got U.S. Congresswoman Colleen O'Bannon, Democratic representative from Virginia and co-chair of the Congressional LGBT Equality Caucus. Thanks to both of you for joining us this evening."

"Oh," Fran said, settling back into the cushions. "You weren't kidding about somebody possibly peeing."

"Senator Prescott, let's start with you. You've proposed a bill that many people say legalizes discrimination based on sexual orientation. How do you respond to that?"

Prescott, a man with greasy hair, a small neck, and barely visible lips, cleared his throat and began to speak in a thick Southern accent.

"Tank, I have to say that those kinds of irrational accusations are made by people who simply don't have all the facts. I don't support discrimination, but it's been proven in scientific studies that children of gay and lesbian parents tend to have more psychological problems, are more likely to develop drug dependencies, and are more prone to suicide."

Fran snorted. "That man is a dick."

"Congresswoman O'Bannon, I'm going to let you address the senator's comments and the allegation that you, as an out lesbian, don't know all the facts. What do you think about that?"

"Is it me, or is Guzman being purposely antagonistic?" Bijal asked.

"I don't know, but your girl looks good."

"She's not my girl."

"Well, Tank, I have to say that Senator Prescott is both remarkably prejudiced and misinformed, and I'm not sure which I find more offensive. It's well-known that a religious fundamentalist group paid for those

*so-called 'studies' he referenced for the sole purpose of producing the
results they wanted. No impartial member of the scientific community
believes those findings to be true. They are deeply flawed and, quite
honestly, motivated by hatred."*

"Ha!" Fran spat as Guzman began speaking again.

*"Senator Prescott, the congresswoman brings up a good point.
Who funded those studies you were quoting?"*

*"Uh, Tank, I don't have that information in front of me, but I can
tell you that the congresswoman is wrong. They aren't flawed. They
aren't bias—"*

Colleen jumped in, and not a moment too soon.

*"Tank, I have that information right here. The Fundamentalist
Alliance for Christ—a group that has for years espoused the practice of
'curing' gays and lesbians and making them heterosexual—performed
the studies in question. So we can assume they may not be the most
impartial folks in the world."*

Tank looked as though he smelled blood in the water.

*"Senator Prescott, assuming that particular data may be flawed,
what other rationale do you have for this bill? Have there been some
specific concerns with adoption by gays in your home state? I mean,
what prompted this?"*

*"Not to my knowledge, Tank. But based on the recent wildfire of
gay-advocacy bills over the last couple of years, we hope this will be
signed into law as a proactive measure, and that Alabama can be a
beacon for the rest of the states on this issue."*

"Oh, my God," Bijal said. "Look at Colleen's face. Here it
comes."

*"Senator, just for my own edification, you honestly feel that what
someone does in the privacy of their bedroom with another consenting
adult is reasonable criteria to determine if he or she is a competent
parent?"*

Prescott squared his shoulders and grinned smugly.

*"Yes, Congresswoman. As a matter of fact, I do. As does anyone
who reveres the scripture."*

"Aren't you a parent?"

"I am."

"Then by your logic, Senator, you need to tell us what kind of sex

you're having, as well as any kind of sex you think you might have in the future."

Prescott's lipless face turned red and he began to sputter. It soon became clear that Guzman intended to uncharacteristically sit by quietly and let the two of them face off.

"Don't be ridiculous!"

"Is it ridiculous because I'm imposing my morality onto you without your permission? Or is it because I'm defining you solely by your sexuality?"

"You're being obscene!"

"Because I'm implying that you have sex, sir? Hardly. I would argue that you and the others who insist on vilifying the LGBT community based on what you assume we're doing in private are far more obscene."

"I refuse to stand for this type of talk. Tank?"

Tank made no attempt to intervene and merely grinned as the back-and-forth continued.

"You don't like being judged on your sexual activities, do you, Senator? It doesn't seem like it's anyone's business, does it?"

"Tank, do you plan to regain control of this interview?"

"And if I told you, Senator, that I intend to assume that you're engaging in some consensual sexual act that I think makes you an unfit parent, and let's say also ill-suited to keep your job, I'd imagine in the spirit of fairness to your own argument, you'd support that, right?"

"I'm leaving if this continues."

"Senator, I think we're all in agreement here. If you're willing to prove to all of us that you're only having the kind of sex that we, as interested strangers, approve of, then I think we can all assent to that kind of a...well, let's call it a purity test."

Prescott began to fumble with the microphone fastened to his lapel as Colleen continued.

"And everyone out there who thinks that LGBT people are depraved or somehow less than others should be willing to take the same kind of purity test. I mean, if we're judging people on what they do in their bedroom, that should hold true for everyone, right?"

Prescott stood up, his mic still affixed to his jacket, and stormed out of frame. There was a large hum of feedback as the small square he had occupied on the screen became empty, before it was hastily removed, leaving only a split screen between Colleen and Guzman.

"*Wow, I guess the senator wasn't prepared for your argument, Congresswoman. I can't remember the last time someone actually walked off the set in the middle of an interview.*"

"*Sorry, Tank. That certainly wasn't my intent. I just wanted him to consider what it's like to be viewed exclusively through the prism of sexuality. No other quality—not race or gender or ethnicity—supposes so much about a person's intimate moments and relationships. And it's so grossly unfair. To use such suppositions to determine if someone gets to keep their job, legally marry someone, or adopt a child is the height of prejudice and discrimination.*"

"*Well said, Congresswoman. And don't worry, you have an open invitation to come on this show anytime. I don't care how many guests you drive away.*"

"*I appreciate that, Tank.*"

"*Coming up next, who's paying more taxes, the rich or the middle class? We just might surprise you when we return from this break.*"

As a commercial began, Bijal was only vaguely aware of the man describing his recent concern over the size of his prostate. She hit the Mute button, and she and Fran sat for some time, neither eating nor speaking. "Wow," Bijal said finally.

"That was *amazing*," Fran said softly, as though she was in shock. "I've never seen anyone…I mean…shit. Dude, that kind of ass-whooping beats brass poles covered with stripper butter any day."

"She was masterful."

"She sure was."

"We are so screwed."

Fran's brow furrowed. "Who is?"

"My campaign. Colleen obviously doesn't operate by the standard political rulebook, the one that says remain above the fray and stick to your talking points."

"You can say that again. She owned that little bastard."

Bijal got up and ventured back to the kitchen to pour herself some whiskey. "Just as I imagine she'll own Janet in our debate on Friday."

"Oh, hmm," Fran said as she chewed.

"Especially on the issues where Janet is being forcibly pushed to the right. Nothing like having your stance inexplicably change and then having to defend it. We're gonna have our asses handed to us."

"Well, if someone has to put their hand on your ass, you picked a damn fine woman to do it. You know, I'm thinking of marrying these spring rolls."

Bijal poured two fingers of alcohol into a glass, paused, then made it three. "This debate is our last stand, Fran. Our poll numbers and our fund-raising have both been steadily declining. I was really hoping Colleen would come off as too liberal or erudite…or wishy-washy. Something we could use, you know?"

"Hang on a second. You yourself have described O'Bannon as smart, charming, and principled."

"Yeah," Bijal said, rejoining Fran on the sofa.

"So why would you even dare to hope she'd come off as some dry, scholarly waffler?"

Bijal sipped her drink, letting the vapor fill her mouth. "I don't know. I guess because she was putting herself out there for such a progressive cause."

"A cause that you support too," Fran reminded her.

"Well, sure, but I still saw it as a risky move. Of course, I had no idea that the guy she'd be up against would be so spineless and inarticulate."

"If I didn't know you better, I'd think you wanted that ignorant ballsack to shut O'Bannon down and be persuasive in his argument to subjugate you."

Bijal felt a sudden pang of guilt. "No."

"That's how you're sounding. Maybe you need to stop for a moment and decide exactly what you're ready to commit to. Are you really prepared to fight against your own principles…or your own best interests?"

"Christ, Fran. Can we not have this conversation again?"

Fran nibbled her sweet-and-sour. "Sure. Right after you explain to me how you can sit right here and root for some shifty-ass bastard who's trying to take away *your* rights."

"I wasn't rooting for him, per se. I obviously disagree with his obtuse draconian position. I just wanted—"

"O'Bannon to screw up?"

"Exactly."

"Maybe announce some pending diarrhea? An STD?"

Bijal stole one of Fran's spring rolls. "Look, I'd just like the ground leveled a little."

"Then maybe you should talk to your candidate and tell her to stop fucking up so much."

"It's that kind of tact and diplomacy that keeps you out of politics, Fran."

"Well, if the massive compromises you're making are any kind of a sign, that's a job I don't want in the first place."

"So instead of trying to make a broken system better, or make a real difference, you'd just give up because at times you have to make concessions?"

Fran picked up the remote and changed the channel back to *The Love Jungle*, but left it muted. "Don't you think you can make too many concessions and compromise your cause?"

"Of course," Bijal replied. "But that hasn't happened here. Janet's still a moderate at heart."

"Have you guys started your debate prep yet?"

"All day long," Bijal said. "It's challenging, but she's improving. She's got a down-to-earth quality that'll help her connect with voters."

"Likability's important, I guess. But you know what trumps it?"

"What?"

"A good old-fashioned ass-kicking. Kablam!"

"Okay, now you're just gloating."

Fran cast a sideways glance. "I suppose you're gonna tell me you didn't get even the teensiest bit aroused at how your sexy congresswoman put her pro-gay foot on that asshole's spindly little homophobic neck and snapped him like a green bean?"

"Perhaps some small nonpartisan part of me found it…exciting."

Fran laughed and turned the volume back up. "Yeah, I'll bet I know just which small nonpartisan part you're talking about too."

Bijal shook her head. "If they ever figure out a way to combine spring rolls and vaginas, you're done for, you filthy woman."

"I'd never leave the house."

CHAPTER TWELVE

Colleen locked her car as her BlackBerry went off. It was her campaign manager. "Hey, Max. What's up?"

"I just wanted to call you bright and early and tell you how much I love you."

"What is it? You sound almost giddy." Colleen began the walk to her congressional office building as she slipped her keys into her bag.

He cleared his throat. "I know I called you last night after your television appearance to tell you how well I thought you did."

"Yeah, that was me. You didn't dream that."

"But I just wanted to touch base and drop a little fact on you—maybe start your day off with a bang."

"Okay," Colleen said slowly. This was decidedly suspicious. Max didn't usually subscribe to theatrics.

"It's safe to say that you went over well, based on the sudden influx of donations we've received in the last twelve hours."

"Couldn't that just be a coincidence?"

"Well, ordinarily, I'd say yes. But considering that the vast majority of them came from out of state, I'm ruling out both kismet and anomalous planetary alignment."

Colleen stepped into a crosswalk as the light changed. "Huh, well, that's certainly an unexpected surprise."

"I haven't told you how much yet."

When he didn't elaborate, she sighed. "Do I need to whisper some secret password first?"

"Nearly four hundred eighty thousand dollars."

"Holy shit! Are you serious?"

"I'm here at headquarters and it's still rolling in, Col. You may need to take Tank Guzman up on his invitation to come back. Maybe we can negotiate a nightly spot on his show."

"I love it when your inner greed comes out, Max." She entered the building and headed toward her office.

"We'll call it *Bitch Slap*, and every night we'll get a new racist, homophobe, or anti-Semite to come on and say stupid shit. You'll make them cry and run away, the viewing public gets a warm tingly feeling in their nonny parts—"

"Their *what* parts? Exactly what kind of feelings are you implying that my appearance evoked in the public, Max?"

"Everyone feels like there's justice in the world, and at the end you get to say, 'You've just been bitch-slapped!'"

"Are you having a mild stroke, Max? Do you smell almonds?"

He laughed. "You think it's too much?"

"You're nothing if not perceptive."

"How about 'you've just been homo-spanked'?"

Colleen was momentarily incredulous. "I'm sorry, are you trying to name a finishing move for me? Is that what you're doing here?"

"You say finishing move, I say catchphrase. Whatever works."

"I may have to homo-spank you if..." As Colleen turned the corner, she saw a group of people assembled outside her office. "Oh, crap."

"What's up?" Max asked.

"A whole gaggle of folks is waiting for me here."

"Friends or foes?"

"Well, I don't see any pitchforks, but no one's holding a fruit basket either. I'll have to call you back later, Max. Wish me luck."

"Homo-spank them!" he said, just before she ended the call.

Colleen slipped her BlackBerry into its holster like a gunslinger and approached the gathering with trepidation. There looked to be a dozen or so people, most of them young, maybe college age. That was a positive sign.

Suddenly, someone in the crowd shouted, "She's here." In what felt like an instant, they had surrounded her.

"Can I help you?" Colleen asked as she valiantly tried to keep moving toward her office.

"We've been waiting for you," a woman with dimples and disturbingly large eyes said.

"I want to speak with you," an African American man said, the urgency evident in his voice and posture.

"So do I," called a voice from the back.

"Okay," Colleen replied calmly. "Everyone come into my office and I'll see what we can do."

She was relieved that no one was shouting at her, and they all seemed agreeable to following her—another positive indication. Over the last couple of years constituents had, on occasion, stopped by her office to speak with her about various issues. Usually they made an appointment first, but sometimes they just turned up. One time an organized group of about ten wanted to speak with her about ending the U.S. military presence in Afghanistan. But she'd never seen an impromptu assembly of this size before.

Her scheduler Penny, whose desk was just inside, was clearly overwhelmed, and her expression was an obvious plea for help. Beyond Penny sat another dozen or so people, looking at her excitedly.

Once everyone was across the threshold, Colleen put her hands up and addressed the entire group. "Hello, folks. Welcome. I'm not really sure to what I owe this visit. Are you all together?" Most started shaking their heads. "All right, are any of you together?" Several looked around at each other, but most had arrived alone, and a few were there in pairs. "Does your visit have anything to do with my appearance last night on TV?"

Suddenly everyone started talking at once.

"Wait, wait," Colleen shouted, trying to gain the floor again. "I can't understand you all unless you speak one at a time. Let's do this by a show of hands instead. How many of you are here because you saw me on Tank Guzman's show?"

Everyone raised their hand.

Colleen exhaled loudly in surprise. "Um, wow. Okay, so how many of you have come here to chastise me and tell me I'm wrong and/or going to hell?"

No one raised their hand. Colleen smiled broadly and felt instantly more at ease. "Well, that's nice to know."

"A couple of protesters were here a little while ago," a sinewy-looking man with beard stubble said. "But we chased them off." He was apparently pleased with himself, and the others chuckled with him.

"How many of you are here because you're looking for a way to help achieve LGBT civil rights?" Colleen asked.

Again, everyone responded in the affirmative. Perhaps Max had been right about how well she'd done against Senator Prescott. If this could serve as a catalyst for something positive, she was more than prepared.

❖

Bijal was sorting through video equipment at her desk, preparing to film the evening's event, as Kristin slumped back down into her chair across from her and sighed.

"Already had a long morning?" Bijal asked.

"It feels more like a long few months." Kristin began to whisper. "Is it wrong that I just wish tonight's debate was over?"

"No, but it might be best if you don't repeat that, just in case."

Kristin looked around to make sure no one else was listening. "I mean, am I the only one who's starting to feel like we just can't catch a break?"

Bijal shook her head and answered softly. "It's not just you, Kristin. But remember that at any time, the tide could turn. Politics is a weird business. Sometimes a shift in momentum can start with a single grain of sand."

"Wow, that's kind of poetic," Kristin said with a grin. "Thanks for the pep talk."

"Anytime." Of course, Bijal didn't elaborate that she was really looking forward to this debate because it would give her an opportunity to see Colleen, whom she hadn't seen in several days.

A couple of times she'd actually considered just *stopping by* the K and K, but she couldn't come up with a reason that wasn't visibly dripping with pretense. Besides, she'd been keeping a close eye on

Colleen's schedule, at least partially to glean any logical detours Colleen could make to Sue's bar, and hadn't spied any real opportunities.

As silly as she felt, this debate at Palmer College would give her an authorized possibility to feed her ridiculous and borderline self-destructive infatuation. Luckily, she just needed to film it from the back of the auditorium. She could remain a detached observer, though perhaps, if she planned it well, she could conveniently bump into Colleen in the ladies' room afterward. Something about that thought felt terribly illicit, perhaps because Colleen was the most forbidden person she could possibly pursue. But maybe there was more to it than that—

Paige unexpectedly rested her full rump on the edge of Bijal's desk and effectively broke her semi-smutty reverie. "Hey, ladies. How are you both holding up?"

"Bijal was just helping me get psyched up for the debate," Kristin replied.

"Really? Did it work?" Paige asked, looking surprised when Kristin nodded. "Then maybe you'd better work some of your magic on me, Bijal."

Bijal set down her tripod so she could give Paige her full attention. "Are you starting to feel discouraged too?"

Paige snorted. "*Discouraged?* Hell, I passed discouraged in the fast lane weeks ago on the way to demoralized hollow shell. At this point, I'd say just feeling discouraged is a pretty good day."

"Wow," Bijal said, taken aback. "You might be past the point where a simple chat can bring you back around." She apparently wasn't the only campaign worker who'd had a slow sinking feeling over these last few weeks. Who knew how many others were in their midst, keeping up a strong façade yet, inside, softly counting the days till failure?

Eliot approached them and Bijal struggled to not openly recoil, silently hoping he was just passing by on his way to someone else's desk. She wasn't certain what about Eliot unsettled her, but the more time she spent with him, the more concentrated her feelings became. "Well, hello, people," he said. "Are we all set for tonight?"

The three of them nodded weakly, though Eliot's sneer implied that he didn't believe their feigned enthusiasm any more than they did.

"We're just a little…worn down," Kristin replied tactfully.

"Understood," Eliot replied, putting his hands in his pockets. "It's certainly not true that this campaign staff isn't pulling its weight."

An awkward silence ensued until Paige finally spoke. "Has...has someone actually said that?"

Eliot's eyes widened for an instant, presumably with the realization that he had just admitted that the NRCC had assumed they were all lazy. "Huh? Oh, are you kidding? Of course not. Never." Bijal was slightly disappointed that yet another career politician had turned out to be such a horrible liar. He quickly turned his attention to the video equipment. "You're testing the equipment before you pack it, right?"

Bijal closed her eyes briefly, hoping they wouldn't obviously roll at her boss's transparent attempt to change an uncomfortable subject. "Yes. Trust me, I'm a pro with this thing now."

Eliot winked in a way that implied a sexual confidence he had no business deluding himself with. "Really? So you're a regular Paris Hilton, huh?"

Bijal interrupted another uncomfortable period of quiet, though this time, completely against her will. "Eww," she replied in disgust. "Um...no." She now understood *exactly* what she didn't like about Eliot—his inherent and intense skeeviness.

"So where's Janet, anyway?" Kristin asked, her expression of shock belying her reasonable inquiry. "I thought we were supposed to do a full mock debate before we headed over to the college."

"She had to stop by her doctor's office this morning," Eliot replied. "I told her that she'd picked the worst day in the world for an appointment, but she promised she'd be quick."

Paige scoffed and crossed her arms. "A quick doctor's appointment? I've never heard of one of those. Is that like a unicorn?"

"Or a trustworthy man," Kristin added, suddenly realizing one was standing there. "No offense, Eliot."

He shrugged. "If I were trustworthy, I wouldn't be in politics."

Bijal started packing the equipment into the camera bag, hoping to end this conversation that had now rapidly gone south. "Maybe we should make that our new campaign slogan, Eliot. We could put it on the yard signs—right under Janet's name."

"Heh." Eliot chuckled. "You're sassy."

Bijal turned to Paige and Kristin in frustration. "Why do people keep telling me that? Is that even a real thing?"

As though to punish her further, Bijal didn't get an answer. Instead, everyone's attention shifted to Janet, who had finally arrived at the office and was shuffling toward them wearing large dark glasses as though she was incognito.

"Well, that took forever," Eliot announced, looking at his watch. When Janet didn't immediately respond, his expression changed. "Is everything okay?"

"We may have a little problem, people," Janet said quietly.

Eliot now seemed to be panicking. "Why? What's wrong?"

Janet removed her sunglasses to reveal that the whites of her eyes were puffy, runny, and the color of Roma tomatoes.

"Ahh!" Kristin blurted.

"Gesundheit," Bijal said quickly, hoping to cover for Kristin's spontaneous eruption.

"Thank you," Kristin replied unconvincingly, her face still registering horror.

Everyone stared, amazed at what they were seeing.

"Is it noticeable?" Janet asked.

"What the fuck is wrong with your eyes?" Eliot shouted, coming unglued all at once.

Janet looked pathetic. "Do you think the cameras will be able to pick it up?"

"Pick it up?" Eliot parroted. "You look like a demon!"

Bijal didn't fully understand how this pleasant day had quickly turned into a fetid mound of warm dung with seemingly no end in sight. "Janet, what is that?"

"My ophthalmologist says it's bacterial conjunctivitis."

"Pinkeye," Paige said.

"Or in your case, festering, oozy blood eye," Eliot added, his voice becoming shrill and accusatory.

Janet continued as though he hadn't spoken. "My eyes started to bother me a little yesterday, but when I woke up this morning I could barely open them. It was like they'd been glued shut. It looks bad, huh?"

"Well, it doesn't look good," Paige replied matter-of-factly.

"Will we need to postpone the debate?" Janet asked.

Everyone turned to Eliot. This was definitely his decision. He ran his palm over his chin nervously as he seemed to frantically mull on it. "I'd rather not postpone. It implies weakness. Did you get drops or anything? Will it look any better by tonight?"

"No to both," Janet said dejectedly. "He said it'll take several days, but it has to clear up on its own."

"Is it contagious?" Kristin asked.

Janet glared in response. At least Bijal assumed she was glaring. Honestly, it was hard to tell. "Don't worry. I'll try not to rub my eyes on any of you."

Paige cleared her throat. "Or rub your eyes and then touch…oh, anything?"

Janet replaced her dark glasses. "So now what?"

"You'll look this way through the weekend?" Eliot asked, his teeth firmly clenched.

Janet nodded. "Apparently."

"Can't you take something to make you look less…diseased? Some kind of eye-whitener?" Eliot looked demented now.

"There's nothing like that," Paige replied with a wave of her hand. "My husband had pinkeye a few months ago. But he didn't have anything like *that*." She wiggled her fingers in Janet's direction.

Everyone was rapidly starting to break down. True, the campaign workers had slowly grown more disheartened as each increasingly scandalous thing had occurred. Bijal suspected that most, like her, were simply operating more out of a sense of duty than from any zeal or expectation of winning. Now that their candidate was poised for what would likely be her last opportunity to appear commanding and informed—to possibly undo some of the recent damage to her credibility—she would appear without any eye whites.

Sensing that Eliot would *not* step up into his leadership role, and that without a voice of reason, the campaign was within thirty seconds of completely imploding, Bijal stood and motioned for everyone to stop speaking. "Okay, that's enough. We've had a good couple minutes to freak out. Let's move on to how we can fix this."

Everyone nodded except Eliot, who was staring at her blankly. "So then, let's hear your 'fix,'" he hissed, using air quotes sarcastically. Perhaps he wasn't the most receptive person when someone else took charge.

"Fine," Bijal replied. "We need to assess the value of this debate. We're all aware that we've had some recent very public, damaging setbacks. At the same time, O'Bannon has gone on national television in what's been generally perceived as a favorable appearance. Her fund-raising has spiked outrageously in the past several days as a result, whereas ours has…not."

"Agreed," Janet said, pulling up a chair.

"So calling off this debate would certainly do nothing to alter our momentum. O'Bannon's clip on Tank Guzman has gone viral on YouTube, and so has Janet's clip talking about Thai food. This may be our last stand. Otherwise our numbers continue to decline and O'Bannon's continue to rise," Bijal explained calmly.

"Is it possible to reschedule it?" Paige asked.

Bijal shook her head. "Calling it off the day of the debate can only look bad for us—like we're unprepared. I mean, we could contact the O'Bannon camp, sure."

"You're right," Janet said. "Everyone will think we're afraid to take O'Bannon on."

"What if you did the debate with your sunglasses on?" Kristin asked.

Paige scoffed. "You don't think that might come off as a little Roy Orbison?"

"Who?" Kristin asked.

Bijal smiled at Paige. "You'll need an example from the last ten years if you want to make your point."

"So Corey Hart is out too?" Paige said.

"I'm afraid so," Bijal said. "Look, if you simply explain to the audience why you're wearing them, you'll be fine. In fact, it might make you appear more dedicated and serious, which is certainly a plus, right?"

"It is, yes," Janet replied with a resolute nod.

Even Eliot seemed somewhat less irritated. Perhaps this event wouldn't be another abysmally appalling festival of shame. Maybe they really could make up some lost ground at this debate.

Bijal clapped her hands to motivate everyone. "Let's get practicing, then!"

CHAPTER THIRTEEN

Colleen locked her car door, and as she gathered her belongings, she spied a familiar blue Subaru about six spaces down from her. Her stomach lurched in anticipation before her brain rudely reminded her that Bijal was part of the opposition and therefore she really shouldn't be considering her a friend, much less a smart, attractive friend whose naked body she might have occasionally visualized.

Perhaps the stress of campaigning was making Colleen more inclined to seek a pleasant distraction. Or had Bijal just really gotten under her skin? Regardless, Colleen thought frequently about her extraordinarily smart and sexy adversary. Sometimes it was her radiant smile, other times something witty she'd said or the way she idly brushed her hair away from her face. But at any rate, all roads led to the same place—a deep attraction with a side of infatuation.

Before she had even started walking toward the college auditorium, Colleen could make out Max quickly crossing the parking lot toward her. The sun was setting, but she recognized his distinctive stride. "I should have known you'd be early," she said, glancing at her watch.

"I'm just eager, I suppose," he said, motioning politely for her to head back with him toward the building.

"Mmm, you seem *especially* enthused now that we've had this sudden influx of donations…not to imply anything, of course. I'm just saying."

He grinned. "We passed the million-dollar mark this afternoon, Col. You have now officially more than tripled the amount in our coffers inside a week, based primarily on your public pummeling of that anti-gay creep. I'm thinking, come hell or high water, we need to get you back on TV."

"But what if the next one doesn't go as well? What if some rabid conspiracist fanatic waving around a crucifix and a farmers' almanac rips me apart?"

He scowled momentarily and rubbed his chin. "What do you think this person's conspiracy might entail? Something to do with when Jesus wants the turnips harvested?"

"Hmm, you know what?"

"You intend to ignore my question?"

"Besides that," Colleen said.

"What?"

"Go ahead and get back with Guzman. Tell him I'd like to come back on his show, but only if I can talk about the Patient Access Reform Act—specifically the Saturday amendment."

"Ah, you want to use a little of your newfound political capital?"

"Maybe," Colleen replied. "We're certainly not as beholden to the Democratic Party for financial support as we were a week ago. Let me know if he's game, okay?"

Max nodded and opened the door to the auditorium for Colleen. "Will do, boss. Oh, and I have a shit-ton of new television ads for you to review too, so we can add your little 'I approved this message' blurb."

Colleen stopped walking and eyed him appraisingly. "Did you keep them positive, like I asked?"

He bit his lower lip, what Colleen knew to be his critical tell. "Most of them," he confessed.

She glared. "You don't take direction very well."

"I just wanted you to consider taking advantage of some of the opportunities for negative ads that Denton has so generously presented us with. You can still nix them if you don't like them."

She shook her head slowly and lowered her voice. "The way I see it, Denton's been everyone's punching bag for the last few weeks, and I just don't feel like piling on. Personally, I hate those vindictive, inflammatory commercials. I think most people do. Don't tell me to vote for you because the other candidate sucks more. Explain what you stand for. Do you disagree?"

"No." He stepped closer so he could speak more softly. "Look, I'll make you a deal, okay? If you check out *all* the proposed spots, I won't say a word to you about them."

Colleen was skeptical. "You won't try to sell me on any of them?"

"Scout's honor."

"Fine," she said, looking around. Bijal had to be here somewhere.

"Oh, and just so you know, this place is already packed." He slid his hand in his pants pocket and propped himself casually against the cinderblock wall. "Not only are the local media outlets set up in the back, but a whole lot of gay folk are here tonight."

"Sue's handiwork, no doubt."

Max shook his head. "This is bigger than that, Col. This goes beyond the standard homegrown backyard LGBT crowd that your events draw. This is more fallout from Tank Guzman's show. Some of these people have traveled to see you because you did the unthinkable and spoke out on their behalf."

"And my own behalf, incidentally."

"Exactly," Max replied. "You're their spokesperson, their best hope for equal rights. If I were you, I'd expect to have a *very* sympathetic crowd tonight."

"Huh," Colleen said, considering the weight of such a statement. "That's kind of cool."

"It is, yes. Take a look for yourself." Max motioned to the auditorium entrance several feet away, and Colleen couldn't suppress her desire for a quick glance.

She shuffled through the propped-open double doors, exhaling loudly when she saw just how crowded it was, with nearly twenty minutes still to go before the debate was scheduled to start. A cursory scan of the crowd showed a lot of familiar faces, rainbow banners, and O'Bannon campaign signs. Max was right that the audience seemed disproportionately in her favor.

In the back, among the media, was Bijal, and Colleen's breath caught as she studied her. Bijal was setting up her trusty camcorder, but she was an absolute vision. Her gray tweed business suit fit her perfectly, the jacket short enough that it afforded a phenomenal view of her impressive butt, made even more spectacular by how flawlessly it was accentuated by her pants—the slacks of ass-angels. Her black hair hung beautifully as she attached the tripod and adjusted the angle. She was, in a word, stunning.

And then Bijal saw her.

Colleen anticipated that being caught staring at Bijal might be awkward, something that might have immediately prompted the average person to sheepishly look away. Instead, she felt bold and unabashed. Perhaps the smoldering expression on Bijal's face made it impossible for Colleen to tear her eyes away. Or maybe it was the rush she got when Bijal licked her full lips sensually.

As Colleen exhaled long and loudly, she heard vague murmuring, but nothing that seemed important enough for her to turn her head. "Hmm?" she mumbled disinterestedly.

"Did you catch anything I just said?" Max asked, standing beside her, droning on for God only knew how long.

"Was it something about a cottage cheese piñata?"

"Not even close. Hey, is that your hot—"

Colleen's paralysis miraculously vanished, and she spun quickly, shushing Max as she pushed him back out the door and into the hallway.

"Your hot Republican sex muffin?" he whispered. "Did you know she'd be here?"

"Max, can you do me a favor and scrounge up a piece of paper and a pen?"

❖

Bijal stood motionless as she watched Colleen suddenly turn and leave the auditorium, her campaign manager in tow. While Colleen was unquestionably striking in her crisp tailored suit, Bijal had sensed something else remarkable, something beyond that.

She had caught Colleen looking at her with what was clearly some mixture of attraction, admiration, and perhaps desire. What she wouldn't give to see that expression again. Preferably up close.

"Wow," Bijal said, fanning herself with her notepad. Her hormones hadn't been prepared for a quick kick in their gland-pants. Hopefully she wasn't blushing.

"Are you all set up?" Eliot asked, startling her so badly she jumped an inch or two. "Good Lord, you're a big bag of nerves," he said.

"Yeah, I guess I am," she replied, trying to calm her thrumming heartbeat.

"Janet's even worse," he said, watching as Bijal verified the charge on her batteries. "I sent Paige to her dressing room to help her get composed and focused. I just hope she's able to."

"There's a lot of pressure on Janet, Eliot. If she can't spark a comeback tonight, this campaign might be essentially over."

"Not necessarily," he said. "We may just have to shift into a different mode."

Bijal tried to read his face, but saw little written there. "As in, smear mode?"

Eliot's brow contracted in thought, but before he could answer, Paige appeared and propped her right hand on her full hip. She blew her bangs out of her eyes in what was clearly frustration.

"How's Janet doing?" Eliot asked, the concern in his voice belying his calm posture.

"She was kind of a mess," Paige said, sighing.

"But you finally got her calmed down?" Eliot asked.

"Well, I had to try a few different methods," Paige explained. "At first, I tried reason. I assured her that in a hundred years, no one would care about this debate or even remember who the candidates were."

"Let me guess," Bijal said. "Somehow that watertight argument didn't put her mind at ease?"

Paige seemed to bristle at the sarcasm. "What's wrong with it?"

"It implies that she has to wait a century for her sense of failure to completely dissipate," Bijal replied. "Other than that, it's awesome."

"Oh," Paige said, momentarily deflated now that someone had explained the flaw in her logic. "Anyway, when that didn't work, I tried to convince her that she was too prepared to fail."

"What did she say to that?" Eliot asked.

"She just kept repeating 'Thai food' over and over. It was exasperating."

Bijal couldn't blame Janet for having a case of the jitters. Things had been going so badly for so long, it was hard to see a nasty case of pinkeye as a harbinger of good fortune. "But you're out here now, so you must have made some kind of progress, right?"

"Eventually, I just broke down and gave her my Valium," Paige replied evenly.

Bijal and Eliot looked at each other in horror.

"You what?" Eliot barked.

"Shh," Paige said as she looked at him in mortification. "Let's not have some kind of incident here in front of the press."

"You're joking, right?" Bijal asked softly. "About the Valium?"

Paige blinked at them blankly. "No, why? I take it whenever I feel a panic attack coming on, and it works wonders."

"So let me get this straight," Eliot said, half whispering and half screaming. "Just before the mayor's scheduled to take on her opponent in their one and only debate, you decided to counteract her anxiety at having blood-red eyes by giving her a tranquilizer prescribed for someone else?"

"Do you know if Janet's ever even *taken* Valium before?" Bijal added.

"No," Paige said quietly. "But she says she has a high drug tolerance. That's why she insisted on taking two."

Eliot's face was now crimson, and veins were protruding from his neck and temples. His hands shook as he struggled to speak. "I…want to…kill you!"

"Eliot!" Bijal intervened, her mind racing with images of local late news stories with graphics that said things like CAMPAIGN CARNAGE running alongside footage of Eliot stomping Paige to death and shrieking expletives. "How much time do we have before the debate starts?"

He glanced at his watch. "About fifteen minutes."

"Should we go ahead and cancel?"

Paige scoffed. "You guys are making a big deal out of nothing. Janet's ready. She's been practicing for weeks. Her nervousness should be subsiding now. It'll be fine."

"You can't know that," Eliot said.

"Look, I have a couple dozen volunteers positioned through the crowd," Paige said. "I've briefed them on when and how to respond throughout the debate. We're all good. You know that debates are all about how you spin them once they're over anyway."

"Do you know how fucking fired you'll be if this goes badly?" Eliot murmured sinisterly.

Eliot was starting to sound amazingly like Donna.

"Relax," Paige said dismissively. "What could go wrong?"

CHAPTER FOURTEEN

B y the time the debate moderator—Dr. Constance Hill, a poli-sci professor on campus—entered and began her opening statement, Bijal was bordering on hyperventilation. She'd managed to momentarily keep her boss from strangling her coworker, but was fairly certain the members of the press nearest them had sensed a budding altercation.

What's more, now that Bijal had spent some time among the attendees, she realized that Colleen's supporters outnumbered Paige's measly twenty-two volunteers ensconced in the crowd, along with all the other conservatives, possibly by as much as three to one.

Bijal had also concluded that God was a Democrat.

Or maybe Janet had taken igneous rocks from Hawaii and now the Goddess Pele was punishing her. Perhaps she'd cut a Gypsy off in traffic and, in return, received the evil eye. Who knew the real story? Regardless, the planets were aligned. The spell had been cast and the bones thrown. Janet clearly had a date with destiny that would culminate in nothing less than her complete and utter ruin.

But she couldn't blame it all on chicken feet and gris-gris. Bijal needed to accept her culpability in this fiasco. They should have canceled this debate earlier in the day when they had the chance. Their gamble of making such a highly visible public appearance when Janet was in less than top form was one that was, at best, a long shot. At worst, it was a disaster from which they'd never recover.

The crowd clapped enthusiastically as Colleen was introduced.

Bijal quickly focused the camera and watched through the viewfinder as the debacle began to unfold, like a beautiful overture that plays just before the bassoonist leaps out of the orchestra pit and cuts you with a scythe…that she happened to have hidden in the tuba next to her.

Bijal noted sadly that her simile sense was still utterly dreadful. Were shitty non sequiturs a genetic defect? Like a deviated septum or feet that smelled like ripened French cheese?

As Colleen strode onto the stage looking confident, poised, and beautiful, Bijal's extraneous thoughts of murderous woodwinds and Camembert extremities dissolved. She made a mental note not to curse, groan, or suck in appreciatively—anything that might be loud enough for the camcorder to pick up. God knew she already had enough problems.

Dr. Hill then introduced Janet, and when she didn't immediately appear, Bijal began to silently count the seconds. Surely it couldn't be taking as agonizingly long for Janet to join them onstage as it seemed at that moment.

Seven Mississippi…eight Mississippi.

"Mayor Janet Denton," Dr. Hill repeated.

Eleven Mississippi…twelve Mississippi. For an instant, Bijal almost expected Dr. Hill to call out "the Family Von Trapp," soon followed by the Nazis' sudden realization that the mayor had fled Virginia up into the mountains, while singing at the top of her lungs. She would never appear for this debate, and that would indeed be the happiest ending of all.

Before Bijal could hum the first verse of "Climb Every Mountain," Janet stepped tentatively out from the wings, wearing her dark glasses and moving at a pace somewhere between a mosey and a slow saunter. As she reached the lectern, she shuffled through her note cards, seeming rather disoriented.

"Good evening, Mayor," Dr. Hill said, though Janet did not immediately respond. "Is everything all right?"

Janet leaned forward, presumably to speak into the mic. But either her irritated eyes, the effect of taking someone else's prescription tranquilizers, or the stage lights bouncing off the lenses of her sunglasses caused her to misjudge its proximity. She struck the head of the microphone with her nose, resulting in a horrific screech of feedback. "I…I have an infection," she announced flatly.

The silence that overtook the auditorium was both awkward and horrifying. Janet was supposed to explain her eyewear with something innocuous, like, "Please excuse my glasses. I saw the ophthalmologist today." Instead, she'd shuffled out like an escapee from a lobotomy clinic and announced that she had some affliction that she had more than likely obtained via unprotected anal sex with animals.

Dr. Hill finally broke the unnerving quiet. "Um, are you prepared to begin, Mayor?"

"Yes," Janet replied. She didn't appear aware of her faux pas. Meanwhile, Colleen looked absolutely aghast, but unlike the majority of people in the audience, she'd somehow been able to fight the urge to gasp and murmur incredulous profanity under her breath.

"Okay," Dr. Hill replied hesitantly. "Uh, let me take a moment to go over the rules that you've both agreed to. I'll take alternating turns asking you questions on social, foreign, and domestic policy. The recipient has three minutes to respond, and the other candidate will have a one-minute rebuttal. It is permissible, and even encouraged, for you to use any part of your time to address each other directly, though obviously if I feel that discourse is becoming unproductive or disrespectful, or has veered off the original topic, I reserve the right to either refocus the discussion or stop you completely and move on to the next question."

Dr. Hill looked at both candidates, more than likely for a sign of acknowledgement. Perhaps in Janet's case, any indication of comprehension. "Are you ready?"

Colleen and Janet both nodded, and Dr. Hill began. "Very well. Mayor Denton, the first question is for you. During her term, Representative O'Bannon has been an outspoken advocate for marriage equality in the state of Virginia, including supporting the repeal of an amendment to the state constitution that limits marriage to heterosexual couples only. What is your stance on marriage equality?"

"Fffuck," Bijal breathed without thinking. Damn, she realized. Between her muttering and the people around her, she'd have a lot of editing to do when this was over.

Janet shuffled her note cards for what seemed like an eternity before finally answering. "Gay marriage is a state issue. And as someone who currently supports our state constitution, I think it's imperative that we allow the voters to have their say. Elections have consequences, and when the people speak, it's our duty as elected officials to heed them."

Though she'd had three minutes to fill, Janet stopped. When it became clear that she was done, Dr. Hill responded. "Um, okay. Well, Congresswoman O'Bannon, you have your minute, plus two minutes and twenty-nine seconds of the mayor's time to rebut."

"May I use the time to respond to Mayor Denton directly?" Colleen asked.

Dr. Hill nodded. "Please do."

"Mayor, I disagree with everything you just said. First, marriage equality should not be left up to the states, because it's a civil right. Putting the civil rights of a minority up for a vote is unconscionable and is nothing more than politicians passing the buck on making a difficult and potentially controversial decision."

The O'Bannon supporters in the crowd began to clap, but when Colleen continued speaking they settled back down. "If we had put desegregation up for a vote in 1954, would a majority have supported it? And what about interracial marriage? If that had been on the Virginia ballot in 1967 instead of decided by the U.S. Supreme Court, do you honestly think it would have passed?

"Second, regarding the state constitution, what you're talking about is the Marshall-Newman Amendment of 2006, one of the most invasive of the recent wave of laws that attempts to define marriage. Not only does it outlaw same-sex marriage, it bans civil unions and invalidates legal contracts, including wills, medical directives, property settlements, and powers of attorney. Just a few months ago, Mayor, you referred to yourself as a moderate Libertarian. How do you reconcile allowing Virginia's electorate to vote away my right to bequeath my possessions to whomever I please? Why are my liberties less important?"

Janet still looked disoriented, and she gazed at Dr. Hill and cocked her head.

Dr. Hill, in turn, looked mystified. "Mayor, you may answer the congresswoman."

"I'm sorry, can you repeat the question?"

Colleen stared at Janet incredulously. It was as though a pod person had taken Janet's place, though perhaps that was an insult to pod people. "I asked how a self-avowed Libertarian—and correct me if something's changed, but the last I knew, Libertarians wanted to make government smaller to keep it from infringing on the rights of the people. Do I understand that correctly?"

"Well, basically, yes," Janet replied.

"What about *my* rights?" Colleen asked coolly. The crowd began applauding again.

Janet squared her shoulders. "The states define everyone's rights, including yours."

"Even though I just explained how the state stripped me of my rights and ensconced their bigotry into the constitution? So if this year the Virginia House of Delegates proposed an amendment that banned marriage between people of different religions, as a Libertarian, you'd have no qualms with that kind of government intrusion?"

Bijal could tell that Janet was struggling with more than just her mental clarity. These were exactly the types of positions that Eliot had coached her on.

"Not if that was the state law," Janet replied. "And not if that was the will of the people. As a representative for Virginia's twelfth district, I should speak for my constituents. That's the whole intent of representative government, to ensure that everyone's voice is heard."

Colleen set her jaw sternly. "Then why do we spend our time telling the voters what we believe? It's not our constituents' job to educate themselves on every bill and amendment. It's ours. It's what we're paid to do. The people don't elect followers, they elect leaders— officials who they expect to listen to all arguments, learn the facts, then vote for what's in the best interest of *everyone*. Not to just support something we think might play well in our district even though we know it's destructive or unethical, or to simply side with those who've made large campaign donations. *Anyone* can do that, and in my opinion, it's nothing more than moral cowardice. It takes courage to always vote your conscience, and that's what these people both want and deserve from us."

At that, the audience erupted into a thunderous ovation of cheering, whistling, and clapping. Bijal was utterly stunned as she watched Dr. Hill try to quiet the crowd.

Colleen had come out of the gate swinging, and by taking advantage of all the time Janet had opted not to use, she'd so far made Janet look like a scattered, calculating, morally compromised sellout with no real vision for the future and a mysterious infection of unspeakable origin.

As calm once again began to descend, a young man near the back shouted, "We love you, Colleen!"

"No outbursts, please," Dr. Hill replied.

"Christ," Bijal said softly. This was going to be the longest two hours of her life.

❖

Bijal and Paige stood off to the side watching Eliot try to spin the debate as a victory for Janet to the local television team interviewing him.

"Tonight was a clear win for Mayor Denton," he said. "She articulated her plans for job growth, a balanced budget, and educational reform. And she showed that she's the candidate who listens to what the public wants."

The reporter didn't look to be buying it. "It did seem that a number of times the mayor was either speechless or confounded, though."

"She was simply being thoughtful. Mayor Denton realizes the weight that words can have and therefore chooses them carefully."

"Mr. Jenkins, what about the confrontation on the death penalty? Mayor Denton didn't even try to respond to that. She just stared off into space."

Bijal winced. That had been an evident touchdown by Colleen. No way would Eliot be able to polish that into anything else. After using the term "pro-life" several times in an answer regarding abortion, Colleen had replied, "Mayor, as someone who professes to be 'pro-life,' how can you support the death penalty?"

It had, as the journalist was now describing, been a momentum breaker. Janet stopped, reached into her foggy cranium as though it was the bottom of her purse, and apparently came out with nothing but a used Kleenex and a lint-covered lozenge. After fifteen or so seconds of silence, Dr. Hill asked if they were ready for the next question, and everyone just moved on. All parties involved seemed to simply accept that Janet had no response and silently agreed to allot the points appropriately.

"Do you think I still have a job?" Paige whispered.

Bijal was torn between wanting to put Paige's fears to rest and the urge to fire her herself. "I don't know," she replied. "It's pretty obvious that the Valium made things worse than they would have been had Janet simply been nervous."

"You know it wasn't my idea. Janet was begging me for it."

"Look, it's not my decision, Paige. You have two choices now. You can either slip out of here while Eliot's busy and just operate like you still have a job—if you don't get a call over the weekend, show up Monday and see if he's calmer. Or you can wait around and talk to him tonight. Make your case and see if Janet will stick up for you. Though at this point, I'm not sure having her take your side will matter much."

"You're right, Bijal." Paige looked back over to Eliot, who was now losing his cool and cultivating a ball of white spittle in the corner of his mouth like some kind of tiny vile pearl. "I'll see you later," she said, dashing up the hallway and out the door into the parking lot.

Bijal hadn't expected that, but at this point, she was ready to do the same. This election seemed to be already over, even though they still had several weeks to go. They simply couldn't make up this lost ground.

With a heavy sigh, she hefted her video equipment over her shoulder and started toward the door, searching her bag for her car keys. It didn't help her state of mind that her silly fantasies about bumping into Colleen in some secluded changing room hadn't borne fruit. Other than the nanosecond of electricity she'd felt when she'd seen Colleen staring at her, this day had been a complete and utter disappointment.

After reaching her car, she unlocked it and started stuffing the camera bag in the backseat. She felt chilled as she started to get into the driver's seat, then noticed something folded underneath her windshield wiper. Hopefully it wasn't yet another flyer for a local masseuse.

"Do these things ever persuade anyone to get a massage?" she asked as she unfolded it. She was surprised to see a handwritten note, in neat and familiar cursive.

B,

You look beautiful tonight—breathtaking, really. So forgive my reckless impatience, but I'd love nothing more than to have dinner with you. If you're busy, or if, unlike me, you have your wits about you, just tear this up. Believe me, I'll more than understand.

But if you're either hungry, craving a diversion, looking for company, feeling gutsy, or any combination of the above, call me on my cell phone at the number below.

Spyxie

P.S. Did I mention how beautiful you look?

Bijal stared at the phone number before reading the note again. If she'd been chilled by the night air before she'd picked this up, she felt no sign of it now. She folded the paper and got in the car and shut the door.

She read it a third time before setting it in the passenger seat. Should she call? Everything inside her wanted to. Everything except the tiny sliver of her brain that handled propriety and conflicts of interest, that is. And that part was rapidly coming around as well.

"Well, just because I call her doesn't mean I'll actually *meet* her," she said, hoping that hearing the words out loud would make them more credible.

She picked up the note, before setting it back down again and putting her key in the ignition. She had nearly turned the engine over before she snatched the note and her phone and rapidly dialed the number. Sometimes she hated her lack of willpower.

"Hello?" Colleen's voice sounded warm and alluring.

"Um…hi. It's Bijal."

"You called."

Bijal was starting to feel foolish. "I did, yes."

"Sorry, I tend to state the obvious when I'm nervous. I'd already convinced myself that you weren't going to."

"Did you say you're nervous?"

"Maybe a little."

"About what?" Bijal asked.

"About approaching you—asking you out while we're still in the middle of this…"

"Steaming bucket of feces?"

Colleen laughed. "You're such a smooth talker. I suppose I should be congratulating you."

"For what?"

"For your victory tonight. I heard your new campaign manager declaring to reporters that y'all won."

Bijal sighed in exasperation. "Do you have no mercy? I was just starting to forget about all that."

"Were you?"

"Well, yeah. See, I got this note from an incredibly hot woman who told me I was beautiful."

"Twice," Colleen added.

"And even though I know that I shouldn't be socializing with her, I can't get past the fact that I really want to see her."

"That's mutual. I've missed having you tail me."

Bijal was giddy at the admission. "So meet me at the K and K."

"I don't think that's a good idea now that I've been on both national and local television. If someone were to recognize me, we'd have a real problem."

"Then doesn't that kind of rule out going somewhere for dinner?"

Colleen mumbled something unintelligible. "I have an idea if you're game. Do you like sushi?"

"I love it, and I haven't had it in months."

"Yeah, I'm thinking your body could probably use a meal that's not fried. I'm on my way to pick up Callisto right now."

Bijal wasn't really sure where this was going. "Where is she?"

"With Hepburn."

"I thought Hepburn was dead."

Colleen chucked softly. "Katharine is, sadly. Hepburn is a husky mix that lives down the road from me. When I work long hours my retired neighbor is good enough to take Callisto to her place to play with Hepburn."

"A nice arrangement."

"Definitely. So what I'm proposing is this. Are you still at the college?"

"You mean the scene of the crime? Yes."

"Good. There's a great sushi place not too far from you. I'll call ahead and order take-out, and I'll pay over the phone. They know me there. I'm a regular. You stop by and pick it up, then meet me at my place for dinner."

"At your house?"

"Is that too forward of me? I just thought we'd have a little more privacy. But if you feel like it's crossing a line—"

"No, it's fine," Bijal said.

"Are you sure? I don't want you to feel coerced or anything."

"I won't, as long as we agree to keep things nonsexual."

After a pause, Colleen replied. "Well, I can certainly agree to do my best."

"That sounds a little noncommittal."

"It does, doesn't it? My head has no problem consenting to that arrangement, but I keep picturing you in that snug tweed suit and I start to experience conflict. You didn't change out of it, did you?"

"No." Bijal felt the blush that must have been spreading across her neck and cheeks.

"Outstanding. Look, we'll compromise. You wear that suit, and you have my word that I'll only ogle you from afar."

"That sounds agreeable."

"I'm glad to hear it. Do you like spicy tuna?"

"Even more than I like spicy shrimp," Bijal replied blithely.

"Then you'll love this place. If you've got a pen, I'll give you directions from where you are."

"Hang on." For a moment Bijal nearly flipped Colleen's note over to write on it, but didn't want to ruin it. In her glove compartment she found a beige Taco Rojo napkin and a pen. "Okay, fire away."

CHAPTER FIFTEEN

Colleen stared at her reflection. She undid the second button on her blouse and then reassessed. "Hmm…too much?" Did it say rosy-breasted maiden? Or scab-ridden whore?

She scowled and suddenly felt ridiculous. What the hell was wrong with her? She was acting like a silly schoolgirl. Next she'd start doodling Bijal's name on her notebook in cursive and writing gothic poetry about unrequited love and the agony of getting her period on prom night.

Callisto started clawing at the back storm door, so Colleen hurried to let her in, glancing at her watch. Based on how busy Sunomono was, Bijal could arrive any moment. And the more time that elapsed after they had agreed to meet at her house, the more uneasy Colleen was becoming. Was this a horrible mistake? Her conscience was certainly telling her that it was.

As Colleen let the dog in, she noticed the dark smears Callisto was leaving on the kitchen floor.

"What the hell?" Colleen knelt down quickly to verify the nature of the filth. "Callisto, what *is* this?" A cursory sniff confirmed that it was fresh mud—only a minor relief.

The dog shook violently, sending speckles of sludge everywhere. Colleen grabbed her by the collar in an all-too-late attempt to minimize the defilement. Callisto had dirt all over her, particularly her muzzle and paws. "Girl, what did you *do*?"

Callisto, clearly startled by Colleen's outburst, dropped what she had in her mouth—what appeared to be an old bone from possibly the Mesozoic era—and now looked suitably contrite.

"You dug this shit up *now*? You couldn't have waited until tomorrow?"

Callisto tilted her head slightly to the left, which was all Colleen needed to forgive her utterly and immediately. "Why?" Colleen asked plaintively as she stood. "Don't you move a muscle, sister."

Colleen headed to the linen closet to get one of her least favorite towels to start scrubbing the filth both off the animal and the floor. She checked quickly over her shoulder that Callisto was still waiting patiently and not spitefully dragging her ass across the kitchen for good measure.

She was sitting, as good as gold. Or, perhaps more accurately, as good as grimy muck-caked gold that smelled strongly of mildew, grass, and, quite possibly, a freshly dead body.

Colleen returned with a towel and began the Herculean task of cleaning Callisto's fur. "Is this some clever ploy on your part so you don't have to share my attention? Is that it?" Colleen brushed her hair out of her eyes as she continued wiping goo off Callisto's chest and stomach. "You *know* I don't have time to give you a bath. That's why you look so goddamn pleased with yourself, isn't it?"

Callisto picked that moment to lick the side of Colleen's face, undoubtedly based on her proximity. "Sure, suck up now."

The doorbell rang, and both Colleen and Callisto froze.

"Shit," Colleen hissed.

A quick examination of things confirmed her worst fear—the kitchen looked like a crime scene in brown. She gazed at Callisto and took a deep breath. "I'll just explain to her that I don't usually live with a layer of silt and clay in my house, and that it's all your fault."

Reasonably confident that the dog had no remaining mud on the pads of her paws for the smearing, Colleen flung the dirty towel into the laundry room and ran to the front hall. When she swung the door open, the sight of Bijal holding a large take-out bag instantly conjured butterflies in her stomach. "Hi."

Bijal smiled broadly. "Hi."

"Come on in," Colleen said, holding the door open.

"You ordered what feels like thirty pounds of sushi," Bijal remarked as she stepped inside. God, she smelled incredible.

"I ordered a variety. Thanks for picking it up."

They stood for a moment in the foyer, staring at each other.

Bijal squinted. "Um, you have a little something on your cheek." She pointed to her own face sympathetically.

Colleen approached the hall mirror and was mortified to see two separate streaks of mud on her face, one on her forehead and the other across her left cheek. It was as though she was moonlighting as a Jackson Pollock canvas. "Fan-fucking-tastic." Without even trying to wipe it off, Colleen sighed and turned, taking the food from Bijal. "Come on in. We might as well get this over with."

"O…kay," Bijal replied, her trepidation apparent.

Colleen led her into the kitchen, where the floor, walls, and cabinets were spattered with crud. "Here it is," Colleen said in defeat. "I was hoping to get this cleaned up before you got here. It's Callisto's handiwork."

Bijal gawked as she took it all in. "Is it…poo?"

"Oh, God, no! It's just dirt! She was out digging in the yard," Colleen blurted. "She came in covered with mud, and she shook." She realized she was gesticulating like an insane person, so she folded her hands in front of her and took a deep breath.

The corner of Bijal's mouth crept upward slowly. "Can we put the food in the fridge real quick?"

"Sure," Colleen replied, taking the bag of food and stuffing it into the refrigerator.

"Okay, where're your cleaning supplies?"

"Under the sink. But you can't clean. You're a guest."

Bijal walked over to the sink and tore a paper towel off the roll, then dampened it under the faucet. "Uh-huh, come here."

Colleen stepped toward her, and Bijal began to wipe the grime off her face. "Thanks for not just spitting on a tissue," Colleen said, humiliated.

Bijal's face was dangerously close to Colleen's, and she looked especially amused. "That would be moving our relationship into a disturbing new stage, I think."

"The tell-mama-all phase?"

"And without stopping at the really good phases that most people hit on the way to that one, yeah."

Colleen swallowed loudly. "And cleaning my house doesn't put us in roughly the same place?"

"Don't get too excited. I'm not grouting your shower or anything," Bijal said, throwing the paper towel in the trash can. "I was just going to help you tidy some of this up."

"Thanks," Colleen said softly.

"What can I use on the floor?"

Colleen retrieved a mop and ran it under the tap before handing it over. She then got herself a damp sponge to start scrubbing the wall.

Bijal pushed the mop in long strokes, until she unintentionally bumped a dirt-encrusted bone with the mop head, sending it skidding to the other side of the room. Bijal warily scrutinized it. "Is this the cause of all this mess?"

Colleen nodded, picking the offending item up. "So it would seem. I think it's from a velociraptor." She took the bone over to the sink to give it a thorough rinse, while Callisto watched in interest. After a cursory blot with a paper towel, Colleen handed the bone back to the dog, who trotted away with it merrily. "Bitch."

"Yeah, I think that's where the word originated, actually."

"Good point," Colleen said, letting her gaze linger on Bijal's hips as she continued to mop. They swayed to and fro in a hypnotic way. "So, would it be completely skeevy if I took this opportunity to tell you about my hot-cleaning-woman-in-a-business-suit fantasy?"

Bijal stopped moving completely. "Well, if not skeevy, it would certainly seem calculated. You know, like you planned this."

"Oh…well, I won't tell you about it, then." Colleen went back to cleaning the wall.

"Interesting logic."

"It works in Congress. Can't we just strike it from the record?"

"That depends," Bijal said. "Can we strike tonight's debate too and just say it never happened?"

"Sure, provided I can ask you a question about it first. Then we'll never speak of it again."

Bijal began to rinse out the mop head with tap water. "Deal, because I'm already starting to block out the details. So you'd better hurry before I mentally replace it with all the lyrics from *West Side Story*."

"How shall I phrase this? Um...how about, what the fuck is up with your candidate?"

"I'm sorry, can you be more specific?" Bijal asked as she washed her hands.

"Denton," Colleen replied. "Does she have a chemical-dependence problem?"

Bijal tore off a paper towel. "No, she has a much more...multi-faceted issue. It involves the NRCC, a mean case of pinkeye, and the ill-advised consumption of someone else's prescription tranquilizers."

"Wow," Colleen breathed. "I'm not sure if that's better or worse than what I assumed, which, frankly, included snorting veterinary-strength narcotics off the ass of a male prostitute."

Bijal whistled in appreciation as she presumably imagined that scenario. "I'm not sure either. Right now, I'm just trying to focus on how to keep our campaign staff coming back to work every morning."

"How's that going?"

"It's hard when your candidate isn't allowed to hold the views that drew you to her in the first place, let me tell you."

Colleen rinsed out her sponge and began to wash up. "That's understandable."

"So when it stops being about the issues, all you have left is a series of public appearances so horrific that we might as well be running a squirrel monkey in a diaper."

"At least the diaper would keep it from flinging poo," Colleen replied, removing the food from the refrigerator.

"You're making an argument for the squirrel monkey?"

"Well, I'm assuming the monkey's not on tranquilizers, right?"

"Ouch," Bijal said, her expression one of amused surprise.

"Sorry, we'll strike that from the record too."

"Then while you're at it, go ahead and strike me flipping you off."

Colleen laughed as she watched Bijal dramatically extend her middle finger. "Done. What would you like to drink with dinner?"

"What are my options?"

Colleen scanned the fridge. "I have diet soda, orange juice, red wine, bottled water, iced tea, and my personal favorite with sushi—cold sake."

"That's all? Just those nineteen choices?"

"I'm afraid so."

"I'll have a smattering of sake, please."

"A smattering?" Colleen asked suspiciously.

"With a glass of water," Bijal added. "I need to make sure I'm able to drive home later."

"I'll let you sleep on my couch if you agree to do my ironing in the morning," Colleen said glibly as she unpacked everything from the take-out bag and arranged it on a serving platter.

"Is this another chore you'd like me to perform in a business suit?"

"No, for the ironing you'd just wear nylons, garters, and a crisp linen apron."

"Is now a bad time to mention that I'm wearing a wire?" Bijal asked.

"Really? Let me know how your diaper-wearing squirrel monkey responds."

"Touché."

Colleen closed the distance between them and her body responded to the energy. She tapped lightly on Bijal's top blouse button. "Is this thing on?"

"God, yes! Oh, you mean a microphone. Nope, sorry. I made that part up. But you can search me if you like."

Colleen had never been so tempted to take someone up on an offer. Bijal's flirty playfulness was beyond distracting—it was utterly entrancing. "I'm afraid that would violate our agreement."

"Oh yeah…damn."

"Come on, let's eat." Colleen set all the sushi and drinks on the dining-room table and motioned for Bijal to take a seat.

"This looks amazing," Bijal said, picking up a set of chopsticks and surveying the spread.

Colleen sat down and poured them both a cup of sake. "To our pact of sobriety and decency," she toasted.

"May it rest in peace—in the plot right next to our restraint."

"And apparently also our dignity," Colleen added before they both took swigs.

"I don't know where to start. It all looks delicious."

"Try this one." Colleen pointed with her chopsticks to an elaborate roll with tuna on the outside. "It's called a Red Dragon roll."

Bijal followed Colleen's suggestion and popped the large piece completely into her mouth. "Oh, my God!" she struggled to say, her eyes rolling back in her head.

"Mmm-hmm, I told you."

"Please don't take it personally if I stop speaking entirely and just unhinge my jaw to devour this like a python."

"I'm not letting you off the hook that easily," Colleen said. "Sorry."

"Do you think we could give polite conversation a try?"

"I know it may feel awkward without bringing up politics, fisting, or dry-humping," Colleen said. "But I suppose some might consider us noble for making the effort."

"I'm game, as long as you agree to stop right away if it starts to sting."

"You mean if one of us gets a rash from all the clean talk?"

"Exactly," Bijal replied. "What are these with the avocado on top?"

"Hmm…I don't remember."

"Just make up a name, then."

Colleen paused for a moment. "Fine, that's the Surly Fellatrix roll."

"So much for keeping it clean," Bijal replied, popping one into her mouth.

"I thought it might be better if we sort of eased into the chastity."

"Good thinking. And I have to admit, this is the best Surly Fellatrix I've ever had."

"Glad to hear it. Try this one with the tempura shrimp in it."

"And that's called?"

"That's the…Frisky Weasel roll," Colleen lied.

"You really know how to sell them, don't you?"

Colleen grinned. "That's why I'm not in marketing. Why don't you tell me a little about yourself? That should be a relatively safe topic, right?"

Bijal cleared her throat, but didn't balk at the request. "Well, let's see. I'm originally from Philadelphia. I got my poli-sci degree at UVA, which is where I met Fran."

"Ah, the roommate with no filter."

"That's the one, yes. Um, my parents met in India and immigrated to the U.S. to pursue their tree-hugging, hand-clapping, sunshine-and-moonbeam dream of American liberalism."

"They sound like *wonderful* people," Colleen said.

"I'm not terribly surprised that you think so. I'm sure they would absolutely adore you."

"You think so?"

Bijal nodded. "Sure, the three of you can bond over entitlement programs and deficit spending and just eat granola and high-five all night long. As you might imagine, the evenings I spend with my parents don't go quite as smoothly."

"Is being conservative your personal form of rebellion? Because that's kind of unusual. Well, except on *Family Ties*."

"I threw them a bone by being a lesbian. Why couldn't that have been enough?"

Colleen grinned at how adorable her dinner companion was. It was official now—she was thoroughly besotted. "Some people are just never satisfied, I guess."

"Exactly," Bijal replied adamantly. "Maybe if I'd had a sibling. You know how in some families one child takes one for the team and becomes a doctor, or goes into the priesthood? Maybe a brother or sister could have realized Mom and Dad's liberal dreams and run off to, I don't know, become a tambourine-playing fanatic who renounces all worldly possessions. Periodically, the folks could go to the airport and shout encouraging things as they watched their offspring hand out daisies to strangers."

"It's nice that you think so highly of progressives," Colleen said, putting another Frisky Weasel on her plate.

"No offense."

"Oh, none taken. I can see why you'd equate flower-peddling, panhandling zealots with a social ideology based on caring for the old, impoverished, and infirm."

"Isn't that charity, not government?"

"'With malice toward none, with charity for all.' Abraham Lincoln, Republican." Colleen added ridiculous emphasis to the final word and rested her chin on her hand expectantly.

Bijal shrugged. "I don't know. He's kind of a bleeding heart in the vast pantheon of Republicans."

"Which is what makes him one of the best you guys ever had so, naturally, you don't want to claim him. He only ended the Civil War, emancipated the slaves, and made it onto the penny, dollar bill, *and* Mt. Rushmore."

"Hold on, I never said I didn't want to claim him. You see how you politicians twist things? You're vipers, all of you," Bijal said, pointing mockingly with her chopsticks.

"Sorry, but coming from a campaign staffer, that's a bit like having a scrotum call you ugly."

Bijal's eyes narrowed playfully. "I'll overlook that you just likened me to a ballsack, because that was a very nice segue to genitalia."

"Thanks."

"Though, next time, can it please not be male? I *am* eating, after all."

"I'll do my best."

"So what about you?" Bijal took another sip of sake.

"You mean my genitals?"

Bijal choked as the liquid went down the wrong way. She coughed and inhaled deeply. "I meant for you to share a little about yourself, like I just did. But if that's where you want to start…"

Colleen sat back in her chair and laced her fingers together. "Since you were an undercover spy, why don't you just tell me what you already know? That way I don't waste any time repeating things."

"Okay, but stop me if I get anything wrong."

"Deal."

"Let's see, your family owns the Arc of Orion distillery, and has since shortly after the repeal of prohibition. You ran the company before running for Congress, then passed it to your brother."

"All true."

"You went to UCLA, presumably so you could burn patchouli, dance barefoot in the streets, and mingle with people named River and Rainbow."

Colleen chuckled. "I love that you equate liberals with hippies. You know that hippies haven't existed in any real numbers for several decades, right?"

"You haven't met my parents. Anyway, you were elected to the House of Representatives to represent a relatively conservative district, yet in spite of that, you're still very outspoken about liberal issues that are unpopular with the majority of your constituents. Candidly, I find that dead sexy, but unfortunately for you, it leaves you rather vulnerable for reelection."

"Wait, can we go back to the sexy part for a moment?"

"Of course," Bijal replied coyly before having another piece of sushi.

"Can you elaborate, please?"

Bijal swallowed. "Well, I've scoured your voting record, campaign website, promises, interviews, and ads, and I've yet to find an instance of backpedaling, flip-flopping, or pandering. You don't seem to do the partisan dance of opportunism that's standard for your contemporaries. You actually put it all out there unabashedly."

"Well—"

"For instance, you support gun control in a state full of hunters. You're pro-choice in a region that leans pro-life."

"Anti-choice."

"Ah, yes. Sorry."

"Tell me, Bijal. Did your research uncover exactly why reproductive rights are so important to me?"

Bijal quickly became serious. "Yes."

"I'm in Congress partly to continue Lisa's work now that she's gone."

"That's admirable."

"So here's my take on what you refer to as the 'partisan dance.'"

"Okay."

"It's total horseshit. And I'd appreciate it if you can explain to me how it's somehow not only acceptable for politicians, based on who they're addressing, to change their opinions like soiled underpants—"

"Ooh, good metaphor."

"—but it's actually *expected* of us. That, coupled with the practice of selling votes to the highest bidder—what I refer to as graft, but what most call campaign donations—is why the American people despise politicians. And in a cruel example of self-fulfilling prophecy, they turn away from politics in disgust, don't educate themselves about their representatives, and don't vote. Therefore lying, crooked assholes without souls get reelected time and again."

Bijal stared at her and said nothing, a tiny crinkle forming between her eyebrows.

"What?" Colleen asked.

"A couple of things, really. Number one, I consider myself, as well as most people in politics, fairly cynical. So when you get all spun up about why things aren't more open, honest, and bipartisan when it pertains to the public's best interest, it reminds me that…well, those aren't things that Janet is saying. Those aren't things that *anyone* in office is saying, to my knowledge, because they're too afraid to actually say what they think. So, in that way, you continue to impress me."

"And number two?"

"It makes me want to jump you…something fierce," Bijal said in a throaty voice.

Colleen was nearly as startled as she was breathless. "Have I told you how much I love your candor?"

"Really?" Bijal seemed pleasantly surprised by the admission.

"Mmm-hmm, it's nice not having to guess what you're thinking."

"Even when it's terribly inappropriate?"

"Oh, *especially* then," Colleen replied suggestively. Her heart was racing.

Bijal leaned closer. "You may be the only person in the world who appreciates that about me."

"Perhaps that's because you don't share such complimentary information with everyone."

"So if I'm saying something less pleasant, like 'hey, asshole, you suck,' that might be why it's not well received?"

Colleen bit her thumbnail in amusement. "I think that hypothesis has merit, yes."

"You have a great vocabulary, Colleen. It illustrates how deliciously brainy you are."

"Hmm, you're no slouch yourself. You know, we probably shouldn't be so free with our praise of each other. We're only making the tension more unbearable."

"Are you implying that it's not really a hundred ten degrees in here?"

Colleen nodded. "Exactly. You're making it a bit of a challenge to keep this platonic—coming in here looking so sexy, filling your mouth with fish in the most provocative manner possible, then casually mentioning that you want to jump me."

The corner of Bijal's mouth quirked upward. "I didn't realize that I was eating any particular way."

"Oh, trust me, you are." Colleen pushed her chair away from the table and picked up her water glass on her way into the kitchen. As she reached the refrigerator, she realized she was being a bad host. "I'm sorry, did you want more water?"

"Sure," Bijal replied, standing to bring her glass over. "More ice would be great too."

They shared smoldering eye contact until Colleen became suddenly self-conscious and pointed to the ice dispenser on the outside of the fridge. "Crushed or cubed?"

"Crushed, please."

Colleen slid the switch over to the crushed setting and watched Bijal press her glass against the levers one at a time until her water glass was suitably refilled. Then Bijal raised the frosty beverage to her lips and drank. How she turned that simple act into something so erotic, Colleen wasn't sure.

Colleen let her gaze drift down to Bijal's neckline where just enough cleavage peeked out from her collar, enticing with the promise of breasts so remarkable that they might sing when her bra came undone. She then let her eyes wander to Bijal's silver necklace, where the clasp had worked its way to the front, near the pendant.

"Make a wish," Colleen said softly, setting down her glass and sliding the clasp around to behind Bijal's neck.

Bijal looked both overwhelmed and out of breath. "I wish you'd just kiss me," she whispered.

Colleen, for once, made no effort to stop and assess the ramifications of her actions. She didn't weigh the pros and cons. She merely accepted the hushed entreaty and met Bijal's lips with hers.

What initially felt foreign was, in an instant, sensual and sublime. She was captivated by the way Bijal's mouth moved against her own, the way she nibbled at her lower lip. Colleen moaned instinctively as Bijal pulled away.

"Oh, my God," Bijal rasped, out of breath. "Why did you do that?"

Colleen's head was still spinning and adrenaline was shooting through her body like lightning. "You asked me to."

"But if I'd known you kiss like that…I mean, how will I be able to think about anything else now?"

Colleen began kissing Bijal's neck, unable to suppress the urge any longer. "You're saying it was too good?" she murmured.

"Mmm-hmm."

"I didn't realize there was any danger of that."

"Mmm-hmm."

"Maybe I can make it bad for you," Colleen offered as she pulled back to see Bijal's face.

"You think?"

"I'll do my best," Colleen said, pressing her lips once again to Bijal's.

This time, Colleen encircled Bijal's waist with her hands until they rested on her arresting bottom, which felt just as marvelous as she had imagined it would. Bijal's mouth opened ever so slightly, which Colleen interpreted as an implicit invitation. She increased the pressure as her ardor began to utterly consume her. She slid her tongue past Bijal's lips and was rewarded with Bijal's tongue in return.

She wanted nothing more than to spend the next forty-eight hours this way—tasting Bijal and feeling all the sensations she evoked.

Bijal drew back again, the desire evident on her face. "You call that bad? I don't think you were even *trying* to make that unpleasant."

"Um…I thought I was. But that was pretty incredible, wasn't it?"

"That was definitely in the top five kisses of all time," Bijal replied, resting her head on Colleen's shoulder and running her hand slowly down Colleen's back. "We may have crossed that line."

"Agreed," Colleen said, enjoying their embrace.

"What do we do now?"

"Try, try again?"

Bijal grinned. "I like that you take pride in your work, I really do. But we should stop before this escalates into something hot, sweaty, and...carnal."

"I'm sorry, was the word 'stop' somewhere in that sentence?"

Bijal's eyes were dark and filled with hunger. "It was," she whispered before kissing Colleen again, this time softly and briefly. "But when can we get together again?"

CHAPTER SIXTEEN

B ijal propped her elbow on the kitchen counter, impatiently staring at the coffee maker and mentally willing it to brew faster.

Fran shuffled out of her bedroom wearing an inside-out bathrobe and fuzzy bunny slippers. She pulled up a chair at the kitchen table and slowly sat, making a sound similar to what a leaky Macy's Thanksgiving Day Parade balloon might make.

"You look like hell," Bijal said.

"Go ahead and bust my balls, but I'll bet my Friday night was ten times better than yours—and that's just counting the parts I can remember."

The muscles in Bijal's jaw tensed. "Fran, despite what you think, you don't know shit."

"I know that last night your boss appeared on local TV looking like an incognito zombie and announced that she had syphilis."

"I'd correct you but, sadly, that's pretty close."

"You don't seem as upset as I expected. What, did you win a bet that she would publicly self-destruct?"

"Yes, I had 'on-air STD admission' in the fuck-up pool," Bijal said sarcastically as she poured her lollygagging coffee and held the hot mug reverently, hoping the contents would not only warm her body, but also nourish her soul.

"Well, congratulations. I hope the prize was a new job."

"Nope, all I won was a sense of impending disaster and a sinking feeling in the pit of my stomach." Bijal filled a steaming cup for Fran and handed it to her before sitting across from her.

"Thanks. You're still in an inexplicably good mood."

"That's because I went on a date last night."

Fran's face lit up. "Thank God! Where'd you meet her?"

"Um...at the debate," Bijal said softly, looking at the tabletop. "She left a note on my car."

"Ooh! Is she hot?"

"Astoundingly."

"And she was at the debate, saw you, and was smitten?" Fran took a sip of coffee.

"So she said," Bijal replied evasively.

"Where'd y'all go?"

"Her place."

Fran looked surprised. "Wow, making up for lost time? Does she have one of those sex swings?"

Bijal shook her head. "There was no sex. Though, admittedly, I can't say it didn't cross my mind."

"What's her name?"

"Huh?"

"Her name," Fran repeated, her tone slightly more stern.

"Um...hmm."

"Oh, Jesus. It was O'Bannon, wasn't it?"

"Or an incredible look-alike."

"What the hell are you doing, Bij?"

Bijal rubbed her forehead in frustration. "We kept it PG-rated. Well, if you don't count the Surly Fellatrix."

Fran stared for a moment with her mouth hanging open. "What happened to your professional decorum? I thought you decided to wait until the election was over."

"It turns out that the main thing that the two of us have in common is a shameful lack of impulse control," Bijal said sheepishly.

Fran sat back, crossing her arms and glaring.

Bijal was somewhat incredulous. "I'm sorry, I'm finding it amazing that the woman who slept with her married statistics professor is sitting here, no doubt covered in dried beer and urine, judging me for just having dinner with someone to whom I'm genuinely attracted."

"Dr. Adams was separated from her husband at the time," Fran said defensively. "And I'll have you know that I learned a *lot* about math from her."

"I'll bet you did. If you're riding on a northbound professor who's had two and a half glasses of Chablis, and her husband is on a southbound train going forty miles per hour, approximately how long will it take you to get expelled?"

"If I'm careful, I won't. And don't try to change the subject."

Bijal took another swig of java. "I'm not changing the subject, just providing a methodical walkthrough of your fragile glass house and very impressive stone collection."

"I'm not the one who claims to have scruples."

"Sad but true."

"And I'm happy to report that I'm urine-free this morning," Fran said, tugging on the lapel of her robe.

"That's three mornings in a row," Bijal said, her voice rife with condescension. "Good for you. Remember, baby steps."

"So back to *your* night of indulgence."

"Again, all we did was have dinner."

"At her place," Fran added with more than a hint of innuendo.

"She wanted to make sure we wouldn't be seen together, now that everyone knows her from TV."

Fran blew into her coffee mug. "She's smooth. I'll give her that. Did it occur to you that she might have a nanny-cam set up to catch you two…fraternizing?"

Bijal nearly laughed. "In an effort to stop the runaway momentum of Mayor Denton's campaign and her magical mystery infection? Doubtful."

"You have a hell of a lot more to lose than O'Bannon does. Everyone knows she's gay, and she's already leading in the polls. If you get discovered, not only do you get outed without knowing how the NRCC will respond, you get to look like some kind of sex spy too."

"Colleen's not like that, Fran."

"How do you know?" Fran asked with a scowl. "It sounds like you're starting to believe her campaign ads."

"Well, she *does* have some very good commercials."

"You're killing me with this shit. Are you serious?"

"No, I'm not," Bijal snapped. "But I *am* serious when I tell you that Colleen happens to have a great deal of personal integrity."

"Which is why she's trying to bang someone who works for her opposition," Fran replied.

Bijal was surprised at how serious Fran was being. "Look, there was no banging. Though, trust me, if she'd really made an effort, she'd have had me."

"Uh…wow. I wasn't expecting that. You're not concerned at all about the possibility that if this comes out, your career is over?"

"Don't think I'm being cavalier about this."

"I'll tell you what I think," Fran said abruptly.

"Okay."

"You've completely immersed yourself in this campaign, to the detriment of your personal life and your mental health. In the haze of fatigue brought on by being overworked, managed by incompetents, and isolated from all other lesbians except for one, you've developed an unnatural attraction for said muff-diver at hand—partially because of the illicit danger she represents."

"Where did all that come from?"

"I fucked my abnormal-psych professor too."

"The obese guy with the prosthetic hand? Dr. Dernwaller?"

"Okay, not really. I just thought you might give my argument more credence if it could possibly have come from someone else."

"Someone whose professional opinion you could have consulted at some point between all the grunting and rug burn? Not really, no."

Fran's eyebrows rose as she no doubt considered that. "Regardless, I think I'm right."

"You usually do."

"You're coming out with me tonight."

Bijal scoffed. "Oh, no, I'm not having you fix me up with anyone. We've gone down that road before too many times."

"What do you mean?"

"Are you joking?" Bijal was almost unable to finish the question because of her laughter. "Have you forgotten the girl you set me up with who called me 'sugar box' all night?"

"She was from the South! They're very cordial down there."

"Yeah, she apparently thought *I* was very cordial *down there*. And what about the one on parole?"

"I don't run people's fingerprints," Fran replied indignantly.

"Remember the one who used to call herself 'Dumplin'?"

Fran laid her head on the table. "Oh, Lord."

"She spent all night listing various inanimate objects that she wanted me to insert into her ass."

"All right, you've made your point."

"You try eating beef Wellington with Dumplin' across the booth, waggling the salt shaker at you suggestively."

Fran took another sip of coffee. "Look, I'm not talking about setting you up. Just come to the bar with me tonight and be with your own people for a while. Once you do, you'll see just how foolish you're being."

Bijal envisioned a gaggle of drunken college-age lesbians spilling beer on her and copping sloppy feels. "I don't think so."

"Come on, what do you have to lose? If I'm wrong, you get to gloat and take some comfort that the cocktail of depression, failure, and celibacy you're currently swimming in hasn't impeded your judgment."

Bijal sighed in futility. "And if I agree to go, I'll stop getting lectures on ethics from the woman who once dated a cop to get her traffic ticket expunged?"

"For your information, that wasn't the only reason."

"Oh?"

"She let me use the cuffs on her." Fran started to tighten the belt on her robe and suddenly stopped. "Why the hell didn't you tell me I had this on inside out?"

Bijal shrugged. "I thought maybe it was dirty and you were just trying to get an extra day's wear out of it."

❖

"C'mon, let's go outside," the blonde said directly into Bijal's ear, gently tugging her from the dance floor.

Bijal nodded briefly, following this new acquaintance to the bar's outdoor deck where a dozen or so women gathered in various clusters.

"You want to sit?" the sporty girl asked, pointing to a small outdoor table for two that was free.

In fact, getting off her feet and relaxing where the thumping bass wasn't so loud that she had to scream to be heard seemed like a great idea. She slipped into a seat and pressed her back against the outside of the building. Her companion, whose name she didn't know, took the other seat and started tapping the bottom of a pack of cigarettes.

Sure, the girl was attractive—in a sort of wiry, all-American, softball-playing way. She was probably in her early to mid-twenties. Possibly even still in college. Bijal struggled to push away the skeevy feeling that notion suddenly evoked.

The shortstop lit a cigarette, then held the pack out. "Want one?"

"No, thanks," Bijal replied. "I don't smoke."

An expression of irritation momentarily crept across the shortstop's face before she replaced it with what appeared to be a pleasant, possibly insincere, smile. She slipped the Marlboros back into her breast pocket. "I've never seen you here. Are you new in town?"

"Nope."

"You're *way* too hot for me not to have noticed you," the shortstop said, contorting her mouth grotesquely in an attempt to exhale her smoke off to the side and not blow it directly into Bijal's face.

"Uh, thanks," Bijal said, finding the compliment dubious and rather transparent. "I've been working a lot of hours lately. Keeps me from going out."

The shortstop winced. "Bag *that* shit."

Bijal was starting to get a decidedly lazy vibe from this girl. "So what do you do?"

"I sing," the shortstop-cum-vocalist replied, obviously intending to impress her.

"Really? Are you in a band?"

"I'm in between bands right now," she said, fidgeting with her lighter. "But whatever, you know? They're all full of fuckin'…dick-cheese…guys anyway."

Bijal's fears about this girl's age had now been confirmed. "I'm not sure what a fucking dick-cheese guy is, but it's perfectly okay if you don't explain." A long silence led Bijal to believe her escort was taking that guidance to heart. "Do you have a day job?"

The singer took a long drag from her Marlboro. "No, me and day jobs don't really click."

"Ah."

"What about you?"

"I'm a political research coordinator."

"That sounds kinda hot," the singer said, her eyes narrowing. "I'll bet you wear a business suit and all kinds of tight shit." She leered at Bijal suggestively, looking like she thought she was a lot more appealing than she really was.

"Sometimes. Are you interested in politics at all?"

The singer laughed. "Hell, no. That's shit's too boring for me. They're all just a bunch of fat old fucks calling each other…"

"Fuckin' dick-cheese guys?" Bijal asked, rapidly losing the will to hide her sarcasm.

"Exactly! With all their blah-blah-blah crap. I mean, good for you that you can keep up with all that gobbledygook stuff, but those dudes are all too shady for me."

"Too shady for you to what?" Bijal asked.

"To fucking hassle with."

Bijal cleared her throat. "Not that I'm defending politicians by any stretch of the imagination, but if you think they're so shady, why let them operate unchecked?"

"Huh?"

"I mean, isn't that kind of like refusing to lock your door because you know your neighbors are thieves?"

The singer shrugged. "They're all the same, so what difference does it make?" she asked defensively.

"But they're deciding how you live your life."

"The hell they are! No one decides how I live my life but *me*."

Bijal was now officially unimpressed. "Except for things like giving you the right to legally marry, deciding if you can be discriminated against in your job or your housing, setting your tax rate on food, gasoline, cigarettes, and other little things like if the country goes to war or not. Luckily, nothing major, right?"

The singer was apparently now just as unimpressed. "I'm getting another beer. You want one?"

"No, thanks," Bijal replied, just wanting this girl to go away and take her frustrating apathy with her.

As she watched her nameless, disaffected dance partner head back inside, she stretched, secure in the knowledge that she wouldn't be back. Idly, Bijal picked up her phone and started scrolling through it.

Had she become one of those serious people she used to make fun of? Was she now utterly unable to make conversation with people who weren't politically minded or ensconced in a shitty, soul-sucking job? What had happened to her appreciation of both diversity and an interest in what other people were enthusiastic about?

Of course, to know for sure, she'd first need to find a person who possessed actual enthusiasm for something.

A cursory glance at her contacts brought her to Colleen's number, still in her phone from the night before. Now there was a woman who seemed to have it all—smart as the day is long, conscientious, pragmatic, and painfully sexy, yet she still had a quick wit and a soft spot for the underdog.

Bijal had no doubt that Colleen wouldn't know what "fuckin' dick-cheese guys" were either.

Unable to prevent herself from briefly sulking at her current predicament, Bijal glanced at her watch before deciding to send Colleen a late-night text message.

I'm sure you're asleep now, but thought u should know I'm suffering withdrawal from civic-mindedness & faggity-ass french fries. - Bijal

The joy from the illicit correspondence was fleeting, however, and it vanished, leaving her empty and a little blasé about her evening. How much longer would she be stuck here? It was only midnight, and Fran undoubtedly intended to stay till last call—unless she first met someone she wanted to leave with.

Bijal had let herself get caught up in Fran's optimistic rhetoric about needing to get out among her own kind and blow off steam. Now that she was here and thoroughly dissatisfied, she wondered if maybe she'd been more accurate in assessing her feelings for Colleen than Fran had given her credit for.

Her phone vibrated in her hand.

I'm still up. Doing prep work for my trip next week. Where are you that has no politics or gay carbohydrates?

Bijal marveled at how silly and giddy she suddenly felt as she typed her reply.

Fran talked me into coming out to a women's bar w/her, and I'm miserable. Where are you traveling?

She would happily spend the rest of the evening doing this, but that only further exacerbated her dilemma of being completely hung up on her boss's political opponent, who just happened to also be her ideological opposite. Well, that wasn't completely true. They did agree on LGBT rights, the courage of one's convictions, and spicy tuna rolls, to name just a few.

Another text message made the device pulsate.

Congressional delegation to the Middle East. Are there too many hippies there for your liking?

Bijal laughed and sent back a very brief response.

Call me.

It seemed to take forever for the phone to ring, and as Bijal answered it, she stood and moved farther away from the dance music. "Hello?"

"Hey."

Bijal's chest fluttered at the single syllable. "Hey."

"You're miserable? Are you there under duress?" Colleen asked.

"Not exactly. Fran thinks I've been too entrenched in the campaign and it's starting to affect my judgment."

"Hmm, and when she says 'judgment,' is she somehow referring to me?"

"Per...haps," Bijal replied tentatively.

"She'll love the fact that you're talking to me now."

Bijal turned and peered through the doorway of the bar to survey Fran on the dance floor. "Well, considering that right now she's apparently trying to count the change in some girl's pocket without using her hands, I don't think she's too interested in what I'm doing."

"Damned oversexed Democrats," Colleen said.

"Don't I know it? It's a wonder you guys can ever get completely dressed."

"Oh, did you assume I had clothes on?"

Bijal's mouth went dry. "Well, until right now I did, yeah."

"Sorry."

"Oh, don't be. You've managed to improve my evening exponentially with only innuendo."

"That's just more of my sorcery," Colleen said, the amusement audible in her voice. "I also do horoscopes."

"Really? Then tell me, what do you see in my future for the rest of this weekend? Because so far, it's been thoroughly underwhelming."

"That depends."

"On what?" Bijal asked.

"On what you're doing tomorrow."

Bijal's pulse throbbed in her temple. "Uh...so far, I think my goal is to focus on forgetting tonight—and large chunks of the last six weeks or so, while I'm at it. Why?"

"If you're game, I promised Callisto I'd take her hiking before it gets too cold. You're more than welcome to join us, depending on how hale and hearty you're feeling tomorrow."

"You mean do something outdoors?"

"Well, I find the indoor trails just aren't as challenging," Colleen replied dryly.

Bijal allowed herself to consider the notion and was momentarily dazzled by the possibilities. "And I wouldn't be chained to the Internet or repeatedly responding to inquiries about my boss's diarrhea?"

"You drive a hard bargain, but I'll agree to those conditions, yes. I'll even throw in a picnic lunch to sweeten the deal."

"Wow, that's kind of romantic, actually."

"Let me guess," Colleen said, sounding suddenly wary. "You hate romance."

"Actually, I think it sounds lovely."

"Is that a yes?"

"Mmm-hmm," Bijal replied coyly.

"Do you have comfortable shoes?"

"Of course I do. Exactly how femme do you think I am?"

"The perfect amount," Colleen said smoothly.

"You're such a politician."

"I'm pretty sure that's an insult."

Bijal felt herself flush. "Trust me, it's not. You're an *amazing* politician."

"Isn't that the equivalent of being, say, the best clump in the litter pan?"

"I do envy your skill with a metaphor."

"Is that an attempt at sweet talk?" Colleen asked.

"No," Bijal said with a small sigh. "I'm just metaphorically challenged."

"What exactly does that mean?"

Bijal pondered how to explain her peculiar disorder. "It means whenever I try to make a point, I end up undermining it by, I don't know, comparing something hot to a head of cabbage, or something dry to a marsupial uterus. It's just bad, and it usually brings the conversation to a violent, jarring halt."

"I can see why. What an unusual condition."

Bijal covered her other ear with her palm in an effort to focus on Colleen. "I think it's safe to say at this point, in full disclosure, that I'm kind of unusual."

"I appreciate the heads-up," Colleen said blithely.

"I've learned to put it out there in advance, so later you can't stage a screaming match with me in the middle of Whole Foods and insist that I'd kept it from you."

"I guess that rules out my plans for a special evening with you in the grocery store."

"Oh?" Bijal asked.

"Uh-huh, I had it all worked out. I planned to start my tirade in the dairy section and have you in tears by frozen foods."

"Thoughtful of you to leave me by the Häagen-Dazs when I'm at my emotional low point."

"Well, I'm not a *monster*," Colleen replied. "So, tomorrow."

"Right."

"Do you know where Brookman Park is?"

Bijal walked to the very edge of the deck. "Sadly, if it's outside the Beltway and they don't have margarita night, I won't know it. But it's the twenty-first century. I can find it."

"It's about forty minutes outside of DC, but the trails there are beautiful. Just meet me in the parking area at eleven. And bring a sweatshirt or something, in case it's chilly. I'll take care of everything else."

"Okay, that works."

"Cool. I'll see you tomorrow, then. Have a good night, Bijal."

"You too. Bye."

"Bye."

Bijal put her phone back in her pocket and looked again at her watch. She needed to get out of here. It was now more than just a mere annoyance. She had somewhere to be in the morning. There were preparations to be made, shut-eye to be had.

Reentering the club, she now found Fran at the bar chatting with a couple of women who looked so much alike they could have been twins. They both were wearing jeans so tight they possibly caused sterility. And both should have purchased tops at least one or two sizes larger, because they clung to every fold of skin in a far from flattering way.

Fran, unsurprisingly, seemed to like that look just fine, and she had a hand resting on the inner thigh of one of the McSqueezy Sisters.

"Fran," Bijal shouted, trying to be heard over the din. She put her hand on Fran's shoulder when she didn't immediately turn around. "Hey, I'm heading out."

Fran looked confused. "What do you mean?" she asked, close to Bijal's ear. "You met someone?"

"No, I'm going home to get some rest."

"What? Why?"

"For the best reason I can think of—because I'm tired."

Fran stepped away from the McSqueezys and focused on Bijal. "What the hell happened?"

"Nothing."

"Look, girl, if you don't blow the cobwebs off your goody basket, it's gonna shrivel up like a raisin."

"Wow," Bijal said in horror. "What a vile image. Thanks for that."

"You're welcome. What happened to that chick who looked like she wanted to gnaw you like a baby-back rib?"

"She spoke," Bijal replied curtly, more than ready for this conversation to be over.

"Well, don't let her do that anymore. Put something in her mouth—whatever it takes."

"Fran, cut the crap," Bijal snapped. "I don't want an easy lay. Sorry, that's just not me. Now I'm going to hop the Metro and go home and sleep, because tomorrow I'm going hiking."

Fran chuckled. "For a minute it sounded like you said 'hiking.' What are you doing tomorrow?"

"I *did* say hiking."

"Are you shitting me?"

"Nope. I'm…whatever the opposite of shitting you is. Pissing you?"

A muscle in Fran's cheek twitched. "You're seeing O'Bannon, aren't you?"

Bijal nodded in determination. "I'm taking a day off and I'm gonna hang out with someone I have fun with, yeah. So don't be mad at me. You stay here and have fun, and I'll see you later, okay?"

Fran seemed to understand. "Okay. Be careful."

"You too. Those girls may not be clean."

CHAPTER SEVENTEEN

A s Colleen pulled into the paved lot of Brookman Park, in front of the sign was a familiar blue Subaru, and stretched out atop the hood soaking up the sun was a familiar raven-haired hottie. She pulled into the space beside Bijal and turned off her car. "You're early."

Bijal's face lit up. "I factored in extra time, in case I got lost, my car broke down, or cannibals waylaid me." She looked perfectly yummy in well-fitting jeans, an open red-flannel shirt over a contour-hugging tank top, and a pair of dark Ray-Bans.

"How fortunate that none of those things happened," Colleen said, getting out of her car and going around to the passenger side to let out her visibly ecstatic dog.

"Well, the first two didn't, anyway," Bijal replied, sliding off her hood and landing soundly on her feet.

"Damned cannibals and their rock music."

Callisto burst out of the car like a cannonball and began dancing around them, no doubt in an effort to speed them up.

"She seems excited," Bijal noted.

Colleen pulled out both a small backpack and a larger one that acted as a picnic basket and set them on the ground as she secured the car. "She can't help herself. Sniffing the poo of woodland creatures is one of Callisto's favorite things in the world."

"Who can blame her? Wow, you brought a lot of stuff. How long are we staying?"

"About four days. Can you help me with the tent?" Colleen asked.

Bijal stared back at her with concern. "Just kidding. I figured we'd probably only be a few hours."

"All this for a few hours?"

"There's lunch, drinks, and assorted basic supplies."

"Ooh, like provisions?" Bijal picked up the small backpack and hefted it to gauge the weight. She was sexy and cute at the same time.

"I guess so. Though today we won't be panning for gold dust or bartering at the old trading post. Are you good carrying that?"

Bijal slid the bag over her shoulder enthusiastically. "Done."

Colleen switched out her regular glasses for her prescription shades and grabbed the larger pack. "Then let's go."

Callisto barked eagerly, and they set off toward the woods.

"So when's the last time you went on a hike?" Colleen asked.

"Um, on prom night I spent the evening out in the woods with a bunch of my friends, drinking two-dollar wine. Does that count?"

"I don't think just being in the woods is sufficient, no. Though being drunk certainly adds to the degree of difficulty."

"Oh, then never."

Colleen chuckled. "Not the outdoorsy type?"

"It's not that I don't enjoy the outdoors. It's just that the outdoors tends to be...dirty."

"So you're saying you're a big priss."

"I wouldn't say priss. I'm more of a—"

"Candy-ass?"

"*Exactly.*" They reached a wooden sign with a map of the different trails on it. "Which one are we taking?"

Colleen realized that Bijal really had no idea what she was getting herself into. "My favorite is the yellow trail, though it may be a little long and steep if this is your first hike."

"My first *sober* hike, thank you. And let's go ahead and take yellow. I'm not some fragile pressed flower who can't walk up a hill."

"The view from the top is really spectacular, and it'll make a nice place to stop and eat."

"Then bring it on."

❖

"Holy shit! How much higher is this fucking mountain?" Bijal stopped, bent at the waist, and put her hands on her thighs as she struggled to catch her breath.

"Do you want to take a break?"

"Well, are we…are we close to the top?"

Colleen looked around as though to get her bearings. "We're over halfway there."

"You're joking, right? It's right behind that ridge, isn't it?"

"No, to both," Colleen replied, walking the few steps back to meet Bijal. "We probably should have taken either the blue or the green trail."

"But yellow sounded like such a…pussy kind of trail. I mean, it's the color of urine…and cowardly gunfighters."

Colleen reached into her pack and produced a bottle of water, which she handed to Bijal. "It's also the color of your gallbladder, which is usually the first organ to fail due to high elevation and extended exertion."

Bijal unscrewed the cap and took a sip. "Christ! Really?"

"No, I made that up. But I love how deliciously gullible you are. It promises hours of amusement."

"Can I blame that on the lack of oxygen?"

"You can certainly try," Colleen said with a grin. "How about this? There's a clearing not too far from here. Let's stop and eat there, okay?"

Bijal was still huffing, but managed to stay upright long enough to drink some more water. "If you're sure you want to stop," she replied, trying to act as though she was actually capable of anything *but* stopping.

"Unless you'd rather wait until you spit up blood."

"That'd only be on the red trail, right?"

"Precisely. You're picking this hiking stuff right up."

"Possibly, though at this point, it could just be altitude sickness."

"You know we're probably not more than seven hundred feet up, right?"

That sounded pretty low to Bijal. "And you start to feel effects at how high?"

"About eight thousand feet."

"So this is just more of my candy-assedness?"

"I'm afraid so."

"That's incredibly humiliating."

"Come on," Colleen said, taking Bijal's hand and tugging her slowly into motion, though thankfully not straight up the mountain this time—off to the right. "It's not too far."

Callisto trotted back to them to survey what the delay was, then snorted in obvious disapproval as she fell in behind them.

"You know," Bijal said as Colleen pulled her along, "I had no idea how out of shape I am. I've obviously been spending too much time sitting at my desk and eating manicotti."

"If it's any consolation, that manicotti seems to be settling in all the right places."

If Bijal hadn't already been sweating so profusely, she might have blushed at the compliment. "Thanks. I'll try to look attractive while I'm on the ground gasping and weeping."

Colleen looked back over her shoulder, her amusement apparent. "Fortunately for you, that's just how I like my women."

"Then you're in for a real treat if we keep walking much longer."

"We're almost there, I promise. It's just beyond these trees."

Bijal continued to allow Colleen to guide her as she focused on where she was stepping. The last thing she needed to do was stumble and twist her ankle. Then it would be like every romance novel she'd ever read, except that neither of them was a double agent, a lonely cattle rancher, or a time traveler trapped in a prehistoric dinosaur land. Wait, was that *Land of the Lost?*

Her fatigue was apparently jumbling her thoughts. How did those things get confused? She didn't recall anyone ever having sex in that cave while a triceratops or Sleestak watched.

"Here we are," Colleen said, as they stopped.

"Wow," was all Bijal could wheeze. Colleen hadn't sold this clearing short. It looked out over a valley striped with trees slowly transitioning to amazing fall foliage. It was striking, stirring, and absolutely spectacular.

Colleen took off her pack and removed a plaid blanket, which she unfolded and set on the grass. "Sit down, Bijal. Drink some more water and unwind."

"Thanks. You know this place pretty well, huh?"

"Well, I used to do a lot more hiking than I do now," Colleen replied as she knelt and started unpacking lunch. "Lisa was very athletic, so I got pretty familiar with the local parks, lakes, and golf courses. Of course, now that I work in Washington there's a lot less opportunity to do sporty things."

It seemed terribly sad to Bijal that for the last several years Colleen and her dog had been wandering around the scrub and prairie lands—or whatever the hell Virginia had—like forlorn nomads. Trapped in the past, Colleen now found herself leaping from life to life, putting things right that once went wrong, and hoping each time that her next leap would be the leap home.

Shit, she was doing it again. That was from *Quantum Leap*.

"Are you all right now?"

"Maybe not *all*, but I'm mostly right. I just need to stop panting like an obscene phone caller and hope my calves quit bunching up."

"This is where a less-sensitive person would tell you that pain is just a reminder that you're alive." Colleen called Callisto over and set down a canvas water bowl for her before giving her a large bone that she removed from a baggie. "Here you go, girl." The dog eagerly took the treat and settled down to give it her full attention.

"Incidentally, the average person in agony is not above limping over to the less-sensitive person and punching her right in the crotch. Just to, you know, remind her she's alive." Bijal reclined on the blanket and stared up at the sky.

"Wow, good thing you're completely incapacitated."

"And probably couldn't stand right now if I had to."

"You might feel better faster if you had something to eat. Interested in lunch?"

"Sounds good. What's on the menu?"

"General Tso's Chicken and Polish sausage."

Bijal jerked her head up quickly. "Um…"

"Just kidding. I packed sandwiches and fruit salad. Would you prefer roast beef or ham and cheese? Oh, and I also brought peanut butter, in case you weren't feeling particularly carnivorous," Colleen said, holding them all up.

"I'll take the ham, if that's okay."

"Absolutely." Colleen found the correct sandwich and extended it to Bijal.

Bijal grimaced as she struggled to sit back up. In resignation, she relaxed her muscles again. "Can you just set it on my body somewhere? I'll get it in a minute."

"I've broken you, haven't I?"

"I'm not broken," Bijal replied weakly, "just recharging."

"Like a solar cell?"

"A wheezing, sticky solar cell, yes."

Colleen poured some of her bottled water over a handkerchief, then wrung it out. "Close your eyes, Bijal."

She followed instructions as Colleen wiped the damp fabric along her cheeks and forehead. "Mmm, that feels nice."

Before she could process any other random television flashbacks, Colleen's lips lightly brushed hers. When the kiss ended, Bijal opened her eyes and was undone by Colleen's blatantly amorous expression.

"Sorry," Colleen said, her tone husky. "I couldn't help myself. You're very alluring when you're all sweaty and wounded."

"Then stick around, 'cause I have *lots* of those kinds of moments." They kissed again, and for the first time in nearly an hour, Bijal completely forgot about her burning muscles and unqualified exhaustion. Instead, the amazing way Colleen's mouth moved against hers was thoroughly monopolizing her mental faculties, and her stomach lurched at the contact. Colleen pulled back again, and Bijal's lust-tinted gaze vacillated from the hunger in Colleen's eyes, to her full and wondrous lips, and back again. "If I were to get really wounded—like, if I needed stitches or something, what might that get me?"

"A trip to the emergency room," Colleen replied, still only inches away.

"That's it?"

"And maybe I'd take off my shirt while I applied pressure to the wound."

"If you're trying to slow my heart rate, you're failing spectacularly."

Colleen gave another smoldering look. "Sorry."

"You're *so* forgiven."

"You should eat."

"You read my mind," Bijal purred, rising to meet Colleen's mouth with her own again.

Colleen softly placed her hand against Bijal's collarbone and forced her back down. "I actually meant food."

"Oh, damn."

"Apparently we've found a cure for your low energy." Colleen backed away and picked the sandwich up and again offered it to Bijal.

Bijal sat up gingerly and took the ham and cheese sandwich out of the baggie. "That may cure a number of ailments. I'm looking forward to doing the research."

"Sadly, that's the part we're supposed to be waiting on, remember?"

"Then you'd better start keeping your lips to yourself, sugar."

Colleen chewed a bit of her roast beef and swallowed. "I'll do my best, but you'll need to stop looking so tempting."

Bijal had another rush of adrenaline. "So maybe what we need is a little bland conversation."

"You start."

"Tell me about this trip you have next week."

"It's a standard congressional delegation, what we call a CODEL. As a member of the House Armed Services Committee, periodically it's in my best interest to travel where our armed forces are. I'll only be there for a few days."

"I'm surprised that you're going in the middle of your campaign."

"My main job is being a congresswoman, not a campaigner. And between you and me, I *hate* campaigning."

"That's understandable," Bijal said.

"I mean, it's just such bullshit—running around shaking hands and kissing babies."

"You could always change it up and kiss hands and shake babies."

"And having to run every two years makes it pretty difficult to stay focused on Washington and the tasks at hand."

"Some might argue that an election every two years forces you to get back in your district and interface with your constituents."

Colleen smiled wryly. "Yeah, well, giving speeches and eating barbecue at a truck stop doesn't really impact the people in my district the way what I do on their behalf does."

"That might depend on the barbecue."

"I'd like to think that the best things I can do to encourage people to vote for me are to consistently do what's best for them and to not be a douchebag."

"Whoa, slow down there, Colleen. You're talking like some kind of crazy radical."

"You think so?"

"Absolutely. Why actually make an effort and accomplish things when you can just sit on your ass and then lie at election time and *say* that you accomplished things?"

"You may have me confused with a career politician. I'm less of a lazy lump and more of a shit-stirrer."

Bijal nodded as she took another sip of water. "I have noticed that."

"In fact, if you want to tune in to Tank Guzman tomorrow night, I'll be back on, stirring my next shit bucket."

"More evisceration of the anti-gay-adoption crowd?"

"No, tomorrow it's all about the Saturday Amendment."

"Really?" Bijal knew the Democrats were pressuring Colleen, and no doubt several other progressives in the House, to pass the bill with the amendment included. But to break so publicly with her party so close to Election Day was a pretty ballsy move. "You're going on TV to oppose it?"

"Yup."

"What changed your mind?"

"I didn't necessarily change my mind about anything," Colleen replied. "I just decided that I feel very strongly about this. It's one reason I ran for Congress to begin with, and I refuse to let anyone try to intimidate me to vote against my conscience."

"Even if the intimidators are your own party leaders?"

"*Especially* if that's who they are. I don't need their campaign support. So I'm just going to put what's really going on out there for public consumption. It'll either resonate with people who are pro-choice, or it won't matter enough to stop it. Either way, I won't be happy if I don't at least find out. If it costs me my seat in the House, so be it."

Bijal studied Colleen for a moment. "Chicks with convictions are hot."

"Hmm, so how's your sandwich?"

"It may be the best ham-and-cheese I've ever had."

Colleen scoffed. "It's okay to be candid. I'll lead you back down the mountain whether you like it or not."

"Trust me," Bijal said. "Candor isn't a problem for me."

CHAPTER EIGHTEEN

Bijal pushed open the door to Denton Campaign Headquarters and hobbled inside. She tried to brush aside the muscle aches, but her thighs and calves burned as though she'd hauled a sack of bricks across the Himalayas, and her back twinged whenever she twisted. Dumping her bag at her desk, she booted up her PC and, rather than wait for it, headed directly for the coffeemaker.

She grabbed the mug that said "2008 Republican National Convention—St. Paul, Minn." and emptied the hot carafe into it.

"Good morning, Bijal," Kristin said from the break-room doorway. "Are you okay?"

"I'm fine," Bijal replied, tearing open a packet of sweetener and fumbling for a spoon. "Why do you ask?"

"Oh, no reason—just that you're walking like a sunburned nudist."

Bijal turned to face her and shifted her weight against the counter behind her. "Yeah, I went hiking yesterday. This is my post-exercise healthy glow."

Kristin looked horrified. "Oh, my God. Really?"

"Mmm-hmm. I thought it sucked while I was doing it, but now the pain has reached a new apex. It's like the Cadillac of physical anguish."

"That's how you chose to spend your day off? Hiking your way to paralysis?"

Bijal took a sip of her coffee and happily let the elixir slide down her throat. "Admittedly, I did it more for the company and less for the gnarled hamstrings."

"Ooh, you mean it was a *date*?"

"Sort of."

"Tell me all about him," Kristin said eagerly. "I'm so ready for some good news."

This was not a conversation Bijal was either prepared for or remotely interested in having. "Maybe a little later. I don't want to jinx it."

"It's that new?"

Bijal nodded and took another swallow of java.

Suddenly, Dan, the office manager, poked his head into the break room. "Ah, you *are* here. Eliot's calling an emergency meeting in his office."

"What time?" Kristin asked.

"Right now," he replied. "And he wants you both there."

Kristin's expression was grim. "Maybe you were wrong and you haven't reached the apex of your pain yet."

"Well, I'm sure he's not calling us into his office to talk about how awesome the debate went."

They both started the slow death march to see Eliot. "Did you look at the editorials and blogs?" Kristin asked quietly.

"Yeah, they were merciless. I couldn't find a single positive analysis, unless you count the crazy guy who said eleven different times throughout the course of his secessionist rant that he wanted to 'do' Janet."

"Eww, I don't think we *can* count that, can we?"

"I doubt it, because I'm pretty sure what he wants to do to Margaret Thatcher is a felony."

They arrived at Eliot's open door and were hastily ushered inside, where most of the campaign workers were already sitting, standing, or leaning. Janet was noticeably absent, which made Bijal wonder if this might be a meeting to talk about her dropping out of the race entirely.

"Dan, shut the door, please," Eliot said.

Dan stepped inside, pulling it closed behind him.

"No," Eliot amended in irritation. "I mean from the *outside*."

"Oh," Dan replied dejectedly. He shuffled awkwardly out of the room.

"I have a few announcements," he said. "First, I want everyone to know that I've fired Paige for her reckless behavior. For those of you who weren't aware, she gave Mayor Denton mood-altering narcotics before the debate, resulting in the complete and utter shutdown of the mayor's mental faculties."

Eliot had apparently assumed he might hear gasps of horror or cries of anger at his rather exaggerated allegations, because he paused dramatically and eyed everyone expectantly. Instead, people just looked warily around the room at each other, as though trying to gauge what might be coming next.

"At any rate, I'm sure most of you are feeling rather disheartened today, based on our disappointing performance against O'Bannon and the slew of negative press that it generated. How many of you feel, at this point, that we should throw in the towel?"

People seemed confused. No doubt they wanted to be honest and admit that, yes, winning this campaign would now take not only a miracle from God, but perhaps also a natural disaster and/or a zombie apocalypse. But most people had already learned that when the boss asks for your honesty, he or she rarely, if ever, actually wants it. No one raised their hand, nodded in tacit agreement, or even twitched an eyebrow.

Eliot pursed his lips. "None of you? Nobody in here feels like we should just accept the fact that we're down too far in the polls to come back in just five weeks?"

Ted, who had recently been moved to oversee the phone bank, bravely held up his hand.

"Aha!" Eliot asserted, his finger extended in accusation. "Then you can go right ahead and leave, Ted."

Ted appeared stunned. "What?"

"We don't need your negativity," Eliot explained. "And anyone else who agrees with Ted can go right along with him."

Ted's brow furrowed and he walked with conviction, stopping only a few inches from Eliot. Ted was tall and imposing in stature. Bijal had little doubt that Eliot was probably very close to his threshold of wetting himself, right there in front of all his direct reports. "You're an idiot," Ted growled. "Maybe not as big an idiot as Donna, but still an idiot." Just when it looked like he might take a swing at Eliot, Ted stomped out of the office and slammed the door.

Eliot sagged in obvious relief. "So can I assume that all we have left in the room are people with positive, can-do attitudes?" People nodded dumbly, having seen the repercussions of answering to the contrary. "Good. Because we need that kind of energy to turn this race around! This meeting is to announce a new beginning for the Denton for Congress campaign. We have a new focus, a new direction, and a new message that's being broadcast to the public starting today in our latest ads. Kristin, hit the lights."

Kristin flipped the switch and the room went dark except for the illumination from Eliot's flat-screen monitor. He turned it slightly so everyone could see and clicked his mouse twice, prompting the ad to start playing.

The ad showed Colleen speaking in slow motion, a popular technique that viewers found subconsciously unsettling and tended to make the speaker look awkward and unattractive. The voiceover sounded menacing.

"Congressman Colleen O'Bannon, radical liberal, is running for your vote. But do you really know everything she stands for? O'Bannon wants gay marriage legalized in Virginia, which mandates teaching our second-graders about things like same-sex marriage, sex education, and transgendered people and their sex-change operations. If you agree that these aren't the values you want forced on our young children, then reconsider your vote for Congresswoman O'Bannon. Does she really represent you? Or is she just another permissive Washington deviant trying to push her liberal agenda? I'm Janet Denton, and I approve this message."

Eliot paused the video at the end and signaled Kristin to turn the lights back on. Bijal stood speechless as the blood rushed to her face.

"This is what I'm talking about," Eliot said. "We're going for broke now, folks. The gloves are off, and we're hitting O'Bannon with both barrels."

"Can I ask a question?" Bijal said, surprised by the sound of her own voice.

"Sure."

"The claim about what would be taught to second-graders—"

Eliot ran his hand through his hair idly. "We lifted that from the ads for Prop 8 in California and Prop 1 in Maine."

"But it's not true," Bijal replied.

"Look, it's a hot-button issue that motivated voters. Everywhere that it's been tried it's been successful."

"Is Janet okay with this tack? I mean, she supports gay marriage too."

A couple people in the office nodded in agreement, but said nothing to back Bijal. Eliot began to glance around the room defensively. "I understand what you're saying. But desperate times call for desperate measures. And, quite frankly, with only a handful of weeks left before the election, things simply can't be more desperate for us. So everyone needs to decide if they're ready and willing to do what needs to be done to get the mayor into Congress, where she can really make a difference."

"So the end justifies the means," someone said from the back, less of a question and more of a statement.

"Yes," Eliot replied. "Because if she's not elected, she won't be able to do any of the things that you believed in enough to motivate you to join her campaign in the first place. Until now, we've enjoyed the fact that O'Bannon has run TV and radio spots that are almost entirely positive and about what she's already done and what she wants to do. Our ads before this wasted too much time branding O'Bannon as 'fiscally irresponsible.' We just talked about her raising taxes. It was practically Sunday school! Everyone needs to understand that every seat in Congress that we lose is an obstacle to the entire party and our ideals, as well as a setback to us doing everything we've promised the public. If we don't fight back in the war against a crippling national debt and massive government expansion, we're just as culpable as the people perpetrating it, are we not?"

The campaign workers all seemed genuinely encouraged now, so Eliot continued with his pep rally.

"This election isn't some piddly little thing, people. This impacts every piece of legislation that comes through the House of Representatives for the next two years. So if you believe in your candidate and what she stands for, you're either here to win or you're just passing time. I'm telling you that from this moment on, we're here to win!"

Everyone responded by either clapping or audibly agreeing.

"Shit," Bijal whispered.

❖

Bijal sat in her car and anguished over her next move. She glanced at her watch and saw that she had only another eight minutes left of her lunch break. She picked up her phone for the eleventh time and studied it with an uncertainty so powerful that she was nauseous and had sweaty palms.

She took a deep breath and typed a message to Colleen.

Please know that I had nothing to do with our latest campaign ad, and I'm very sorry.

She pressed Send before she could possibly second-guess herself further.

How had she ended up here? She'd originally gotten interested in politics because of the low caliber of elected officials, both local and federal. Every other week someone was getting caught stealing, taking a bribe to do something utterly reprehensible, or cheating on their spouse with a staffer/paid escort/gay prostitute. Politics didn't have to be like that. If we just worked hard enough to remove the corrupt officials, we could replace them with ethical people who would neither compromise nor sell out their principles.

Now here she was working for a candidate who'd allowed herself to be scared into doing those very things.

Her phone vibrated suddenly, startling her in multiple ways. Did she really want to see the response?

Already saw it. I'd like to say it didn't faze me, but I can't. It's loathsome and irresponsible.

Bijal quickly entered a reply.

I tried to argue against it, but the ads were already distributed by the time I saw it this morning. They're desperate and see this as their last chance.

It took less than a minute this time to receive Colleen's response.

That doesn't justify incendiary lies. So your strategy has become "If we can't win on merit, just make shit up that will get people angry enough to vote for us"?

Bijal was becoming more despondent as she feverishly pressed the keys to answer.

They feel threatened enough to take a page right out of the Proposition 8 handbook.

Bijal's lunch break was now almost over. Though she desperately wanted to see how Colleen would respond, she was so upset and patently embarrassed by betraying her principles that she didn't think she could withstand any more terse text messages. Then it arrived.

Even more reprehensible to use propaganda that was used to discriminate against your own community in an attack against me. How do you sleep at night?

Bijal turned her phone off and got out of her car. As she walked back to her desk, she couldn't blame Colleen for being angry. This campaign had become exactly what Fran had predicted. Anyone with an ounce of integrity would march right in to Eliot's office and tell him to fuck off. But Bijal couldn't do that—not without at least speaking to Janet first.

CHAPTER NINETEEN

Doug Patel, the media specialist for the O'Bannon campaign, stared through the camera viewfinder. "And cut," he called, making a slashing motion with his hand.

"How was that?" Colleen asked, feeling fairly confident about it.

"Perfect," Doug said. "You're a natural."

Max stood nearby with his arms crossed, staring in interest over Doug's shoulder. "I told you this would be a breeze."

"Yeah," Doug said with an affable grin. "But just so you know, everyone says that and it's almost never true. Luckily our subject wasn't horrible."

"Thanks for setting the bar so low for me," Colleen said, taking out her BlackBerry and scrolling through her e-mail.

Doug's face froze. "That came out wrong."

"I was hoping it was unintentional," Colleen replied without looking up. "Do you need anything else?"

Doug watched the commercial as he played it back on the camcorder. "I'd say we're good. In fact, that last take was so first-rate, we can use it unedited—just a single shot that slowly pulls in tight."

"Excellent," Max said. "I want to see your first cut the second you have the graphics and music incorporated."

"You know what I'm thinking?" Doug stopped the playback and spun in his chair to face Max.

"What?"

"Let's not have music. Have it just be the congresswoman talking to the voters—no gloss. In fact, maybe we put the sponsorship message at the beginning so we don't lose the impact at the end."

Max smiled broadly. "Ooh, nice! Does that sound good, Colleen?"

It wasn't that Colleen didn't care, but the prospect of being done with this was the best news she'd had all day. "Whatever y'all say."

"Were you even listening?" Max asked as he yawned.

"For most of it. Sorry, Max, but I have to head over to the television studio to get ready to film my spot on *The Tank Guzman Show*. Then, first thing in the morning, I jump on an international flight."

Max raised his hands in feigned surrender. "Okay, you win. You officially have too much to do. Don't worry, I'll send you the ad as soon as it's ready for your approval."

"Thanks, guys." Colleen stood and gathered her belongings.

"Try to mention the campaign website at least twice when you're on TV," Max said.

Colleen paused long enough to respond. "Max, my goal is to encourage the public to get involved with the Patient Access Reform Act, not to campaign. Sorry, but I won't be prostituting myself tonight."

"You could just sort of toss it in at the end," Max said hopefully.

"Nope, won't happen."

"Maybe just the phone number?"

Colleen shook her head slowly. "Get me the ad as soon as possible, so I can approve it before I leave in the morning, okay?"

"You're ignoring me again?"

"Mmm-hmm," Colleen replied, heading out the door. "Thanks again!"

They waved good-bye as she headed out to find her car. She unlocked the driver's door and got inside before stopping to once again consider the impetus of this impromptu commercial—Denton's inflammatory and deceptive attack ad.

She really wished Bijal didn't work for that campaign. But as much as she sensed that Bijal hadn't been a party to all their shifty schemes, Bijal *had* been the one with a video camera rooting through the mud in Colleen's front yard.

She shut her car door and tried to massage the tension headache out of her temples. Perhaps she'd been impulsive to get involved with Bijal before the election. It wasn't like her to act recklessly—but it had been so long since she'd found anyone this alluring.

Unfortunately, as disappointed and burned as she felt politically, she was just as saddened that things were now awkward between her and Bijal.

She turned the key in the ignition and the engine started.

❖

Bijal sat dejectedly at a dimly lit booth in the Cheshire Grille, a place not too far from her apartment that served delectable comfort food and strong mixed drinks. Glancing at the door, she saw Fran walk in and make a beeline for her.

"Hey," Fran said, sliding in across from her. "What's up? Your text had a lot of punctuation."

Bijal groaned and took another sip of her libation. "A bad day at work."

"I thought those were the only kind of days you have anymore."

"Pretty much."

"What happened now? Did Denton slap a nun?"

"Nothing that forgivable."

The server arrived with a menu, which Fran quickly waved away. "No, thanks, Chuck. I already know what I want. I'll have the meat loaf and a light draft beer."

Chuck nodded. "And for you?"

Bijal grimaced. As much as her appetite had left her for a sunnier climate, if she was drinking, she needed to eat something substantial. "I'll take the chili and cornbread, and another whiskey, please."

"Will do," Chuck replied, then spun away toward the bar.

"Okay." Fran propped her chin in her hand. "Lay it on me."

"As of today, we're running a deceptive, contemptible anti-gay ad."

"And?"

"What do you mean 'and?'" Bijal snapped.

"Okay, don't get all pissy about this, but look at the base of your party, honey. Their mutual hatred of other people is the glue holding them all together."

The muscles in Bijal's neck tightened uncomfortably. "I'm not supposed to get pissy about that?"

"No, because it's true."

"It's *not* true, Fran. It's a Democratic talking point. The Republican Party was originally founded on the principles of advancing the middle class, small businesses, and civil rights. We can and should still be about those things."

Chuck appeared with their drinks then vanished again.

Fran picked up the frosty mug and gave it a taste. "Well, then, someone needs to tell the folks in charge, 'cause they're the ones running on an anti-gay, anti-immigrant, anti-affirmative action, pro-corporate conglomerate, pro-gun platform."

"So you're saying that because I don't subscribe to the ideology of the far right of my party, I should just walk away from it? How would a mass exodus of the moderates improve things exactly? Don't you believe in a two-party system?"

"Sure."

"As long as the party other than yours is reduced to a small pocket of angry, socially regressive people who can be easily mocked, right?"

"It sounds bad when you say it."

"Because it is! This isn't how things are supposed to work. Politicians are supposed to *stand* for things, not make up ridiculous lies that appeal to the most frightened and base aspects of human nature. Government should not be like *Lord of the Flies*. It's supposed to make our lives better and safer."

"Bij, why aren't *you* running for office?"

"Huh?"

"I'd vote for you."

Bijal shook her head as she downed what was left of her first whiskey so she could economically transition to the next. "You would not."

"I would! Because you're sincere, which makes you better than ninety-nine percent of the people currently seeking office in *all* parties."

"Including Janet Denton, apparently," Bijal said cheerlessly.

"So she totally Nixoned out on you?"

"I'm not sure. I haven't even seen her since we got our new marching orders this morning."

Fran's left eyebrow arched. "Hmm, so it may be more your new campaign manager or the NRCC?"

"I don't know, Fran. Ever since I signed on I've been giving Janet a pass. First I blamed Donna, then I blamed the NRCC. But it's Janet's voice at the end of this appalling ad saying she approved it, not anyone else's."

"It's that bad?"

"Like *Hindenburg*-oh-the-humanity bad, yeah."

"Wow, what's it say exactly?"

"It calls Colleen a 'deviant' and spews some ridiculous shit about how if gay marriage is legalized, it'll force schools to teach second-graders about strap-ons and donkey shows."

"Damn, did you say anything to anyone?"

"I said it wasn't true and mentioned that Janet supports gay marriage just as much as Colleen does."

"Did you walk out?"

"I thought about it...but no."

"What's the plan now?" Fran asked seriously. "Swallow your ethics?"

"I plan to try to talk to Janet tomorrow, to find out if she's completely onboard with this. I mean, Colleen wouldn't entertain something like this for a second."

"Aha."

Bijal started to speak, but just then Chuck delivered their food. Once they'd assured him they didn't need anything else, Bijal said, "What did that 'aha' mean?"

"That's what this is really all about—what Colleen would approve of."

"That doesn't even make sense." Bijal tore off a piece of cornbread in irritation.

Fran jabbed her meat loaf forcefully with her fork. "You had no qualms creeping around and following your opponent like she was

Lindsay Lohan with no panties on, hoping to catch her doing something gay."

"I did so have qualms—all kinds of crazy qualms. I was practically swimming in…qualminess."

"But apparently not quite enough to tell your bosses to take their witch hunt and stuff it up their fat, bigoted asses."

"They would just have gotten someone else to do it. Maybe I was fighting them via sabotage. Did you think of that?"

"Or maybe you can't admit to yourself that not only do you no longer support your candidate, but at this point, you don't even qualify as impartial."

Bijal stared at Fran. "Bullshit."

"Bij, listen to yourself. You're clearly in the bag for O'Bannon, which I'm sure is exactly what O'Bannon wants. Honestly, what could be handier than a sympathetic insider in the opposition's camp who just so happens to be fascinated by your rack? You don't think she might be using you?"

"No, I don't."

Fran continued her conjecture. "And now in response to your shitty ad, all she has to do to mount a valid defense is to out you—show what a collection of hypocrites y'all are with your fake outrage against gays."

Bijal suddenly had a sinking feeling in her gut.

"You see where I'm going with this?"

"I think so. Hopefully Colleen wouldn't do that."

"But Denton would if she was in the same position, wouldn't she?"

Bijal ran her hand through her hair as she pondered the possibilities Fran was posing. "This completely sucks."

"I believe I predicted some kind of suckage quite some time ago, did I not?"

"Yeah, yeah, what do I do now, though?"

"Whatever you do, don't contact O'Bannon."

"Um…"

Fran looked incredulous. "Jesus, are you under *hypnosis*? What the hell?"

"I just wanted to give her a heads-up," Bijal explained, regretting the admission as soon as she spoke the words.

"Which is completely what a loyal Denton supporter would do, right?"

"I can't help it if I had a momentary pang of conscience when my boss decided to suddenly ally with the Klan."

"Uh-huh." Fran was clearly not buying it.

"Look, maybe my expectations of Colleen are totally unreasonable. For all I know, she could be just as shady as everyone else in this town. It's possible I've been nothing more than a naïve idealist who never should have entered politics without the blanket assumption that I'd have to sell my soul just to cheat someone into office whom I neither support nor respect."

Fran chewed, then swallowed. "I don't disagree with any of that."

"So, yes, I texted her about it, but she'd already seen it."

"How'd she take it?"

"Bad."

"*Hindenburg* bad?"

"Well, I didn't hear her voice, but it sure seemed that way."

Fran sat back and stared at Bijal for a moment. "Now what?"

Bijal rubbed her tired eyes. "I wish I knew. Part of me wants to tell Eliot to fuck off and just storm out on principle. But then I couldn't pay my bills. And what, do I just go back to waiting tables for the rest of my life and hope the tips will cover my student-loan payments? Or do I adjust my scruples to be more realistic and stay in the fight to try to make a difference? Do I quit before I'm outed and unwittingly take down not just myself, but the whole Denton congressional campaign as well? Or do I refuse to let them make my sexuality an issue—because it shouldn't be?"

"You sure have a lot of questions. Regardless, I think you need to stop this little side fling with O'Bannon."

"I think she beat me to it," Bijal said morosely.

Fran cleared her throat. "Not to be callous, but you really should take advantage of the opportunity. Every time you two interact, you compromise yourself."

Bijal buried her face in her hands. "I know. You're right."

"And maybe when this is all over you can look her up and ask her out—once there's nothing left to hide."

"Doubtful. I think I blew it," Bijal replied wistfully as she stood up. "I need to run to the restroom. I'll be right back."

She had painfully hobbled only a few steps when Fran stopped her. "What the hell happened to you?"

"Hiking."

"I told you that healthy shit will kill you."

CHAPTER TWENTY

B ijal stared at her monitor as the video clip ended. She'd watched Colleen's *Tank Guzman Show* appearance from the previous evening twice already since she'd gotten to work and could find little to use from a campaign perspective.

Colleen had apparently accomplished exactly what she'd intended by going on national television to talk about the pending bill. She'd been very specific about why she opposed the Saturday Amendment, explaining that pro-choice and pro-sex-education voters needed to understand exactly what effects the legislation would have before the House rushed it through a vote next week.

This was essentially the last piece of major business on the docket before the House adjourned prior to the election, and Colleen was taking a big risk by publicly crossing her party's leadership and trying to pressure other progressive Democrats to do the same. If she succeeded in peeling off some of the representatives who'd pledged a "yes" vote, as well as eroding some of the public support of the bill as written, she could claim a huge victory. But either way, she'd just made a lot of very powerful enemies, many within her own caucus.

Janet came through the front door, encumbered by her enormous purse and hiding behind her trusty sunglasses. She apparently wanted to go unnoticed, not addressing anyone as she slunk by them on the way to her office. Bijal quietly stood and followed her, trying to be just as unobtrusive.

Janet tossed down her bag and glasses and threw herself into her desk chair. With a tired groan, she slowly spun to see Bijal lingering in her doorway. "Oh," she said with a start. "Good morning, Bijal."

"Good morning. I'd ordinarily have given you a few minutes to settle in, but I know you have a hectic schedule today, and I thought I'd get you while I could. You have a minute?"

Janet glanced at her watch. "Sure, though I don't have much more than that. Come on in and close the door."

Bijal did so and took the chair directly across from her. "I know you've had a lot to deal with over the last month or so, and that we're running out of time to make up the ground we've lost."

"But?"

"But I have a real problem with this new ad we're running."

Janet nodded slowly, as though she expected the contention. "I know it may not feel right," she said.

"Because it's *not* right, Janet. It's reprehensible."

"Look, this campaign is bigger than one thirty-second commercial, and while I certainly understand your feelings—"

"I don't think you do understand. I was really excited to work for you. Not just because this was my big break into politics, but because you believe a lot of the things I do. You're a moderate who opposes government overreach and inefficiencies, regardless of what may be polling well. When you and I met, you supported civil unions, and that meant a lot to me."

"Bijal—"

"It meant a lot to me because I'm gay, Janet. I'm a lesbian."

Janet's red eyes were immense and unblinking. "Uh…"

"While it's possible that you lied to me initially, you've now decided to endorse a statement that's shamefully homophobic and inflammatory—one that sends a message that the LGBT community is subhuman or abnormal to the degree that children need to be shielded from us. Is that what you really think?"

"No," Janet replied softly, appearing still somewhat stunned. "This is just politics."

"I'm sorry, but it's clearly more than that. I need to know if you have a problem with gays—one that impacts my job."

"What do you mean?"

"I mean, am I any less qualified now that you know I'm a lesbian? Will I get a pay cut? Be fired?"

Janet looked mortified. "God, no, of course not! Why would you even think that?"

"Why *wouldn't* I think that, Janet? You're obviously fine with me not having equal rights. You have no issue with using me as your boogeyman du jour to frighten voters into thinking that all gays want to destroy democracy and eat the flesh of the righteous—all in the hopes that they scurry out to the polls to cast their ballot for the candidate who'll keep them safe."

"I'm very sorry about all this," Janet said, her voice tinged with what sounded like a combination of depression and fatigue. "I meant it when I told you that I support civil unions. I don't believe in discrimination of any kind."

"Then why have you let yourself get pulled so far off-message?"

Before Janet could craft an answer, they heard a knock.

"Come in," Janet called, making Bijal wonder if Janet was secretly thankful for the interruption.

The door swung open, revealing Kristin, wearing a rather serious expression. "Y'all need to come see this."

"What?" Janet asked.

"O'Bannon's camp has just issued a response to our latest ad. We've got it all cued up for you."

Bijal followed Janet out to the main office area. Carl, who'd been given Ted's old job after Eliot inexplicably fired him, was sitting at his desk, his mouse finger at the ready. "Everyone here?" he asked.

"Eliot's not here yet," Janet replied. "But let's not wait for him. Go ahead."

The rest of the staff gathered around Carl's screen as he clicked Play. After the sponsorship message, the camera simply showed Colleen sitting, looking both stoic and beautiful.

"Hello, I'm Congressional Representative Colleen O'Bannon, incumbent candidate for Virginia's twelfth district. I believe that a politician should run a positive campaign that focuses on what he or she stands for and will work toward. Unfortunately, my opponent is now running an attack ad that's not only virulently homophobic, but

also provably untrue, clearly intended to appeal to your emotions and your need to protect your children. I've asked several independent fact-checking organizations to evaluate Mayor Denton's claims, and I encourage you to visit their websites, now displayed on the screen, to review their findings. Just as important, though, I suggest that you consider the character of an elected official who would purposefully lie in an attempt to scare people into voting for him or her. If you think you deserve honesty and transparency from your government, then demand it. Your politicians owe it to you."

The video ended and everyone stood for a moment in silence.

"What, they didn't play 'The Battle Hymn of the Republic' in the background?" someone in the back asked.

Several people tittered nervously, perhaps too uncomfortable with the reality of Colleen's accusations to respond any other way. Bijal locked gazes with Janet, who swallowed loudly but said nothing.

❖

Colleen had already taken her seat on the plane scheduled to take off from Dubai and land about four-and-a-half hours later in Kabul, Afghanistan. The trip to Dubai had been long and taxing. But at least it was on a commercial aircraft. This last leg of the journey would be aboard a C-130 Hercules military transport plane—a far less luxurious ride.

"Shit," she muttered as she recognized that she still had no signal on her BlackBerry. It was frustrating not to be able to access her e-mail. Cut off digitally from her congressional office as well as her campaign headquarters, Colleen had immersed herself in the documentation she'd brought outlining the CODEL—where they were going, who they were meeting, and what they were ultimately hoping to accomplish.

"Colleen," someone called. Looking up, Colleen recognized the smiling face of Congressman Steve McAllister, an affable Republican from Ohio. "Of course you're working. Why wouldn't I have assumed that?"

"Hey, Steve. I *would* be working, if I could get a signal."

"Yeah, I haven't been able to get one either. Mind if I sit next to you?"

"Not at all. Take a load off."

Steve slipped his carry-on bag off his shoulder and sat beside her. "The flight out of DC seemed like it lasted forever. Did you get any sleep?"

"Not enough," Colleen replied wistfully. She had tried to nap several times during the nearly thirteen-hour flight, but her mind had been racing and wouldn't let her relax. Even her most random ruminations somehow ended up transitioning to thoughts of Bijal. Those seemed to start out pleasant enough—the tone of her rich voice, her warm mahogany eyes, her full lips, the knee-weakening way she kissed.

Then, like a terrible boomerang of despair, somehow everything wondrous would fade into the twisted, unpleasant confines of their ugly political battle, and she was left feeling a horrible fusion of arousal and anguish. The combination was neither satisfying nor tolerable.

"How's your election coming along?" Steve asked, little realizing the pot of viscous shit-soup he was stirring.

"From a polling perspective, fine. From a mud-slinging perspective, it completely sucks."

Steve scoffed. "Come on, you must be sitting pretty after your opponent called the Department of Justice the 'Justice League of America' last week. That was *hilarious*. He's a real Einstein."

"Sorry, you've got the wrong Einstein. That guy's running against Bob Gutierrez. I have the anti-gay pants-shitter as my opponent."

Steve laughed loudly for several seconds before visibly restraining himself. "Right! How could I forget? Wait, when you say 'antigay,' does that mean she played the gay card on you?"

"Like a dealer in Vegas."

"Ouch, sorry."

It was a genuine comfort to Colleen, albeit a wee one, that Steve seemed to empathize with her. "That means a lot coming from someone who's running unopposed, Steve," she joked.

"Look at the bright side. At least you weren't pretending to be straight and they outed you."

"True, but I'm in the wrong party for that."

Steve feigned horror. "Ooh, well, that may be, but you're in the right party if you plan to embezzle."

"Well, maybe someday we'll get as good at covering up our financial irregularities as you guys are."

Steve dipped his head discreetly, "Hey, speaking of irregularities, I flew in to Dubai with Zeller. Have you seen him yet?"

"No, why?"

"I passed him in customs. Apparently he—"

As Steve spoke, Congressman Harlan Zeller—Georgia Democrat and horse's ass—walked onto the plane with a woman who could best be described as a truck-stop-bathroom-stall lay who was past her prime, but more than likely still smelled of diesel fuel and urine. "Harlan!" Colleen shouted, trying diplomatically to interrupt Steve's gossip. "How are you?"

Harlan stopped in front of them, but Colleen couldn't look away from the bleached blonde in the gold lamé miniskirt beside him. Though clearly in her mid to late forties, she still had a visible tattoo on her upper arm of Hello Kitty sitting on a toilet, melting heroin in a spoon.

"Hey there," Harlan said. "I don't know about y'all, but I'm about as tired as a bag of beat dicks. This trip is grueling."

Steve stood politely and extended his hand. "And is this Mrs. Zeller?"

Colleen had tried to stop Steve before the question came tumbling out of his mouth, but even humming the word *no* and subtly shaking her head had no effect.

"Hell, no!" Zeller cackled. "You obviously haven't met my wife. This is my aide, Cha Cha Staines."

Colleen and Steve were both momentarily struck mute. Was he serious? "Nice to meet you," Colleen finally managed to say.

Cha Cha whined a wordless greeting and nodded pleasantly. It was not beyond the realm of possibility that she spoke a language other than English—or possibly no language at all.

"Go on and head on back, darlin'," Harlan said, slapping Cha Cha playfully on her bottom. "Good Lord, honey, your jugs are out. Wrap those puppies up before any of our fine fightin' men come onboard and want to rub 'em."

She responded with a nasally giggle before making a futile attempt to pull at the sheer fabric of her clingy blouse. "Sorry."

Harlan and Cha Cha shuffled to the back of the plane and sat as far away from Steve and Colleen as possible.

"Holy shit," Colleen muttered.

"I'm glad he's a member of your caucus," Steve said softly.

"I'd rather not claim him, if it's all right with you. Did he say she was named after vaginal discharge?"

Steve laughed loudly and shook his head. "Maybe."

"What is he thinking? Why would you bring your mistress into a war zone? And what'll happen when we get to Afghanistan? Do you think either of them have the foggiest notion of the societal restrictions on women there?"

"I'm pretty sure your boy Harlan sees this as a fun trip he can take with a"—his voice trailed off as he clearly struggled for a noun that wasn't disparaging—"lady other than his wife."

"In the words of every Star Wars movie, 'I have a really bad feeling about this.'"

CHAPTER TWENTY-ONE

Because she was unable to think about anything else for more than a few minutes at a time, Bijal had sent Colleen a couple of text messages over the last two days to test the waters. When the first one went unanswered, she sulked, fearing she had indeed alienated the most attractive and scintillating woman she'd met in years.

The following day she texted Colleen again and obsessed over her wording—wanting to masterfully walk the fine line between sounding needy and just seeming earnest. Again she'd gotten no response. It was only after she went to Colleen's website that she remembered about the CODEL to the Middle East and realized Colleen probably wasn't in range of cellular phone service.

CODELs in classified locations weren't allowed to broadcast their location in real time, as doing so was considered a threat to security, so perhaps Colleen wasn't even allowed to have her phone with her.

Bijal pushed back from her work desk and stretched before reaching for her coffee mug. She really needed to let this go. Worrying and fretting all day wasn't getting her anywhere other than a bleak and oppressive dwelling somewhere near the intersection of Sleepless Boulevard and North Anxiety Drive.

Perhaps when Colleen got back, Bijal could send her flowers. She shook her head at how tired and clichéd that sounded. What could she do that would, instead, be charming? Refreshing? Conceivably captivating?

Maybe she could have an adorable puppy delivered to Colleen's house, with a note on its collar about how much Bijal missed talking to her. She could name the animal after someone else from Xena, to perpetuate her canine theme. Um…who else was a character in that show? Chlamydia? Why did that name sound familiar? Wait, wasn't that what her college roommate contracted after staying out all night with three members of the school lacrosse team?

She sagged in her chair. Scratch that idea.

Maybe she could send her a fancy invitation for an evening on the town—a lavish dinner somewhere and possibly a carriage ride. Did DC have horses? If so, she'd never seen one, though downtown she'd certainly smelled shit often enough for her to *hope* horses were nearby.

The familiar chime sounded, signaling that she'd received an e-mail. Setting her coffee back down, she pulled up her in-box to see that it was an automated alert—one she'd set up to notify her when something was posted online about Colleen.

Opening the e-mail, her stomach dropped at the title of the article: "Explosion in Afghanistan May Have Hit Congressional Delegation."

Clicking the link, she scoured the brief piece for details. A bomb had gone off in or near the location where Colleen's CODEL had been. They were reporting both injuries and fatalities, though the identity of anyone had not yet been confirmed.

"Holy shit," Bijal muttered softly.

Frantically, she began to search the Internet for additional details, combing search engines and news outlets. No one seemed to have any more information for the moment.

Bijal stood, her legs rather wobbly. She wandered in a haze toward Janet's office, knocking and waiting for a response for what seemed an eternity. Her pulse was pounding in her temples.

Eliot opened the door. "What's up?" He stared at Bijal for a moment, then said, "Oh, God. What's wrong?"

"Um, a bomb apparently hit O'Bannon's congressional delegation in Afghanistan." Bijal's voice cracked as she struggled to keep it together.

"Are you serious?" Janet asked. "Oh, my God!"

Bijal nodded and looked back at Eliot, who motioned for her to step inside.

He shut the door softly and crossed his arms nervously. "Is she dead?"

"They don't know. They're still trying to identify the bodies."

Eliot drew in a long breath. "This is very bad."

Bijal felt a momentary kinship with Eliot. Perhaps compassion and altruism had finally broken through the political artifice.

"What do we do?" Janet asked.

Eliot sat down, rubbing his palms repeatedly on his thighs. "If O'Bannon's injured, she'll have the public's sympathy for her harrowing ordeal."

"What?" Bijal was astounded.

"And I need to look at the Virginia Election Code to see how they'd handle it if O'Bannon dies this close to Election Day. Chances are the Democrats will replace her with someone else, and unless whoever they choose is awful, they'll be the odds-on sentimental favorite. The best thing that can happen to us is for O'Bannon to emerge totally unscathed—safe, but because she did something reprehensible, like she hid behind a group of schoolchildren and let them take the brunt of the shrapnel."

Bijal was now livid. "What is *wrong* with you?"

"What?" Eliot seemed genuinely confused.

Something inside Bijal snapped. "People were killed, for God's sake! Do you two really not see what's wrong with this campaign? What's been wrong all along? We have no humanity. At every turn, where we could have taken the path of inclusion or sensitivity, we consciously chose not to. We dance around public opinion daily, pretending we've always held some particular view or other, hoping that no one will notice that we don't have the courage of our convictions. Now we have the gall to take a horrific terrorist attack that may have killed our opponent and try to spin it so it looks best for *us*. And while we wait for the details of who's dead and who's maimed, we'll continue to run our vile television ad full of hateful lies. *That's* why we're behind in the polls."

As Bijal's angry words evaporated into the ether, a stunned stillness fell over them. Bijal braced for the inevitable string of profanity that would surround the declaration of her termination—like a fluffy kaiser roll of four-letter words that enveloped a meat patty of poverty and despair, with maybe a pickle slice of failure for garnish.

"She's right," Eliot said.

Bijal was certain her heart stopped for at least a second. "Really?"

He rubbed his jaw and squinted. "We should stop running the gay-marriage ad until we get confirmation of O'Bannon's health. Rao, go ahead and get on that. And let me know if there's any news one way or the other."

Astoundingly, the words that had been flowing without impediment from Bijal's mouth just moments earlier had now vanished, leaving her an empty husk, just whistling in the breeze. She glanced at Janet, glimpsing what was possibly guilt and dejection on her face before turning and leaving the office.

❖

"Bij, wake up." Fran shook Bijal's shoulder gently. "You can't stay out here all night."

Bijal, sprawled on the sofa, groggily sat up and rubbed the back of her neck. "What time is it?"

"A little past eleven," Fran said, moving toward the kitchen. "I know tomorrow's Saturday, but you haven't slept much lately. You should at least *try* to get some sleep."

Bijal wiped her eyes, then glanced at the television that she'd at some point lost consciousness in front of. Seeing Colleen's name zip across the crawl, she pounced on the remote control and turned up the volume. "Holy shit!"

Fran returned—orange juice in one hand and a sticky bun in the other. "What's up?"

"It's Colleen. I think…I think she's all right."

"Thank God." Fran took a seat beside Bijal and they watched together as a reporter posted at the U.S. Capitol Building spoke into the camera.

"Again, we're waiting for a spokesperson from the U.S. congressional delegation to Afghanistan to make a statement and brief us on exactly what transpired when the bomb went off. The most recent update says that none of the casualties were part of the delegation, though we've heard conflicting reports regarding whether any of the party was among the injured."

The shot switched to a different angle, showing a podium with several microphones mounted to it. To Bijal's great relief, Colleen stepped into view with a familiar-looking congressman next to her.

"Two of the three members of Congress from the delegation have emerged—Steve McAllister from Ohio and Colleen O'Bannon of Virginia. It looks like Congresswoman O'Bannon is about to address the crowd. Let's listen in."

"Good evening. Let me first thank everyone for coming out so late. Regarding our overseas CODEL, here are the facts. On day two of our trip, on the outskirts of Kabul, a car bomb exploded as our convoy was passing through the area.

"There were two fatalities, both locals who were not with our party. Four other civilians were injured, two critically. Of those individuals, only one—Ms. Staines, who was traveling with Congressman Zeller—was part of our delegation. She was struck by some shrapnel, received medical attention on the scene from U.S. Army personnel, and was dispatched upon arrival in Washington to a local hospital. Her condition is currently listed as stable.

"Our trip was immediately terminated following the incident. Therefore, the events planned for the last two days of the CODEL were canceled, though we're hoping to reschedule them at some point—if not with us, then perhaps with other members of the House Armed Services Committee as opportunities arise.

"I'll take a few questions now, if you have some."

Colleen looked somewhat tired but seemed alert and somber.She began the press conference by calling on a reporter in the front row.

"Congresswoman, do you believe, as representatives of the U.S. government, that you were targeted? Or is this incident more of a case of unfortunate timing?"

"Currently, the U.S. government is working with the Afghan police to gather information about the bomber, but as of our latest update, there was no evidence that we were specifically targeted. We hope to know more later. Bob?"

"Thank you, Congresswoman. Can you provide us with more information regarding Congressman Zeller's staff member who sustained the injury? Um, Ms. Staines, I believe you said? What is her job title? Has her family been notified?"

"To my understanding, Ms. Staines isn't technically classified as a staff member. It would be more accurate to say that Ms. Staines was simply traveling with Congressman Zeller."

Fran's head snapped to the side. "What the hell does *that* mean?"

"Congresswoman, are you saying the married congressman was traveling with a woman who isn't his wife and isn't employed by him?"

"Uh, I have no knowledge of whether or not Congressman Zeller has ever compensated Ms. Staines for her company, so I can't address the issue of 'employment' per se. I can only confirm that she is neither his wife nor technically a member of his staff."

"You're saying she may be a prostitute?"

"I haven't seen her résumé, so I can't corroborate her occupation."

"Oh…my…God!" Bijal was wide-awake now. That was certain.

The volume in the press room had become so loud that Colleen was struggling to regain enough control to continue fielding questions. Everyone was speaking over each other and clamoring to be heard.

"Easy, everyone. One at a time. Elizabeth?"

"Just to clarify, are you saying that Congressman Zeller took his mistress on a government CODEL to a war zone, where she was ultimately injured?"

"Again, I don't have any empirical evidence as to the level of intimacy between Congressman Zeller and Ms. Cha Cha Staines. You'll need to ask one of them for specifics. Terry?"

"Did anyone else travel with a companion, either in the capacity of employee or…otherwise?"

"No."

"Where is Congressman Zeller now? Is he at the hospital?"

"He stated he was going home directly to hug his wife and children."

Another crescendo ensued at that revelation. The members of the press were acting like frenzied piranhas, either horrified by Zeller's behavior or simply ravenous for a story this salacious.

Fran swallowed a mouthful of glazed pastry. "You know, I'm really starting to like your girlfriend."

"Why is she doing this?"

"Because Harlan Zeller is an asshole."

"You just don't like him because he's a conservative Blue Dog Democrat."

Fran shook her head once. "It's more because he's a shady bastard who's been bought off by corporate conglomerates to sell out the environment and bend over small businesses to take it in the—"

"Shh!"

"Congresswoman, are you concerned that being so candid about Congressman Zeller's travel companion so close to Election Day may torpedo the reelection chances of a member of your own party? Especially with so many seats in the House in play?"

"In my opinion, politicians should speak honestly and act with integrity at all times. So if you're asking if my party or I would willingly mislead the public or collude to protect someone's unethical behavior in the hopes of retaining a seat in Congress, I can say with great certainty that the answer is no."

"Are you saying that Congressman Zeller has behaved unethically?"

"I don't have enough facts to make that determination."

"To your knowledge, does the congressman have a sexual relationship with Ms. Staines?"

"Again, I can't speak specifically to the nature of their relationship. I had not met Ms. Staines prior to this trip. Perhaps some inquisitive journalists will do some research to ensure that her presence on the CODEL was justified and proper. I'm merely stating that in the two days during which I spent significant time with both of them, I saw no real evidence of propriety. Maybe someone else did."

The reporters then started shouting at Congressman McAllister, who looked both mortified and terror-stricken. Colleen pulled him in front of the microphones, and he grudgingly spoke to the press in a timid voice.

"Um, I haven't prepared a statement."

"Congressman, did you see any behavior by either Representative Zeller or Ms. Cha Cha Staines that might imply they had an inappropriate relationship, or that she was on this trip in a role other than staff support?"

"Uh...I..."

"Congressman, why won't you answer? Are you protecting your peer? Is this part of the Washington culture of complicity?"

"I'm not protecting anyone. There did appear to be some over-familiarity, but nothing I could swear to. Um...thank you!"

McAllister flew off the dais like a rocket, bumping into Colleen in the process. He grabbed her by the wrist before turning to thank the press one more time—an assurance to them that they would take no further questions. In a flash, they had left the room.

❖

"Colleen, what did you just do?" Steve said in a nervous sort of shriek-whisper. "You threw Zeller under the bus?"

"I told the truth. That's all. If Zeller's under a bus, he crawled there himself."

"Your caucus is going to destroy you!"

Colleen was tiring of this. "I'm not here to cover the ass of a guy like Zeller, Steve. And if it's more important to my party to hold a single seat in the House than it is to have principled people in office who do their jobs, then we don't deserve to have a majority, do we?"

Steve seemed to consider that point. "Heh."

"Am I right?"

He stood with his arms planted firmly on his hips. "O'Bannon, you're one hell of a woman. It'll be a real shame when they crucify you over this."

Colleen shrugged. "So be it. But at least I'll have a clear conscience."

"And balls of steel," Steve said reverently.

"I'm out of here. Go home, Steve. Be with your family."

"Thanks. For what it's worth, I really hope you're right."

"Me too," Colleen replied. She waved good-bye and headed toward the exit.

CHAPTER TWENTY-TWO

Colleen started her clothes dryer as she heard her BlackBerry go off from the kitchen table. She wiped her hands on her jeans and walked over to pick it up with great trepidation. Unsurprisingly, it was another request for an interview with the press.

She grumbled in disinterest and set the device back down on the counter. It had been only hours since she'd been languishing without e-mail access. She laughed as she realized how stupid she'd been then. She should have been enjoying the quiet information void she'd been nestled in. She'd now been back home for all of an hour, it was after one in the morning, and she couldn't get the goddamn phone to stop beeping at her.

Of course, she *had* told the press a little bit ago that a married congressional representative had been busy playing grab-ass with an erotic dancer that he'd stupidly taken into a war zone on the taxpayer's dime, accidentally getting her blown up for good measure. *That* little detail, she supposed, provided further justification for all this late-night pestering.

Sure, she could turn the phone off, but then she wouldn't know if Bijal had tried to contact her—though good sense told her she'd be better off putting their liaison on hold. Colleen had seen upon reentry into friendly airspace that Bijal had sent her a couple of cautious and apologetic text messages. But Colleen still hadn't made up her mind about the merits or the wisdom of replying, not to mention what she would possibly say to her.

It seemed hypocritical to shove a peer into media quicksand for having an inappropriate relationship when, admittedly, she was doing the same thing. Granted, she wasn't cheating on anyone, and she hadn't misappropriated government funds to facilitate her tryst. Technically, she and Bijal hadn't had sex, though God knew that Washington, DC had spent enough time and money in the '90s trying to define what "sex" actually was. It was nevertheless unlikely that anyone had thoroughly classified and cataloged all the various sexual acts and settled on their parameters with any great certainty or consensus.

Ultimately, however, the most important factor was the question of ethical impropriety that their friendship—more accurately, their budding romance—called into question. True, neither of them had revealed anything about the other's campaign of any real value. There had been no quid pro quo for secrets or strategies—no blackmail, graft, or unscrupulousness of any kind. Well, unless you counted Bijal's crawling-through-the-dirt-with-a-video-camera-that-wasn't-filming-anything mission. And, honestly, that was an odd combination of cute and pathetic.

Colleen chuckled at the way Bijal had managed to simultaneously evoke both sympathy and arousal that evening. Sure, Bijal had been lounging in Colleen's living room mostly naked while her clothes dried, so that invariably played a significant part in it. After all, Bijal was stacked in ways that Colleen couldn't help but appreciate. Had anyone else from the Denton camp been spying on her, Colleen was fairly certain she'd have called the police, the media, and quite possibly the Super Friends to capture and expose the Denton campaign for the carnival of corruption that it was.

Somehow, with Bijal everything was different. And even though things had taken a rather nasty and personal turn within the election, she just couldn't maintain her anger when it came to Bijal. As Colleen considered her feelings, she recognized it wasn't simply that she *hoped* Bijal had nothing to do with the disreputable ads. Deep down, Colleen truly *believed* her and hadn't even entertained the possibility that it could be otherwise.

The magnitude of that kind of trust stunned her. She let her index finger trail idly down the front of the BlackBerry as she again considered sending Bijal a message.

"You have no self-control at all," she said, forcing herself to leave the room.

A sudden rumble of thunder made her thankful that she'd gotten home before this unexpected electrical storm. From the sound of it, the rain was due to start pouring any minute, which ultimately would make sleep even more elusive. She wished she'd gotten in early enough to pick up Callisto. As it was, the house seemed unsettlingly empty.

Another clap of thunder was followed by something that sounded like faint knocking. Was it possible that Mrs. Skelton was still awake and had brought Callisto by? Hurriedly, Colleen headed to the front door and opened it.

In her haste, she neglected to flip on the porch light, but it took only a moment to recognize Bijal's silhouette when a flash of lightning in the distance illuminated her. Also momentarily evident was a hunger in Bijal's eyes that caused Colleen's stomach to lurch.

Though the logical thing was to speak—to greet Bijal in some way—neither of them uttered a sound. Another cluster of electricity lit up the sky, causing the hair on Colleen's arms to stand on end as she exhaled steam into the cold night air.

A crack of thunder suddenly split the night and Bijal sprang forward, no longer suspended in time and space. Their mouths collided passionately as Colleen grasped Bijal by the waist and pulled her close. Their kiss was ravenous and they paused only long enough for her to pull Bijal inside and shut the door before pinning her against it and resuming her ardent exploration of Bijal's lips.

Bijal's hand moved up to Colleen's cheek and through her hair as she pulled away and looked breathlessly at Colleen as though she meant to devour her. "I missed you."

Colleen trailed her mouth down Bijal's inviting neck, nipping lightly as she made her way to Bijal's collarbone.

Bijal uttered a long murmur of approval. "I was petrified you weren't coming back."

"I'm sorry you worried," Colleen said, lifting her head and staring into Bijal's unfathomable sepia eyes. "I should have sent you a message as soon as I could."

"I hope it's all right that I came by." Bijal punctuated her sentence with a masterful kiss. "I know it's late and I should have called first, but I *really* wanted to see you."

Colleen's entire body was humming, and Bijal's husky admission accelerated her roughly idling libido. "Come with me," she whispered, entwining her fingers with Bijal's and tugging her into the living room. After several strides, Colleen faced Bijal, struggling like hell to gather her thoughts through the fog brought on by Bijal's striking features and lusty expression.

All those reservations she'd been poring over just minutes earlier…what the hell had they been again? God, Bijal was beautiful, and her inviting bee-stung lips had a gravitational pull that rivaled a supermassive black hole. "I'm glad you came. I can't stop thinking about you."

Okay, so that hadn't exactly been the gentle refusal that Colleen had intended it to be. But she could still do this. It was only a matter of weeks before the election would be over and the two of them could freely embark on a romantic relationship without risking accusations of misconduct or fear of reprisal. It really was the only responsible thing to do.

"I want you so much," Bijal purred provocatively.

Colleen, blindsided by a devastating surge of desire, wasn't able to catch her breath long enough to utter even the most feeble argument for abstinence. Instead, she was only capable of a low growl. She pressed Bijal gently against the back of the sofa and encircled Bijal's waist with her palms.

Bijal slowly caressed Colleen's neck, the fingers of her left hand continuing upward to lightly brush Colleen's jawline, her thumb running along Colleen's lower lip reverently. "Do you want me?"

"God, yes." Colleen eagerly met Bijal's tantalizing mouth with her own, formally abandoning her previous fantasies of steadfast resolve. The feel of Bijal's tongue as it stroked hers enflamed her ardor beyond its limits. Without hesitation, she grasped the back of Bijal's thighs and lifted her so she was sitting on the back of the couch. Bijal wrapped her legs around Colleen's waist as their kiss deepened.

In a desperate need to feel the silken heat of Bijal's skin, Colleen grabbed the buttoned edges of Bijal's blouse and impatiently ripped it open. She was rewarded with the phenomenal feel of Bijal's pert nipples through the satin and lace of her navy blue demi-cup bra.

"Oh, fuck," Bijal breathed, grinding against Colleen erotically.

In an instant, her shirt and bra were both off and Bijal's hands were frantically pulling Colleen's shirt up over her head.

Colleen couldn't decide which part of Bijal's body she wanted to focus on. Her breasts were on extraordinary display before her like legendary spheres of wonder, and as much as she wanted to lavish upon them all the oral attention they so richly deserved, she couldn't tear her mouth away from Bijal's for more than a second or two. "Christ, I'm ready to explode."

Bijal bit her lower lip seductively. "But I haven't even touched you."

"Keep kissing me like this and you won't need to." Colleen began fiddling with the fly of Bijal's pants, but, thankfully, Bijal took over and had them undone in a flash before shifting her attention to Colleen's jeans.

The feel of Bijal's firm thighs and undulating ass were driving Colleen to the brink of hunger. Colleen pushed them both over the sofa until they landed squarely on the plush cushions below. Bijal was now sprawled on her back, and before she knew it, Colleen was braless on top of her.

Again, Colleen was conflicted. She wanted to spend countless hours becoming familiar with Bijal's curves and valleys, but she couldn't remember *ever* being this hot. If she didn't come soon, she might shatter into a billion tiny pieces of magma-filled frustration.

Bijal slipped Colleen's jeans down her hips and tossed them onto the floor before mercifully slipping her fingers inside Colleen's panties. Her touch was sublimely evocative, and Colleen moved instinctively against her.

"God, you're so wet," Bijal whispered appreciatively.

Colleen shifted her weight to her hands and her mouth descended on Bijal's. Her breathing became ragged as a familiar current began to gather throughout her body. "Mmm, harder," she said desperately. She wanted Bijal to be assertive and primal with her and, thankfully, Bijal took direction well.

Not only did Bijal increase the force of her strokes, but she entered Colleen briefly with at least two fingers and then withdrew again.

"Please...don't stop," Colleen said.

"No chance of that," Bijal replied, plunging inside her again.

"Fuck, you feel so good." Bijal seemed to be everywhere Colleen needed her to be—filling her, yet never leaving her clit. The pressure was agonizing and blissful at the same time.

"I love how you move against me," Bijal said. "But I really want you to come...all over me."

Colleen rode the rush that Bijal's words evoked. "I'm so close."

"Good," Bijal said, her fingers pumping like pistons. She nipped at Colleen's lower lip boldly and ran her thumb in circles across Colleen's nipple. "'Cause I need it, baby. Please."

The sound of Bijal begging her to come was all the stimulation Colleen required to push her over the rapturous edge. Her body gave in to an exquisite ache that then ruptured into pleasure. She was vaguely aware of crying out as she shuddered, before resting her head on Bijal's shoulder and marveling at the aftershocks coursing through her. "Oh, my...God," she muttered.

"Okay?" Bijal asked, massaging Colleen's back sensuously.

Colleen lifted her head. "That's an understatement."

"Did I wear you out already?"

Colleen pondered the question for less than a second before the sight of Bijal half naked beneath her enticed her into further exploration. She closed her mouth around a nipple as she lightly traced the side of Bijal's breast with her fingers. After feeling the nipple harden beneath her tongue, she switched to the other, previously neglected one. Bijal's hands wove through Colleen's hair, wordlessly urging her to continue.

Though Colleen would have happily stayed like that until her jaw locked, Bijal was ardently rotating her hips against Colleen's stomach. Feeling Bijal's arousal and urgency, she traveled down farther, to Bijal's unzipped pants. Methodically, Colleen peeled them off and draped them over the back of the couch, then did the same with Bijal's damp panties.

Once Bijal was completely naked, Colleen stopped long enough to appreciate her magnificent bounty.

"What?" Bijal asked.

"You're so beautiful," Colleen replied, running her fingers slowly up Bijal's thigh. "Let me taste you."

"God, yes."

Colleen needed no further coaxing. Kneeling on the floor, she positioned herself so she had unimpeded access. Bijal's pelvis continued to rotate, perhaps unconsciously, seeking the rhythmic contact she craved.

As Colleen brought her mouth to the inside of Bijal's thigh, then to her labia, she realized just how slick with want Bijal was. Colleen moved her mouth against the hot and hungry flesh that glided across her lips and could tell from Bijal's countermovements that she wanted it rougher, faster. Colleen complied, even lightly using her teeth.

Bijal responded to Colleen's increased force by jerking her hips harder. "Oh, yeah. Suck me."

Colleen took Bijal's clit into her mouth and worshipped it, alternating between long strokes with her stiffened tongue and small tight circles. Bijal's hand found the back of Colleen's neck and stroked it lovingly. Colleen slid her hands around the small of Bijal's back as she continued to lick her with a deep, focused craving.

Bijal's breathing became shallow and she begged for release. "Please, baby. I need to come. Yeah, like that."

Suddenly, Bijal's body began to tremble. She called out loudly before going completely rigid, then limp like a rag doll.

Colleen gathered Bijal to her as she settled back down onto the couch cushions and kissed her good and hard. "Are you all right?"

Bijal nodded and propped her head in her hand and stared down at Colleen. "That was amazing! Remind me exactly why we waited so long to do this?"

"I have no idea. I mean, I knew before you got here, but now a profound desire to fondle every part of you has replaced that space in my brain." Colleen cupped Bijal's ass appreciatively and squeezed it.

"You're well on your way, I'd say." Colleen captured Bijal's left breast in her mouth and began tonguing it. "Oh, shit," Bijal groaned, closing her eyes. "Your mouth is…mmm."

Colleen released the nipple and moved back up Bijal's body, studying her rapturous expression. "Can I make a confession?"

"As hesitant as I am to give you this kind of power, it's safe to say that as long as you keep doing that thing with your tongue, you can pretty much do whatever the hell you want."

"Do you know the first time I fantasized about your prodigious rack?"

Bijal looked amused now. "When it was smeared with mud in your front yard?"

"Well, yeah, then. But that wasn't the first time."

"Ooh, really? Tell me when, so I can make sure I wear whatever it was I had on again."

"In the elevator, the first time we met."

Bijal gasped. "You sneaky little bitch. I have to say, you hid it very well, because I still managed to walk away from that encounter feeling utterly ashamed and mortified."

Colleen kissed her. "If you like, I can try to make you feel that way again."

"Is it wrong if that threat turns me on a little?"

"Horrifically wrong, though, sadly, I don't think that even cracks the top ten of the most troubling aspects of our relationship."

"You sure know how to sweet-talk a girl."

Colleen was utterly besotted by this gorgeous naked woman on her sofa. "Come to bed with me, Bijal," she breathed into her ear.

"Christ, that's the hottest fucking thing anybody's said, *ever*."

Colleen stood, pulling Bijal into her embrace. "Not necessarily. Go ahead. Try and top it."

"I'd rather top *you* and…ride you like a parade float."

Colleen was unable to suppress her laughter. Bijal hadn't exaggerated one bit about her metaphorical impairment. "And will you throw candy to onlookers?"

"If that's what you want to call it, baby. Sure."

Colleen took Bijal by the hand and led her to the bedroom. "God, I love how smutty you are."

"You ain't seen nothin' yet."

❖

Bijal shut the door as she entered her apartment, tossing her keys on the kitchen counter as she breezed by.

"Bijal?" Fran emerged from her bedroom, wearing yoga pants and a football jersey. "Where the hell have—" Fran froze in mid-sentence and mid-stride. "Jesus Christ on a cracker! You filthy whore."

Bijal stood stunned. "What? Is it written all over my face?"

"Well, you do look mysteriously satisfied, but it's actually written all over your boobs."

Glancing down, Bijal realized that Fran was talking about the T-shirt Colleen had loaned her to wear home. It read I'VE JUST CUT OFF THE FLOW OF BLOOD TO YOUR BRAIN. YOU HAVE THIRTY SECONDS TO LIVE. "Oh, yeah. Well, I wouldn't wear the one that said 'Proud to be a Liberal.'"

"You wore a Xena T-shirt on the Metro?"

"This is from Xena?"

Fran rolled her eyes. "You're an awful lesbian. What did you think it was from, pro wrestling? I'll probably regret this, but dare I ask what happened to the blouse you were wearing when you left last night?"

Bijal held up the shopping bag she was holding. "Um, I lost a button."

"That must be one massively critical button."

"Or maybe it was six or seven," Bijal added hastily, tossing the bag onto the floor. "But it turns out that riding the Metro without any buttons is largely frowned upon. The only ones who support it are the chronic masturbators and the pants-shitters."

Fran crossed her arms and studied her for a moment. "If this was *Law and Order: SVU*, you know what I'd already know about you?"

"What?"

"That you went over to that woman's house last night and fucked her until your bits were sore. Though, admittedly, if this were *SVU*, then you'd have killed her in a creepy way, like using a strap-on made of dynamite."

None of this was making sense to Bijal. "Wouldn't an exploding strap-on have killed me too?" She rubbed her eyes in fatigue.

"You think I didn't think of that? It was a murder/suicide, you sick bitch. I told you to get help." Fran walked into the kitchen and grabbed some bottled water out of the fridge.

"Sometimes I think you're completely insane," Bijal replied, sagging into the sofa.

"I'm right about that first part, though, aren't I? Are your bits sore?"

"Maybe a little, but that's not why I went over there, Fran."

Fran took a long sip of water. "Of course not. I'm sure you just popped by to talk to her about why you two shouldn't be talking."

"Well…"

Fran sat beside Bijal and raised an eyebrow. "You jumped her, didn't you?"

"Like she was a goddamn hurdle, yeah. It was incredible."

"Did you get her out of your system?"

Bijal grinned wickedly. "No, but I sure tried like hell."

Fran appeared unimpressed. "Uh-huh."

"Over and over," Bijal said. "And let me tell you, pretty speeches aren't the only thing that mouth of hers is good for."

"Jesus! You've finally snapped, Bij—like a dry piece of kindling. I knew you were stressed out and overworked, but I wasn't prepared for your foray into the Congressional Penthouse Forum."

"Sorry, I'm sleep-deprived."

"Yeah, so I hear. Can I just ask a quick question?"

"Mmm-hmm." Bijal sat back and got comfortable. For Fran, a twenty-minute rebuttal often accompanied her quick questions.

"What the fuck do you intend to do now?"

Bijal shook her head. "I've been thinking quite a bit about that, actually, and you know what? I can do this, Fran. I can *totally* do this."

"Do what?"

"I can do my job well and date Colleen at the same time."

Fran was clearly skeptical. "You think so?"

"Well…yeah, I do. I've been agonizing over this for weeks, and now I realize I don't *have* to choose. I haven't shared any proprietary secrets. I came out to Janet at work. She knows how I feel about that anti-gay ad, as well as a host of other things I disagree with."

"Does she also know you're riding her opponent like a merry-go-round?"

Bijal tapped her forehead lightly in frustration. "A merry-go-round! That's so much better than a parade float!"

"Huh?"

"Never mind. Look, the point is that I took a stand with Janet and came clean with her. If she thinks I might compromise the campaign, then let her fire me."

"Wow," Fran said. "That must be some amazing pussy."

"Oh, my God, it is. But it's more than that. I mean, Colleen's smart, principled, funny, and sexy. I think I…love her."

"What?"

"I know! I haven't even said those words out loud since the tenth grade—to Tim Crudup. Trust me when I say that the phrase 'ended badly' is a monumental understatement."

"Was he the one who ditched you at lover's lane and left you to walk home with only some of your clothes on?"

"Unfortunately. At any rate, this relationship feels right to me. I'm so—"

"Happy?" Fran suggested.

"Well, yeah." Bijal marveled at how unexpected it felt.

"You know, I've given you a lot of shit over this, Bij, because I care about you and I worry. And maybe I was a tiny bit jealous that you selfishly nabbed the hottest piece of liberal ass in town, when you could have stayed on your own side and chosen someone from the pool of smokin' conservatives…hmm, scratch that."

Bijal laughed. "You're such a partisan bitch."

"Anyway, let me say that I'm really glad for you. I kinda like this new bright-eyed, blissful Bijal."

"Aw, thanks," Bijal cooed, giving Fran a hug.

Fran rubbed Bijal's back before releasing her. "So, you're gonna give some details about last night, right?"

"I have one word for you—multiorgasmic."

CHAPTER TWENTY-THREE

B ijal went over the raw polling data one more time. She couldn't see any positive way to spin these numbers, and less than a month out from the election, they painted a very bleak picture.

In looking at likely voters, without factoring in political-party affiliations, Colleen was pulling 52 percent of the vote to Janet's 29 percent, with 8 percent for Phillip Taylor and 11 percent still undecided. So even if Janet somehow secured *all* the undecided voters, she still didn't have enough to win. Breaking it down further into partisan groups, according to these numbers, Colleen had the support of 88 percent of district Democrats, 64 percent of Independents, and 32 percent of Republicans.

Looking at the voter comments, she couldn't deny that Colleen's trip to Afghanistan had positively influenced her polling numbers. Many viewed just her presence in a volatile war zone as brave and admirable. Others saw her open exposure of the malfeasance and hypocrisy of a member of her own party as a sign of personal integrity, though a small number of Democrats criticized her for what they viewed as sabotaging the party's chances of holding that seat in November.

For his part, Harlan Zeller had been spending the last week making speeches—insisting, at first, with his wife by his side, that his relationship with Ms. Staines had been "maliciously misrepresented" by those who, in his opinion, "by the nature of their own ungodly lifestyle, had an axe to grind with those openly in favor of the superiority of traditional families."

Thankfully, the media had smelled enough blood in the water that they'd been encouraged to investigate. So when, less than twenty-four hours later, they discovered Cha Cha Staines was not only currently an employee of a DC strip club called Lickety Split's, but was a headliner known for her participation in a three-woman dildo dance/performance known to regulars as the Red Rocket Rump Spectacular, Zeller walked back his accusations of moral authority and tearfully declared to the press that he'd "strayed from the path of Jesus."

However, it was only when his wife called a separate press conference to announce that she was leaving Zeller and taking their two children with her because she couldn't "look at his fat, lying, scheming, perverted face one more day" that Zeller resigned from office. Of course, his very public combustion had only boosted Colleen's numbers further—the cherry on top, if you like.

Bijal's cell phone vibrated beside her, startling her as she examined the text message she'd just received from Colleen.

> Good news—the Saturday Amendment is officially dead. The bill just passed the House without it. :-D

Bijal felt genuine pride for Colleen's success, and she admired the way Colleen had used her resources and noggin to show her party leaders that she was no ideological pushover. She said what she stood for, and she stood for what she said.

> Congratulations, honey! Does this mean we'll be celebrating tonight? 'Cause I'd love to see you if you're not spending tonight schmoozing and fund-raising.

Bijal pressed Send and held the phone while she waited for a response. She had to admit that the last week or so had been more emotionally and sexually fulfilling than she had been prepared for— and certainly far more intense than any relationship she'd had in some time.

It was a bit maddening, really. She got butterflies in her stomach when the phone rang, the instant they were reunited, when Colleen would say her name...or when she saw a car that looked like hers. She sighed, feeling suddenly ridiculous. Was this what all those '80s power ballads were about? Was this love? Could she take Colleen high enough? Did every rose really have its thorn?

Her hand vibrated.

> I'd love to celebrate with you. I only have one obligation until tomorrow. I'll be on Tank Guzman tonight talking about the passage of the bill, but I'd definitely rather be on you.

Bijal hurriedly tapped out a reply.

> That makes two of us. Tell me what time to meet you, and I'll make sure I wear something with snaps. ;-)

"Hey, Bijal. How's it going?"

Bijal turned to see Kristin beside her, looking tired but affable. Bijal set down her phone in a manner that she hoped reeked of nonchalance. "Well, I'm doing fine. But these numbers totally suck."

Kristin scowled, making the bridge of her nose crinkle. "I was afraid of that."

"Yeah, at this point, based on this data, I'd say that Colleen O'Bannon could be caught conspiring with terrorists to eat orphans and we still couldn't pull within the margin of error."

"Yikes! I mean, I knew it was bad, but I've still been holding out hope, you know?"

"I know, trust me. But it's starting to seem insurmountable. Have you heard about the problems fund-raising?"

Kristin shook her head and sat on the edge of Bijal's desk. "With Janet out making appearances all this week, I haven't heard much about anything."

"Let's just say that the well is running dry."

"Seriously?"

"Don't get me wrong, we still have some wealthy contributors who're inspired to give even more because they see us struggling. But most folks are hesitant to bet on the horse bringing up the rear. It's caused some challenges."

"I did notice that we didn't start back in with our ads like I thought we would after O'Bannon returned to the States. Is that a problem with funds, do you think?"

"Possibly, but I can't say I'm sad to see that horrible commercial go." Bijal's phone vibrated alive again, and though common sense told her to ignore it, the giddy feeling that began in her chest and disappeared somewhere in her pants made that feat utterly impossible. She glanced at it quickly, trying to feign an air of quiet dispassion.

> You and your snaps should be at my place at 9. Bring some champagne, and if you want a couple hours of my undivided attention, a marrow bone. More instructions to follow.

Bijal chuckled softly before remembering that Kristin was watching her. She fought to wipe any trace of amusement from her face as she slid the phone into her bag.

"So, you never did end up telling me about your date last week. Is that still going on?"

Well, so much for nonchalance. Clearly Bijal looked just as goofy on the outside as she felt on the inside. "Yeah, it's still going on."

Kristin's tone took on the quality of a gossipy teen. "Is it hot and heavy?"

"Yeah, actually, it is."

"What are you waiting for, then? Tell me all about it."

"What do you want to know about her?" Bijal waited, watching Kristin's expression change as she fully realized the weight of the chosen pronoun.

"Her? As in, your hot and heavy dates are with another woman?"

Bijal nodded, trying to gauge what was coming next. Somehow, this never really got easier. "That's what I mean."

"Wow," Kristin said, seeming floored.

"And what does 'wow' mean exactly?"

"Um, just that…I'm surprised. I didn't realize you're—" Kristin looked around them conspiratorially. "Gay," she whispered.

"Don't worry about it."

"Sorry, I'm totally oblivious, I guess. I just don't know any gay people," Kristin explained nervously.

Bijal stared at her for a moment. "Well, you know me."

"Sure, I do," Kristin replied, just a little bit too enthusiastically. "I mean I just didn't pick up the signs."

"Signs?"

Kristin nodded rapidly, obviously ill at ease with this topic. "My bad."

"Well, it was probably my fault. Next time I'll make sure I'm wearing flannel, sporting a mullet, blaring Melissa Etheridge music, and packing my strap-on underneath my tweed skirt. Are those the kinds of signs you're looking for?"

Kristin's eyes were wide and her pupils constricted. Distress was written all over her face as Bijal waited for a response.

Janet entered the office through the front door, walking to the center of the room and clapping her hands to get everyone's attention. "Excuse me, hello. If everybody could please give me just a moment."

All activity ceased, and several dozen campaign workers hung on Janet's next words expectantly.

Janet cleared her throat, then took a deep breath. "Thank you. I have a few announcements to make, and I want you all to hear everything at the same time—no multiple versions, no rumors. First, as of today, Eliot Jenkins is no longer affiliated with this campaign. He and I just had too many differences of opinion when it came to how this camp should operate, and, honestly, I let him have his way far too many times. Well, not that he had his *way*, but you know what I mean." Janet looked directly at Bijal. "I let him dictate things that deliberately contradicted my stated values and positions, and that was a mistake— hopefully, my last, at least when it comes to this race."

Bijal smiled at the acknowledgment. Perhaps the anti-gay ad had not made its way back on the air because Janet had finally come to her senses and recognized it was the right thing to do.

"That being said," Janet continued, "we'll receive little, if any, assistance at this point from the NRCC. Which leads to my next piece of news. Our finance manager has made it clear that due to sharply declining donations and unexpected expenses, our coffers are basically empty. For all of you paid staffers, today will be the last day I can afford your salary. I realize that you've all put my election and its daily chores ahead of your own lives in many instances, and I want to thank you deeply for your remarkable dedication and loyalty, even in the face of mishaps and falling poll numbers. For those of you who can't stay on, I absolutely understand. But for those of you who possibly can, I invite you to keep working with me for the next few weeks. Help me get my message out—the message I should have been sending all along—and see this through to the end."

Bijal was thoroughly caught off guard. She'd never expected a layoff. Though, sadly, the notion wasn't without portent or plausibility. In all her research, perhaps she should have looked closer at the watertight integrity of the very ship in which she was sailing.

Campaign workers began to mill about in shock, the mood shifting to that of general malaise and confusion. It was one thing for people to work on a losing team and be compensated, but when asked to simply volunteer and then take a beating, that was quite a different issue.

Janet approached Bijal and Kristin, who still sat speechless. "If only I'd been that eloquent and direct when I'd started this damn thing."

"It's not over yet," Bijal said.

"Is that what your new numbers say?" Janet asked.

"That's what *I* say," Bijal replied firmly.

Janet looked contrite. "I'm sorry I put you in a position where you doubted the value of your contribution, Bijal. I let my aspirations overshadow my integrity."

"It happens," Bijal said with a shrug.

"But it shouldn't. Let me know if you're able to stay on in any capacity, okay? Both of you."

"I'll…see what I can do," Bijal said.

"Me too," Kristin added. "I just need to figure out some things."

"Thanks," Janet said. "I appreciate everything you've both done." She turned and went into her office, shutting the door and leaving everyone else to work out their future.

Kristin nudged Bijal good-naturedly. "Hey, I'm sorry about what I said earlier—about seeing signs."

"It's okay. I shouldn't have made that comment about the strap-on. That was out of line."

"No, I deserved it. I'm a complete idiot."

Bijal grinned. "No, you just probably need to get out more."

CHAPTER TWENTY-FOUR

On Election Night, Bijal stood among the crowd in the hotel conference room, listening to Janet give her concession speech. Her loss didn't surprise anyone who'd been paying attention, but she had managed to reemerge as a candidate with her veracity reclaimed. Though, of course, to the voters, it simply looked like insincerity and flip-flopping. But at least to those in the know, she regained honor, if not victory.

"Hey," Kristin said. "That's a hell of a speech she's giving. Did you help out with that?"

Bijal shrugged. "I may have thrown a phrase or two into the mix."

"Uh-huh, right. So now that it's over, what's next?"

"Starting tomorrow, I'll be working for *QPolitic* as a staff writer," Bijal replied happily.

"I have no idea what that is, but congratulations!"

"They're an online political magazine that focuses on gay issues."

Kristin's joyful expression suddenly seemed to lose a little of its genuineness. "Oh."

"I'll be their new sex-toy-and-lubricant correspondent." Kristin's face remained frozen, with the exception of her eyebrows, which she, more than likely, was simply unable to control. "I'm kidding," Bijal said finally.

Kristin laughed at her gullibility. "Sorry."

"It's okay. I probably should have picked something less believable."

• 253 •

"True. Though if that *had* been true, you could've gotten Harlan Zeller as your first interview."

"Touché."

"So where's your girlfriend? I thought I'd finally meet her."

"She's working late tonight."

"Really? What does she do?"

"She's…in politics too. So it's kind of a busy night all the way around."

"Oh, that's too bad," Kristin said, sounding as though she meant it.

"But it's kind of nice that you wanted to meet her."

"I'm trying to expand my horizons."

"By doubling the number of lesbians you know?" Bijal asked.

Kristin smiled. "Exactly."

At that moment, the crowd burst into applause and Janet waved her way from the podium toward Kristin and Bijal, who were now both clapping excitedly as though they'd been listening.

"That seemed to go over well," Janet said brightly.

"It was great, Janet," Kristin replied. "I only wish it'd been an acceptance speech."

"You and me both," Janet said. "But, honestly, this was the only speech I bothered to write."

Bijal felt an obligation to reassure her. "Live and learn, though, right? There's always next time."

"That's right," Kristin added. "Imagine how much smoother things will go without the learning curve we had this time."

Janet shook her head slowly. "I'm not so sure there will be a next time."

"No?" Bijal asked.

"I'm still walking funny from this time," Janet joked. "But never say never, I guess."

"There you go," Kristin said. "Leave your options open."

"I really owe you both a huge debt," Janet said, changing the subject. "You hung in there when things were at their worst, even when I stopped paying you. I can't tell you what that means to me."

Bijal glanced at her watch. "You're welcome, Janet. Though as much as I hate to say it, I need to run."

Janet pouted. "You don't want to stay and enjoy what's left of the campaign funds?"

"I would, but I have to go meet my girlfriend. I did want to stay through your speech, though."

"Oh, well, thanks again for everything." Janet pulled Bijal into a big hug.

"Thank you," Bijal said earnestly as she stepped back. "I learned a lot."

"Like, before you speak, always make sure your mic isn't live?" Janet asked.

Bijal chuckled softly. "*Especially* that."

"Let me know if you ever need a reference," Janet said as Kristin and Bijal embraced. "In case you're applying for a job with someone who's never heard of me—because, otherwise, my word might not be worth too much."

"I'll keep that in mind, Janet. Good luck to both of you." Bijal waved good-bye as she headed for the door.

❖

As Bijal entered the K and K, she was surprised at how packed it was. Sue clearly knew how to market an event. Bijal waded through the throng until she managed to squeeze between two women seated at the bar. Bijal gestured until she got Sue's attention. "Hey, is Col here yet?"

Sue was expertly filling two mugs with draft beer at the same time. "She sure is, honey—beat you here by about five minutes. She's in the office changing out of her Sunday-go-to-Congress clothes. Go on back."

"Thanks." As Bijal wove her way through the crowd of lesbians, she was temporarily stopped by the sight of Fran on the dance floor. She was bending at the waist and rubbing her ass enthusiastically across the crotch of none other than Flayme Coverdale, fisting aficionado. "No fucking way," Bijal muttered.

With absolutely no interest in being covert, Bijal shifted course toward Fran, finally getting her attention by waving her arms around like she was trying to signal a rescue plane.

Fran whispered something in Flayme's ear, then slunk over to where Bijal was standing. "What's up?"

"You *do* know who you're dancing with, right?"

"I sure do. She signed a copy of her book to me. And let me just say, I flipped through it and that's some *hot shit*!"

Bijal rubbed her forehead. "Well, be careful. And remember, if it looks like it's too big, it probably is."

"If what looks too big?"

"You'll see."

Fran's eyes lit up. "Ooh! Then I better get another drink." Fran headed back to the bar as Bijal forged ahead to the office, eagerly knocking.

Colleen opened the door just wide enough to see who was there. "Hi," she said warmly. "C'mon in."

"Are you decent, Madam Congresswoman?" Bijal stepped inside and shut the door behind her.

"I am, but that can easily be rectified," Colleen replied smoothly as she unbuttoned her blouse and slid it onto a hanger. "Did you see my speech?"

"No, I was on my way here. Give me the highlights."

Colleen put on a more informal blue button-up shirt as Bijal openly ogled her. "Something something, implement my socialist agenda... indoctrinate your children, blah blah blah, government takeover. You know, the standard Democratic stuff."

Bijal laughed. "You're *so* antagonistic." She took a step closer and wrapped her arms around Colleen. "It's a good thing you're hot too. Otherwise I might be less inclined to jump you."

Colleen kissed her deeply, then nibbled her way down Bijal's neck. "In spite of all my liberalism and snarkiness?"

"Mmm-hmm." Bijal marveled at Colleen's innate ability to reduce her to a small puddle of frothy longing.

"Just how strong is this inclination?"

Bijal ran her tongue along the outside of Colleen's ear. "Would you like to see the polling data on that?"

"Oh, I definitely would." Their mouths met again as Bijal traced Colleen's breast with her right hand. "That's...very compelling evidence, Ms. Rao."

"I'm pretty sure I need to do some more in-depth research," Bijal said lustily.

"A deeper dive?" Colleen asked, her tone rife with innuendo.

"So to speak."

Bijal kissed Colleen hungrily, becoming rapidly more aroused as their tongues melded.

"I don't mean to skew your findings," Colleen breathed, pulling back only slightly. "But in full disclosure, I love you."

Bijal's chest tightened and she felt suddenly flushed. "I love you too."

Colleen squeezed Bijal's hand. "Maybe we should go out there and be social, because if we stay in here much longer with you looking at me like that, I might be forced to pin you to the wall and tongue you like an after-dinner mint."

"I'm sorry, were you trying to make a case for *leaving* this room? Because that wasn't terribly persuasive." Bijal nipped Colleen's lower lip playfully.

"God, you're sexy. How about this? Let's mingle for about thirty minutes, dance a little, then cut out of here."

"Deal," Bijal replied, straightening Colleen's collar. "Hey, speaking of dancing, Flayme Coverdale appears to be successfully wooing my roommate."

Colleen tucked her shirt into her pants and checked her appearance in the mirror. "Really? Did you give her a heads-up?"

"That she might end up a little later as Flayme's personal hand puppet? Uh-huh. That's apparently not a deterrent for Fran."

Colleen raised a single eyebrow. "Are you worried?"

"About Fran? No, she's a big girl."

"Yeah, I'd imagine she'd need to be to get any enjoyment out of it."

Bijal winced. "Yikes! You just made me clench a little."

"Sorry."

"All ready?"

Colleen paused for a moment. "More important, are you?"

"What do you mean?"

"Are you prepared to step into that room as my date? No more sneaking around?"

"Totally. Are you prepared to tell people your girlfriend's a Republican?"

"Whoa, easy. Let's not go crazy with this honesty thing."

Bijal brushed a stray lock of hair out of Colleen's face. "I don't know. Your Democratic friends might just be envious. Everyone knows we Republicans are wild women in the sack."

Colleen grinned. "Good point. You do look particularly sultry tonight."

"Thanks. I chose this clingy blouse just for you."

"You spoil me." Colleen took Bijal tenderly by the hand and opened the office door. "So you won't mind if I introduce you to colleagues as Mistress Chesty von YumYum, Republican operative and dominatrix?"

"Not at all…Congresswoman Spyxie Sugarbottom."

"Quite a mouthful."

Bijal moved closer to Colleen so she could be heard above the thumping dance music. "Truer words were never spoken."

About the Author

Colette Moody is an avid fan of history and politics. When she isn't doing research or crafting scenes for her next romp of a novel, she can be found doing one or more of the following: watching classic films, irrationally screaming at news commentaters on the television, meticulously recreating cocktails from the 30s and 40s, or planning her next trip to Disneyland. By day, her alter ego toils at what she fondly refers to as her "crap job." She lives in Virginia with her very naughty dog and her only slightly less naughty partner.

Parties in Congress is Colette Moody's third novel, but only her first contemporary one. Her first book, also for Bold Strokes Books, was the rollicking pirate tale *The Sublime and Spirited Voyage of Original Sin*, followed by *The Seduction of Moxie*, a bawdy Prohibition-era tale.

Books Available From Bold Strokes Books

Dying to Live by Kim Baldwin & Xenia Alexiou. British socialite Zoe Anderson-Howe's pampered life is abruptly shattered when she's taken hostage by FARC guerrillas while on a business trip to Bogota, and Elite Operative Fletch must rescue her to complete her own harrowing mission. (978-1-60282-200-9)

Indigo Moon by Gill McKnight. Werewolves Hope Glassy and Godfrey Meyers are on a mercy mission to save their friend Isabelle after she is attacked by a rogue werewolf—but does Isabelle want to be saved from the sexy wolf who claimed her as a mate? (978-1-60282-201-6)

Parties in Congress by Colette Moody. Bijal Rao, Indian-American moderate Independent, gets the break of her career when she's hired to work on the congressional campaign of Janet Denton—until she meets her remarkably attractive and charismatic opponent, Colleen O'Bannon. (978-1-60282-202-3)

Black Fire: Gay African-American Erotica, edited by Shane Allison. *Black Fire* celebrates the heat and power of sex between black men: the rude B-boys and gorgeous thugs, the worshippers of heavenly ass, and the devoutly religious in their forays through the subterranean grottoes of the down-low world. (978-1-60282-206-1)

The Collectors by Leslie Gowan. Laura owns what might be the world's most extensive collection of BDSM lesbian erotica, but that's as close as she's gotten to the world of her fantasies. Until, that is, her friend Adele introduces her to Adele's mistress Jeanne—art collector, heiress, and experienced dominant. With Jeanne's first command, Laura's life changes forever. (978-1-60282-208-5)

Breathless, edited by Radclyffe and Stacia Seaman. Bold Strokes Books romance authors give readers a glimpse into the lives of favorite couples celebrating special moments "after the honeymoon ends." Enjoy a new look at lesbians in love or revisit favorite characters from some of BSB's best-selling romances. (978-1-60282-207-8)

Breaker's Passion by Julie Cannon. Leaving a trail of broken hearts scattered across the Hawaiian Islands, surf instructor Colby Taylor is running full speed away from her selfish actions years earlier until she collides with Elizabeth Collins, a stuffy, judgmental college professor who changes everything. (978-1-60282-196-5)

Justifiable Risk by V.K. Powell. Work is the only thing that interests homicide detective Greer Ellis until internationally renowned journalist Eva Saldana comes to town looking for answers in her brother's death— then attraction threatens to override duty. (978-1-60282-197-2)

Nothing But the Truth by Carsen Taite. Sparks fly when two top-notch attorneys battle each other in the high-risk arena of the courtroom, but when a strange turn of events turns one of them from advocate to witness, prosecutor Ryan Foster and defense attorney Brett Logan join forces in their search for the truth. (978-1-60282-198-9)

Maye's Request by Clifford Henderson. When Brianna Bell promises her ailing mother she'll heal the rift between her "other two" parents, she discovers how little she knows about those closest to her and the impact family has on the fabric of our lives. (978-1-60282-199-6)

Chasing Love by Ronica Black. Adrian Edwards is looking for love— at girl bars, shady chat rooms, and women's sporting events—but love remains elusive until she looks closer to home. (978-1-60282-192-7)

Rum Spring by Yolanda Wallace. Rebecca Lapp is a devout follower of her Amish faith and a firm believer in the Ordnung, the set of rules that govern her life in the tiny Pennsylvania town she calls home. When she falls in love with a young "English" woman, however, the rules go out the window. (978-1-60282-193-4)

Indelible by Jove Belle. A single mother committed to shielding her son from the parade of transient relationships she endured as a child tries to resist the allure of a tattoo artist who already has a sometimes-girlfriend. (978-1-60282-194-1)

The Straight Shooter by Paul Faraday. With the help of his good pals Beso Tangelo and Jorge Ramirez, Nate Dainty tackles the Case of the Missing Porn Star, none other than his latest heartthrob—Myles Long! (978-1-60282-195-8)

Head Trip by D.L. Line. Shelby Hutchinson, a young computer professional, can't wait to take a virtual trip. She soon learns that chasing spies through Cold War Europe might be a great adventure, but nothing is ever as easy as it seems—especially love. (978-1-60282-187-3)

Desire by Starlight by Radclyffe. The only thing that might possibly save romance author Jenna Hardy from dying of boredom during a summer of forced R&R is a dalliance with Gardner Davis, the local vet—even if Gard is as unimpressed with Jenna's charms as she appears to be with Jenna's fame. (978-1-60282-188-0)

River Walker by Cate Culpepper. Grady Wrenn, a cultural anthropologist, and Elena Montalvo, a spiritual healer, must find a way to end the River Walker's murderous vendetta—and overcome a maze of cultural barriers to find each other. (978-1-60282-189-7)

Blood Sacraments, edited by Todd Gregory. In these tales of the gay vampire, some of today's top erotic writers explore the duality of blood lust coupled with passion and sensuality. (978-1-60282-190-3)

Mesmerized by David-Matthew Barnes. Through her close friendship with Brodie and Lance, Serena Albright learns about the many forms of love and finds comfort for the grief and guilt she feels over the brutal death of her older brother, the victim of a hate crime. (978-1-60282-191-0)

Whatever Gods May Be by Sophia Kell Hagin. Army sniper Jamie Gwynmorgan expects to fight hard for her country and her future. What she never expects is to find love. (978-1-60282-183-5)

nevermore by Nell Stark and Trinity Tam. In this sequel to *everafter*, Vampire Valentine Darrow and Were Alexa Newland confront a mysterious disease that ravages the shifter population of New York City. (978-1-60282-184-2)

Playing the Player by Lea Santos. Grace Obregon is beautiful, vulnerable, and exactly the kind of woman Madeira Pacias usually avoids, but when Madeira rescues Grace from a traffic accident, escape is impossible. (978-1-60282-185-9)